Tomazina

Her Book

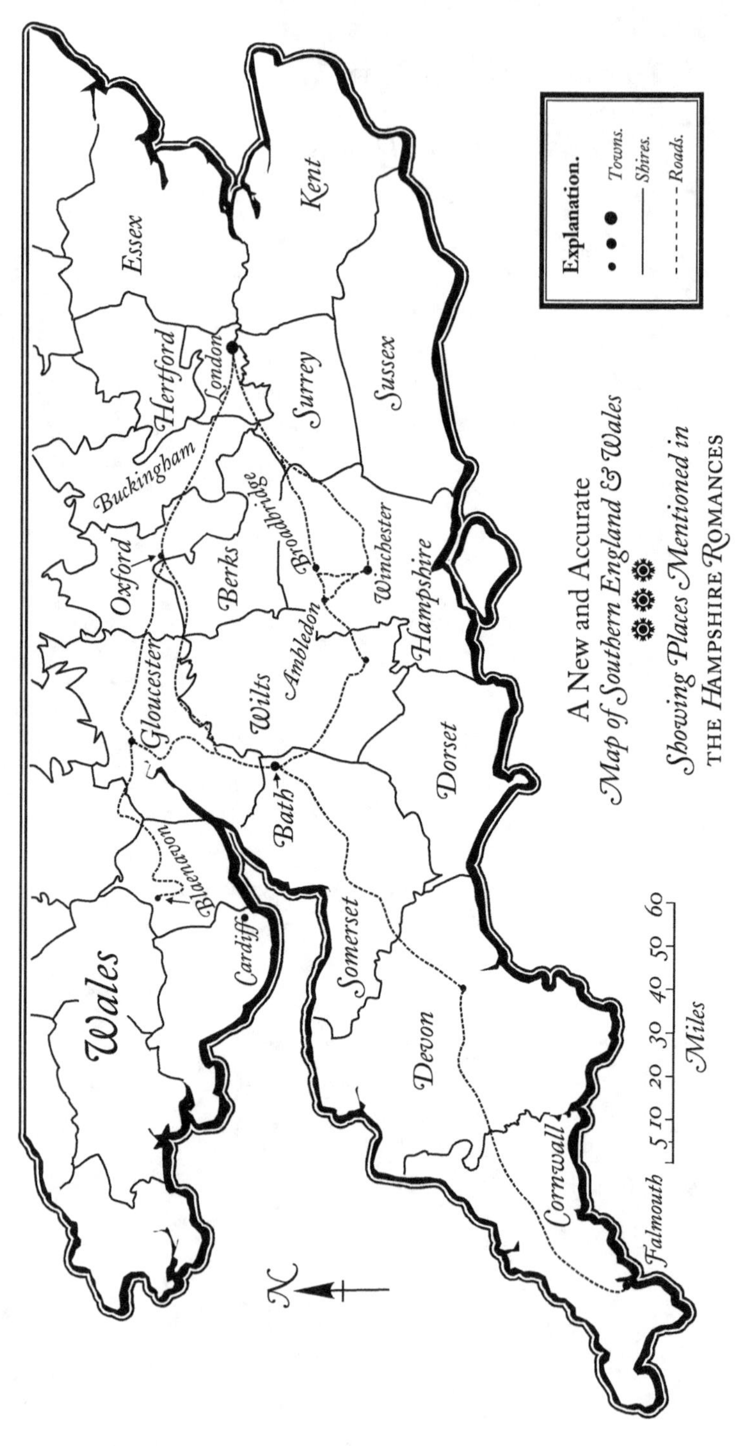

Explanation.
Towns.
Shires.
Roads.
A New and Accurate
Map of Southern England & Wales
Showing Places Mentioned in
THE HAMPSHIRE ROMANCES
Wales
Essex
Kent
Hertford
London
Buckingham
Surrey
Sussex
Oxford
Berks
Broadbridge
Winchester
Hampshire
Gloucester
Wilts
Ambledon
Dorset
Blaenavon
Cardiff
Bath
Somerset
Devon
Cornwall
Falmouth
N
5 10 20 30 40 50 60
Miles

Tomazina's Folly

or

Love Unsought

by Stuart Shotwell

In Five Volumes: This Being the Fourth, Containing

Act 4

Love sought, is good: but given unsought, is better.

—Shakespeare

MERMAID PRESS OF MAINE

This is volume 4 of 5.

Publication Data
Shotwell, Stuart (1953–).
Tomazina's Folly/Stuart Shotwell
p. cm.
ISBN 978-1-941864-00-5 (volume 1 : alk. paper) — ISBN 978-1-941864-01-2 (volume 2 : alk. paper) — ISBN 978-1-941864-04-3 (volume 3 : alk. paper) — ISBN 978-1-941864-02-9 (volume 4 : alk. paper) —ISBN 978-1-941864-05-0 (volume 5 : alk. paper) —1. England—History—19th century—Fiction. I. Shotwell, Stuart (1953–). II. Title. III. Hampshire Romances, the.

Conceived, written, edited, designed, typeset, and produced by Stuart Shotwell. Jester illustration on chapter openings: Patrick Tuller.

The cover illustration is from a hand-colored steel engraving, after J. P. Neale, of Dogmersfield Park, Hampshire, 1831. The original print is 12.7 cm × 7.62 cm and is in the collection of the author.

This book is distributed directly from the publisher at www.stuartshotwell.com. Mermaid Press of Maine regrets that it is not able to acknowledge, consider, or return manuscripts submitted in any form.

Act 4

Still Herself

I charge you, O daughters of Jerusalem, if ye find my beloved, that ye tell him that I am sick of love.

—Song of Solomon 5:8

Chapter 39

In the other life . . . all the spirits are known by what they love.
And as long as [God] keeps them fixed in that love, they are not
able to act contrary to it, because to act contrary to it would be to
act contrary to themselves.

—Swedenborg

To offer oneself, wholly, under promise of further irrevocable vow, to one's beloved and to be rejected—say if
there is anything more bitter in all of youth.

Thus Tomazina felt, standing at the window in the parlor at Hanley Wold, watching Samson Esterbroke ride away
from her on that day at the end of May.

She felt annihilated, made nothing; made to doubt the
worth even of her bare life. It was as if she were not in the
world at all; as if she were only a phantom in some other
realm who thought, delusively, that she walked among beings of flesh and blood—a fairy, an inhuman foreigner; and
of course no one wanted such a creature here. It seemed her
entire being had grown dim, as if it were an illusion; as if she
might ask of her reflection, *Who are you?* And the answer
would come back: *No one.*

That was her first response—to be crushed into a silence
of thought and a numbness of feeling. When the enormity
of what had just transpired had sunk into her mind, she
could not even weep, she actually stopped in the midst of
sobbing, and all her thoughts and feelings went blank and
seeming-dead.

She went out of the house, hatless and gloveless, and walked on the hill, avoiding the gardeners and the laborers on the estate, whom she had always enjoyed visiting before; she drifted along alone, finally pausing in the high cover that was the park at Hanley Wold, and looking about her almost as if she did not recognize the place.

The thought came to her, very stark and cruel: *You will never have what you desire.*

And she thought, *No; and why should I? Why should I be allowed to love? So few ever are. I must find some other consolation, some other meaning in life than this . . . this joyous dream I have had over these past weeks—these past years—of being loved passionately and of loving, of being wife and mother. This is* my *sacrifice, this is the death-within-life I shall offer up to the order of things, until I utterly perish from the earth—to suffer the disuse of all my power to love a man.*

And it seemed an irony of ironies that she, Tomazina Comstock, who had dreamed since she was a girl of the high commerce of man and woman in the marriage bed—that it should be she of all women to whom God chose to deny this fruition of hope.

I suppose I shall survive, she said to herself dully. *Oh, I shall prop myself up with philosophy—I shall go to bed with books by men who now are dead, and they shall be my lovers—dead men, dead minds, I shall be wife to them. No, I shall not kill myself. I do not at all feel the way I did a year ago. This is all too cool and clear a feeling—not hot and muddy as that passion was. I knew all along that Samson loved another—if love it can be called, which I deny!—and I bent my own neck beneath this blow, willingly; so I shall bear it.*

For a long time she stood without moving, and these thoughts blew through her like a icy breeze.

But then, through the grace of God, it was as if her flesh could not stand the loss of Samson, and her body rebelled against the numbness of her thoughts. She remembered the sweetness of touching him, of putting her hand on his shoulder, and then of leaning against him, the wild daring of kissing his coat—the sweetness of it, ineffable. She burst into sobs so violent she could not stand; she stumbled forward and fell onto the floor of the park, and she heaved great heavy sobs out of her chest as if she were regurgitating a poison in every breath; and she wept until she was sick with weeping.

This was just the first stage of her grieving, this mixture of mental numbness and physical agony; and it returned now and again, even after she moved into the next stage.

Which arrived when she went back to the house and dressed for dinner. She grew angry. For Tomazina Comstock, wrath had always been a rare and transient emotion; not so now. She put on her finest gown; she brushed her hair until it gleamed and had Susan dress it to perfection; and she stood in front of the mirror and she glared at her beauty as if she were glaring at Samson Esterbroke himself, as if she were saying to him, *How dare you reject me?* Her color was high, in her face and on her throat and in the top of her breasts where they showed over the bust of her dress. She did not feel half-invisible now; she felt more real than life itself.

Who needs you, Samson Esterbroke? she said inside herself. *Only let me decide I want a man—any other man—and by all that is holy, I shall have him!*

She did not let herself think about how she did not want any other man; for that time she let her bravado act as an anodyne. She went down to dinner and conducted herself with a mixture of such obvious suffering and defiance of her own cares that the Hanscoms did not know what to think. The sobs came back later, when she was alone, and only when she had gone numb again did she fall asleep.

The third stage was similar to the second, only she was not angry at Samson, but at Isabella Doronne. It began on the journey back to Hampshire, in the carriage with the Hanscoms; and she was sure she must have perplexed them to the absolute pink of puzzlement, for she sat upright as a caryatid, staring out the window with an unseeing eye, thinking such furious thoughts as *Isabella Doronne! Am I, Tomazina Comstock, to be bested by the likes of her? Am I to have the love of my life stolen away by a chit of a girl? The day shall come—let her be ever so blonde—that I shall ask for her golden head on a platter and Samson shall bring it to me! I shall find a way! Have I not brains enough? Have I not wiles enough? Do I not love him more than any woman has loved a man on this good green earth since the day the Shulamite took her lover in her arms? See if I do not conquer! I shall tread her beneath the heel of my slipper like the insect she is, and my love shall thank the day I rescued him!*

This mood—what a fine mood it was! It kept her from crying all the journey home. She envisioned a thousand meetings in future, when she was married to Samson, and they together happened upon Miss Doronne in the company of some lordling or manufacturer or planter home from the Indies—how they would condescend, the two of them, in speaking to her kindly, and how they would laugh later at how she had obtained all that she deserved. She pictured herself teasing Samson from time to time about his infatuation, until he had to sternly beg her to stop provoking his disgust at his own former words and actions. She plotted ways in which to trap her rival into revealing the emptiness of her personality, or into flinging herself at some man thought to be rich and only later (after Miss Doronne had entered into matrimony with him) found to be impoverished and even cruel. These fantasies were sickeningly petty, but it was better to yield to them for a while than to make herself a spectacle to the Hanscoms and to everyone they met on their journey by sobbing through mile after mile.

These and more were her first reactions. Ultimately, when she had arrived in Hampshire again, a greater sobriety of thought settled upon her, and she found that in truth she was not silent or numb or choked with grief, she was not angry or vindictive or crazed with jealousy.

No, she was Tomazina—still Tomazina. She still loved Samson. She still hoped that somehow, someday, he might see his error and learn to love her. She did not plot hurt against him or anyone, least of all Isabella Doronne; her Christianity recurred to her, and she prayed for them all— for Samson, for herself, and even for Miss Doronne.

In this mode, she decided upon three things.

First, she had only herself to blame. She could look back on that last conversation with Samson and see how the deeply fixed qualities of her character had led her to destroy her own chances—and those qualities were her impulsiveness and her sexual hunger in particular. In that conversation she had abandoned the plan that her intellect had sketched out in quite plausible detail, all for a wild hope that she could force Samson to acknowledge his feelings for her then and there. And somehow, by taking the blame on herself in this way, she made her burden more bearable. If she had blamed Samson—and there was indeed much to blame him for, including blindness, stubbornness, and even, some might say, a failure to behave properly toward her—if she had had to remain angry at him and feel betrayed by him, she would have found it difficult to go on living. It was easier to release him, as she had released Edmund before him, from any complicity in her pain.

Second, she refused to become like Mr. Burck. She had been the victim of his kind of self-importance, and she would not make Samson such a victim. Samson had told her that he did not wish to marry her, and told her as clearly as he could under the circumstances. She would not pursue him. In the more realistic moments when she pictured herself meeting him again, she imagined herself only politely exchanging greetings with him and then trying to escape. That was not to say she did not also have fantasies in which he returned to her, in which—fantasy's palette being pure exaggeration—he stormed his way into her presence and begged forgiveness for what he had done; but these daydreams were soured by the wiser view that he had made his choice, for better or worse, and that she could no more succeed with him now than Mr. Burck could succeed with her. At times she actually felt an increased dislike of Mr. Burck for showing her the obnoxious effect of such stubbornness. His example had made her sure what she must avoid at all costs. As for Samson's pursuit of Miss Doronne, it had this excuse, this mitigation: He had reason to think he might still succeed. Miss Doronne still flirted with him, still teased him, still tried to keep him in reserve. Despite her refusal, he still had reason to hope for her, however mistaken might be his belief that she would make him happy.

Third, she would, as she had early in the process decided she must, utilize her philosophy and her religion. She had learned a great deal from the Hanscoms; and greatest of all was how to bear up under this woe and loss. She saw clearly that what Samson chose to do was not within her power to control. She had loved, once again, where love had proved to be impossible; she had proved, once again, that love cannot conquer all. Love can only extend as far as the hand that proffers it; and if from that hand it falls into the dust, unmet and disregarded, then that is an end of it, for it has no wings to fly farther.

She felt like someone who has received a terrible bodily injury, to whom the mere state of consciousness entails a constant reminder that yes, the limb is indeed missing, or yes, the eyes have lost their powers. Samson was now lost to her, as irrevocably as some part of her that had been severed and buried. She had seen at once that the pain she felt now was infinitely greater than the pain she had felt in the final throes of her passion for Edmund; and yet, look—here was no frenzy of infatuation, no terror that she would slay herself, no madness that would drive her to attempt such destruction. She asked herself why this was so, and the answer she received was that her love for Samson was too great to dishonor with girlish insanity and thoughts of suicide. In loving Samson she had taken a long stride closer to God; and closer to that presence, she felt its support. Her love for Samson had not been godless, it had not left her without reserves or preservation. She felt honored by it, not dishonored. It made her want to live, not die. It made her want to look about her and see what help she could offer others, even if she herself could not possess what she wanted. Somehow, in fact, it was exactly *because* she could not have what she wanted that she wished to help others.

If she could have taken some anesthetic, some draft or dose that would have made her *not* feel the pain of her loss, she would not have done so. In those days, in fact, she watched in a kind of horror as others drank wine, even in the most moderate fashion. She knew instinctively that it is not possible to kill deep sorrow without also killing great joy; and that ultimately, to rob oneself of any emotion, either bad or good, cannot lead to happiness. The very concept is a paradox. Every joy has roots deep set in pain; and if you rip out the roots, the joy will die with them.

And so, bearing these three gifts with her, she entered into the final and most difficult stage of all: The Waiting.

For this has been one of the great curses of women in all the human ages, and especially of ages before ours: to live, merely waiting; to live in suspense. First a woman waited for the great change that would take her out of her father's house; then she waited for a child, patiently or impatiently, for nine months—time after time, child after child, she waited. She waited among tedious chores and squabbling children for her husband to return from his working day, hoping he would be kind. She waited for him to come home from war or journey, and oftentimes her waiting never ended. She waited in dread over a sickbed in which he or a child lay seemingly about to die. If her husband was cruel, she might wait for some accident of fate to rescue her from his drunken hand, and oftentimes then her waiting ended only in her own death. Or she waited at the end of her life, when her husband, whether bad or good, had gone on before her, and she counted up what she had done and left undone, wondering what was to come.

Or, like Tomazina, her doom of waiting might be to love a man and wait, wait to hear some word of him, wait for some chance she could seize to effect some change, wait fearing the news that he had chosen another, wait impotently, distracting herself as best she could with work in her home and family.

She felt in those days like the lovers in Dante's whirlwind, but she was whirling through the world alone, looking for Samson in the wind.

For when the wind blew, the real wind in the world, she raised her head and listened to it and thought of Samson. When the fleeting sun shone on her head and warmed her, she thought of Samson. When the dark stole in, by immeasurably slow degrees in that northern summer, she thought of Samson. In reading, in worshiping, in bathing, in taking her meals, in waking, in falling asleep, in talking with others, in brooding by herself, she thought of Samson.

She did doubt; she did wonder, as the days crept by, if he really would ever realize he loved her. She wondered if she should take another for her husband, and the thought clung to her like an odor one cannot shed.

But she loved on.

She could not help herself. That was the way it always was with her: she could not help herself.

She remained who she always had been—Tomazina; that unique amalgam of impulse and thoughtfulness, passion and introspection, sensuality and intellectuality, self-assertion and self-doubt, piety and unwitting sinfulness.

And, remaining Tomazina, she loved on.

❀ ❀ ❀

At least she could cry freely during her homecoming, and no one suspected the pain that was the root of that emotion. Everyone wept at least a little: there were definitely tears in her father's eyes, and he held her in his embrace for a full minute, almost as if he meant to make sure that she would never leave again. And Vita wept too, though Tomazina could see that she was vexed that she had made no progress in the matter of Hugh Ashleigh even during Tomazina's long absence. Mrs. Comstock was all coarse tears, alternately making much of Tomazina and reproaching her for being away, petting her and grumbling about how she had come home before Vita was settled. Ursula wept quite genuinely, and then went and sat apart in a chair, as if she did not expect anyone to care how glad she was that her favorite sister had come home, and did not blame anyone for not caring.

One blessing in her return was that Mr. Comstock was forced to shed his uncertainties about the Hanscoms. He was deeply impressed by her physical recovery; so much so, in fact, that he followed Mr. Hanscom back out to the carriage after they had bidden one another goodbye, and there took his hand a second time and thanked him profusely.

To see Rose Elizabeth she must travel to Priedpie Hall. She arranged that she should do so first thing the next morning. Her father proposed that all the family should go together, but Tomazina managed to overrule him and persuade him that she wanted to go alone, with only the gig and a steady boy to drive it for her. This concession was won only with promises to return that same day, or if she was pressed to stay at Priedpie, to send the boy home with the gig to let them know, and to return by morning of the next day at the very latest. And so she went by herself to this long-postponed reunion with the person she loved best in all the world—after Samson.

As the gig drove up the sweep toward Priedpie Hall, she saw Rose Elizabeth walking by herself on the lawn. A pang went through her, remembering the days at Asbury Valence when the two of them would pace the forecourt at Pilgrim's Rest together for hour after hour, chatting about nothing, or telling one another their dreams of future life. In none of those dreams had either of them thus walked alone.

Rose Elizabeth did not see the gig, and if she heard it she paid no attention, perhaps thinking it was some tradesman; and so she did not notice Tomazina until the boy had let her down and she had begun walking across the grass.

They did not run to one another, as they might have in younger days. But by the time they met in the middle of the lawn, their eyes and cheeks were bright with tears. They said nothing at first, and for a long, long moment; they embraced silently, and gripped one another as if to defy Death itself to ever unclench them.

"Oh," said Rose Elizabeth then, in a voice that broke, "you smell so fresh! I had forgotten how you smell, dearest! So fresh, so fresh!"

And for some reason Tomazina did not understand, this only made Rose Elizabeth weep the more.

At length Tomazina held her sister at arms' length; she wiped away Rose Elizabeth's tears with her handkerchief, and she examined her up and down. "You look splendid, dear," she said, "healthy as a new rose; and I suppose you *are* a new Rose."

"Indeed I am," said Rose Elizabeth. "The old Rose is gone forever, for better or worse. And *you*—you look like the *old* Mazie—you have got all your curves back. The last time I saw you, you needed only some bristles to make you a broom; and now you are as fetching as can be."

"I have been very happy in Gloucestershire," said Tomazina, wondering at herself even as she said this, for it was true despite the sharpness of the pain she carried.

"But you do not want to go back," said Rose Elizabeth.

"I would live there all my life if I could," said Tomazina.

"Oh, do not say that," said Rose Elizabeth, stricken at the thought. "Oh, Tomazina, I need you here. The thought of you is all that has kept me going sometimes."

"Is being married so very difficult, then?"

Rose Elizabeth looked about as if afraid of being overheard. "Come with me," she said. "Let us sit down somewhere quiet, and I shall tell you about it."

They went together to a bench on the far side of a broad boxwood shrub. Although they were concealed behind it from any eyes at the house, they themselves could see the house through a gap in the greenery, and Rose Elizabeth periodically looked in that direction as if making sure that they were still alone. Tomazina realized that her sister had deliberately chosen this spot because no one could approach them without their knowing of it.

Rose Elizabeth held her hand, but for several minutes she did not say anything.

"Well?" said Tomazina after this time.

"I do not know where to begin," said Rose Elizabeth.

"Does he treat you badly?" asked Tomazina, imagining the worst. "Has he hurt you?"

Then it all came out in a rush.

"Oh, no, dear! Nothing like that. It is only that I know him now, as I did not before. It is strange. I love him as much as ever; and he loves me, I know he does. It is just that he is not as great a man as I thought he was. He is petty at times; he drinks a little too much, he quarrels with people for no reason, he holds silly grudges, and sometimes he is stingy about giving money to people who help us. When we travel, he refuses to give a coachman his shilling in a most embarrassing way if he thinks that he has been knocked about in the coach more than he ought to have been, or that the coachman has not whipped up his team enough; and a thousand other things like that. Sometimes he is moody and short with people; and I do think he is a little arrogant about his place in life, and forgets that those below our station are human beings who have feelings just as we do. I often have to go along behind him repairing the damage, soothing hurts—and applying a little of my own ready cash in the effort."

"Is he like Edmund's brother, then, proud and conceited? Do you feel compelled to steer his conduct all the time, as Mrs. Percy does?"

"Oh, no, he is not as you have described Mr. Christopher Percy. There is nothing I could do to *manage* him, certainly. He is utterly his own agent. I can only follow along in his wake helplessly, sympathizing with those who are shocked at his behavior. But do not misunderstand me: he is not so *very* bad; no, no, he can be very sweet and generous at times. It is only that he has not the greatness of soul that I imagined he did."

Tomazina thought to herself that this was not surprising; for in her experience, there were only a very few men indeed—about the biblical ten—who redeemed the entire sex from the imputation of foolishness, if not outright brutishness. But she was pained at her sister's confession.

"Perhaps, dear," she said, "that discovery is the fate of all women when they marry, with only very few exceptions. Perhaps that is simply the way most men are, and we deceive ourselves about them or simply fail to see the facts until after we have wed."

"I have thought so, too," said Rose Elizabeth.

"And truth to tell, we are bound to disappoint our husbands similarly," said Tomazina. "We cannot say that we are not petty and moody ourselves, especially at particular times. That cannot fail to make a man feel he has got a very troublesome creature on his hands in compensation for all his affection. Besides, we must look worse to them than we really are: They do not understand the things that mean so much to us—and when one thinks of those things, one can see why. We love to talk of the silliest matters, you must admit; and what men can never understand is that it is not the silly matters that interest us, but the talking of them. My heart leaps up when I think of all the cozy times we four have had together, rattling away at a great pace about sheer nothings. And men, for their part, have their own silly matters, and love the talking about them—coursing, and shooting, and fishing; and we blame them for that, just as much as they blame us for prattling together about *our* interests; and neither side is willing to admit that it is the *company* we love most of all, and the gossip just an excuse for having it."

Rose Elizabeth agreed to all this with her silence. In all likelihood she had had these very thoughts herself, and took them for granted by now.

"So I suppose," added Tomazina, "though of course I know nothing of it, that being disappointed in one's spouse must be a kind of stage that one just gets through somehow as best one can, like a kind of stretch of rough water; and there is smoother sailing on the far side, once you have got it over with."

"I suppose," said Rose Elizabeth, but as if she were not really listening, or as if this very humble and practical observation were overshadowed by a consideration far more complex and serious. Indeed, after stealing a look through the boxwood again, she said: "But there *is* something else."

"What is that, dear?" asked Tomazina.

"Well . . . *why did Mama never tell us more?* She has borne ten children—she cannot be ignorant of the facts."

"What facts in particular do you mean? I mean—I know what you are talking about in general. But what is it that you find you did not know and wish you had?"

"Do you remember that I had it in my head that men and women never . . . never tried to make babies more than once a month?"

"Oh, yes, I do recall that. And I tried to persuade you it was not so."

"Well, you were right. I find that one is required to *do it* a great deal more than once a month." She stole another look through the boxwood. "In fact, Mr. Ashleigh has asserted it as his right to . . . have relations of that sort *once a week*. And I must confess that I do not know enough to say whether this is common or excessive."

"Or perhaps even less frequent than is commonly the case," said Tomazina.

"Less frequent!" cried Rose Elizabeth. "Do you think it is possible?"

"If what I heard from our cousins through the wall at Brackensom is any indication, once a week may well be comparatively seldom."

"Lord! I never thought of *that*. It is almost inconceivable to me that anyone should *want* to . . . to do that *at all,* let alone once a week or more."

And suddenly it seemed to Tomazina as if, in the interval between their seeing one another, she and her sister had grown very far apart. That difference had always existed between them, but there was never anything to bring it into evidence. Her sister loathed the very sort of sexual fulfillment she herself craved; and somehow, despite all her love for Rose Elizabeth, this made a space between them, a gulf of cool difference.

Another thought occurred to her, and she said: "Do you remember, Rose, reading Chapman's *Odyssey?*"

"What an odd question!"

"Yes, but just answer me: Do you recall it?"

"Yes, I do; but I could not now tell you much of what I read."

"There is a passage there that I thought very striking at the time. What were we then, fifteen or so? And still I remember it. It is when Ulysses is visiting Circe, and she is about to cast a spell on him. He pulls forth his sword and holds it at her throat, and she yields. And then she does a most curious thing. She says to him that they must . . . that they must lie together in the way of a man and a woman."

"Why do you talk of this repugnant thing, Mazie?" said Rose Elizabeth in disgust.

"But do you recall why, dear? Do you recall what she says about why they must do it?"

"No, I do not, I am sure."

"I recall the very words, they struck me so at the time. She says 'when the bed we prove,' we do it so that 'we may believe in one another's love.'"

"Believe in one another's love!"

"Yes. It is one of those strange things one finds in Homer—very naive; as if merely sharing a bed would make them trust one another. And yet, there *is* something true in it, something deeply true. I think that if a man and wife do not enjoy their marriage bed, they do not trust one another; and if they do enjoy it, trust blossoms between them. And that is why the Bible always talks of a man *knowing* a woman or a woman *knowing* a man. They cannot truly know one another until . . ."

Her attempt to explain died on her lips. The expression on Rose Elizabeth's face did not suggest that she was receptive to this line of thinking.

"Of course," Tomazina added hastily, "I realize that I know nothing of it, except what I have read in books; but I have heard Mariah say something about . . . about the need for it."

"I cannot understand *what* you are saying," said Rose Elizabeth, hopelessly, shaking her head. "I can only think that that has been part of the difficulty. All we knew about the subject was what little we could glean out of books. And it has proven not enough—nowhere near enough to prepare me for the reality."

"But do you not find you grow used to it?" Tomazina asked.

Rose Elizabeth gave a shudder. "Grow used to it! God forbid I should. I do my duty—I do as I ought. I let Mr. Ashleigh . . . take his pleasure. It is as God has ordained it should be. God willing, I shall have the more children for it."

"And so you think as Vita does, then, that there is nothing in it for the woman?"

"Oh, Mazie, I have conclusively proved it. No woman could possibly enjoy *that*. If there were any way to have a child without submitting to it, I would urge you to pursue that course. I would never wish you a husband after what I have been through, except that . . . except that I do love him—I do love Mr. Ashleigh; I do. If it came to it, I would lay down my life for him. Is it not strange? And he does love me, although he compels me to submit to this . . . to these *relations.*"

She looked through the boxwood again. "He has usually been drinking," she said. "I think it would help if he had not been."

"And there is absolutely no pleasure in it for you?" asked Tomazina again, sadly this time.

"No; it is extremely painful."

"Oh, Rose—maybe it will get better with time."

"Mazie, you do not know what it is like. No woman of us takes life seriously, I think, until she has experienced . . . *that.* It is almost as if God has purposefully left us blind so that we cannot see what we must endure in marriage—for how else could generation take place?"

"Maybe if you talk to Mariah, she could tell you something that might make it better, easier."

Rose Elizabeth looked at her in horror. "I would not make my conjugal relations the subject of talk with anyone but you. You are my heart's blood, and I know you will never say anything to anyone."

"Of course not," said Tomazina hastily.

Rose Elizabeth peered through the boxwood again.

And now Tomazina looked into the sadness in her sister's face, and suddenly she cried, "Oh, how this grieves me!"

"No, no," said Rose Elizabeth, putting her hand on Tomazina's arm, "do not fret about me."

"But you say you love him—do you love him? That is something; indeed, that is something great—to love someone, even if he is a man of many faults."

"Yes," said Rose Elizabeth.

They were silent for a minute. Then Rose Elizabeth said: "There will be good times and bad times—that is the way of all flesh, you know. Mr. Ashleigh and I shall have children together; and the children will supply the loving-kindness that Mr. Ashleigh sometimes lacks. I shall have plenty of love, do not fear for that. And even more importantly, I shall have plenty of scope to give love—not just to Mr. Ashleigh, but to our children, to say nothing of our dear parents and all my sweet sisters. So there is no reason to be sorry for me."

And yet Tomazina could not help but be sorry; but she did feel the force of Rose Elizabeth's assertion that such was life, and the way of it—that most people make matches with those ill-suited to them; or rather, that there are not enough truly good souls among either sex for such people to find one another and be happy together. Or perhaps it was that people simply did not know how to make their way together a happy one, once they did marry. Perhaps it did not really matter much, for most people, whom they did marry, as long as they found their way to mutual kindness and respect afterward. Obviously that was the difficulty Rose Elizabeth and her husband were undergoing now.

Despite these sour thoughts, she felt it was necessary to encourage her sister's positive outlook. "Yes," she said, "when you hold your first babe in your arms, you will beg me to forget that we ever had this conversation this day. You will say that it was all worth it."

Rose Elizabeth laughed. "No doubt I shall," she admitted. "You must remember, I am still, even after a year, only a young bride. All this is new and strange to me. I should not have said anything—I should not have frightened you. If my hopes of children come true, that will indeed reconcile me to everything. I should indeed endure *it* not just once a week but every night of the week if that were what was required.—Besides, I think that once I am with child, I might offer good reason for an intermission in these relations." Now, however, she looked a little worried. "But I do think it a little odd that I am not with child yet."

"Oh, but remember Susan Pinkham—she went two years after her marriage without a child. And that little thing we met in church in Asbury, Alice what-was-her-name; she was barren for three years and then gave birth to an enormous boy."

"Yes," said Rose Elizabeth, still looking worried, "that is another thing: when I have a baby, it must be a boy."

"Oh, bother," laughed Tomazina. "You shall have a thousand boys. Let Mr. Ashleigh wait a bit for his first boy. Give him a great lovely girl to worry his head over."

"Oh, but things would go so much more smoothly—if only it were a boy I had first."

"Well, there is no way of knowing, and so no point in worrying."

"That is a new philosophy for *you*, Tomazina. You worried yourself almost to death in the course of the year before you left, and now *you* tell *me* not to worry."

"At Hanley Wold I learned how not to worry. Mr. Hanscom teaches the skill there; it is no more difficult than learning to sew."

"I wish you could teach me!"

"Maybe I can, Rose; maybe I can."

"But tell me everything about Gloucestershire—everything that happened there."

Tomazina looked into her sister's eager and loving face, and she knew then that she would not be able to tell her what she most ought to tell—about loving Samson Esterbroke. There was something about doing so that was impossible. She had kept too many secrets from her sister already; she feared that to tell even one would unravel all the rest. She had her sexual hunger; Rose Elizabeth would never understand that. She had her old love for Edmund Percy. And she had her new love for Samson, which had grown out of those other secrets somehow and was intertwined with them. Maybe someday she would find a way to tell just so much and no more; but now she was frozen, unable to speak, unable to utter a truth that was only half of the whole.

Fortunately, there were still many things with which to distract Rose Elizabeth from the unshareable, at only a moderate cost to her own peace of mind. Of these things she compelled herself to speak instead. There were the Hanscoms and their generosity, which she soon brought Rose Elizabeth to approve and admire; there were Captain Thirrlews and Mary and all the children; there were Mr. Carver and Mrs. Cudworth and the rougher denizens of Hanley Wold, in particular the gardeners; and there was Gloucestershire itself, and the beauty of coomb and ridge. She even thought that some cautious discussion of Miss Doronne was called for. And there was Mr. Burck, of whom she now could speak despite his being such an odious caricature of herself; for her former inhibition against retailing that man's failings broke down when she was speaking confidentially to her sister person to person.

She talked of these things, and they *chatted*, and even laughed together, as in the old days; and before they finally rose to go inside, she felt less distant from her sister than she had, and the barrier that the act of knowing and loving men had brought into their lives did not seem to mean so much.

❁ ❁ ❁

Everyone has had the experience of encountering a woman grown up into new beauty. Often one has known her as a child, and sees her again after an interval of a decade, or perhaps an interval of only those few but critical years when the transformation occurs. For some reason, there is something very gratifying in this—in discovering that a formerly lanky and awkward being has become beautiful. Perhaps this testimony to the mere process of blooming gives us hope, or we are struck by the poignancy of knowing that this new butterfly is in herself just an ephemeron.

Now, Tomazina had not by any means been a girl when she left Hampshire; but she had so changed from what Mr.

Ashleigh had known of her that her reappearance at Priedpie Hall mimicked the effect of such a girl grown mature. She had lost her pale and greensick look, to say nothing of regaining her figure; and there was a new knowledge in her eyes, of matters of the heart and of matters sexual, that made her face infinitely more interesting to look on. She had acquired that form of beauty that is enigma.

He was sitting in his favorite chair, reading the Winchester paper, when Tomazina and Rose Elizabeth entered the room from the lawn. Perhaps he heard the scuffle of an extra pair of light-shod feet, or perhaps he put down his paper and looked up only idly; but when he laid eyes on Tomazina, the effect was electric. He stood up, staring; and he muttered, "By Jove!"

"Look who has come back to us, dear," said Rose Elizabeth. Her tone, for all his complaints of her husband, was rich with affection for him, and with happiness at being able to please him.

"Come back to us!" repeated Mr. Ashleigh somewhat purposelessly; and then he attempted to give point to the remark by saying, "I should say she has *not* come back to us, for this was not the lady who left us! Miss Tomazina—Miss Comstock, I must say—how blooming and splendid you look! They have treated you well in Gloucestershire."

"Indeed they have, sir," said Tomazina.

He came forward and shook her hand, staring at her very frankly.

"Rose, my dear," he said, "I always thought your sister was handsome, but this new look is rather overwhelming. I shall send a boy down to Hugh at once."

"Oh, no, please, sir," said Tomazina, a little alarmed at how quickly his mind went to certain possibilities.

"No, he will never forgive me if I do not summon him straightway. You would not want to be the means of a division between brothers, would you, Miss Comstock?"

"No, Mr. Ashleigh, but—"

"Nor between sisters either, I think," he said significantly. Then he went and pulled the bell cord for a servant, simultaneously shouting for the man, as if he did not trust the bell to work. The two sisters stood by, Tomazina a little embarrassed and anticipating no good from this excitement about her return, and Rose Elizabeth, beaming at her knowingly. When orders had been given to have a boy run all the way to Ransome Field and spare no effort to find and summon Mr. Hugh Ashleigh, Mr. Ashleigh turned back to them and became the genial host.

"You have had breakfast I suppose, Miss Comstock? Would you like something more? Rose, dear, ask Phinney to put a little something together for your sister—but you are here so early, Miss Comstock, you must need a little refreshment. And you stay to dinner—how long can you stay? Will you stay a week with us? Perhaps you would honor us with a month; we would be very pleased to have you here—would we not, Rose?"

"Oh, yes, yes," said Rose Elizabeth happily.

"I am afraid you cannot talk me into that, sir," said Tomazina. "I must stay with my parents still; though I am very honored at your kindness."

"Oh, parents, bosh—that is what I say. Rose and I shall not be happy until we have you at Priedpie, or *very close by*. Seven miles is much too long a drive. You will certainly stay over this night."

"I am afraid I ought not, sir. I returned only last night, and I would slight others if I did not make certain visits in Broadbridge tomorrow."

"Well, start out from here. You shall have the barouche landau. You and Rose shall go together—eh, Rosie, would that not be fun? Hugh and I might go with you ourselves, eh? It would be jolly. I do believe the weather will hold; the barometer is high and steady, for once in this miserable spring. Nothing more fun than a ride in the barouche landau on a fine June day, with not just one, but *two* pretty women!"

Though Tomazina protested this plan, she was soon won over by Rose Elizabeth's eager pleadings. Still she had misgivings. If Mr. Ashleigh were to so easily commandeer her time, she would only long to go back to Hanley Wold the sooner, where she was as close to being mistress of herself as she had ever been.

Her anxiety on this point was compounded when Mr. Hugh Ashleigh arrived, as he did, in remarkably short order, slightly breathless from what must have been a very rapid walk up from Ransome Field. If Mr. Ashleigh himself had been pleased at the sight of her, Mr. Hugh Ashleigh was speechless with admiration.

There is something in such homage that must be pleasing to anyone. To be frankly stared at in wonder; to see a little blush of color in the cheeks of one's admirer; to hear a hesitancy in the speech, or even some silliness that marks the preoccupation of the beholder—these tokens cannot fail to have their effect. Mr. Hugh Ashleigh had somewhat the air of a boy gawking at a pretty cousin. She rose when he entered the room, she gave him her hand when he extended his; but she could not get him to speak for several minutes, much to the amusement of Mr. and Mrs. Ashleigh, and to her own discomfiture. He only looked at her, and colored, and smiled, and shook his head in a peculiar way, as if trying to shake off cobwebs; and after what seemed an age, he finally stammered a polite greeting, and she drew her hand out of his, and curtsied, and sat down again. He remained standing before her, his eyes roving over her face in a kind of stupefaction, until Mr. Ashleigh, laughing, seized him by the shoulders and compelled him to sit in a chair.

"By Jove, Miss Comstock, I think you may be sure of your effect on my brother," he said. "I have never seen a man so taken in my life. Hugh, are you going to act like an empty noddle, or are you going to be civilized, and speak up, and entertain us all properly?"

"I beg your pardon," said Mr. Hugh Ashleigh to Tomazina. "You look so—so very blooming, Miss Comstock."

And why should I not? she thought. *I am in love, sir, though not with you.*

"It is the good Cotswolds air," she said.

"Ah, but nary so good as Hampshire air!" said Mr. Hugh Ashleigh.

"You shall not convince me of that, sir," she said. "And your own praise of my looks give testimony against your claim."

"But let us have no more talk of the Cotswolds, or Gloucestershire, or any odious folk who took you away from us. You are back, and here you shall stay. We shall thank *whomever* for this wondrous restoration of your health, but we shall not let you go again."

Tomazina thought that the Ashleigh brothers were all too prompt at ordering ladies about; and though she had not planned to remind Rose Elizabeth so bluntly of her plans, she was driven by impulse to answer: "But as I told Rose Elizabeth in my letter, I return to the Hanscoms' at the end of the month."

"You did say that, Mazie," said Rose Elizabeth, "but you cannot have meant it!"

"It is impossible," said Mr. Ashleigh. "You must change your plans. We will have none of that, Miss Comstock."

"I am sorry, dear," Tomazina said to Rose Elizabeth. "I do mean to go back. For the time being, it is the only place I can be happy. You would not have me waste away again, would you?"

"Anything but that—anything but that. You know I would give you up if I had to, to save you from that. You had us so frightened, Tomazina."

"I assure you your sister has been endlessly concerned about you, Miss Comstock," said Mr. Ashleigh. "You must not think of leaving her again. You will tax *her* health by doing so; and you cannot wish that, now, can you?"

"And what is in Gloucestershire that you cannot find here, Miss Comstock?" asked Mr. Hugh Ashleigh.

Unfortunately, this question brought a little color to Tomazina's cheeks, and her three interlocutors seemed instantly suspicious.

"There is philosophy, sir," she answered him. "Philosophy—a good soup-plate full at every meal. It has strengthened me; it has fortified my religion. It is a sustenance I do not obtain in sufficient quantity here in Hampshire."

"But that is mere bluestocking nonsense," said Mr. Ashleigh. "What you need, Miss Comstock, is what any young woman needs—a husband and home and children. Then you will be happy, wherever you are. Philosophy is something you only need when you are alone—is it not so, my dear Mrs. Ashleigh?"

"Absolutely," said Rose Elizabeth loyally.

"Tell me, Miss Comstock," said Mr. Hugh Ashleigh, "what sort of company did you see when you were in Gloucestershire?"

"We seldom went out into society, to tell you the truth," said Tomazina. "The Hanscoms are somewhat retiring; and that suited my disposition. Of course we went to Lord Esterbroke's, when summoned; and to Stoutly Hall, a very handsome estate, the home of a couple nearby, the Forbeses; but aside from those places, we saw little else."

"Does not Mr. Esterbroke still own his family's house there?" asked Mr. Ashleigh in a prying manner. "I think his lordship said something about that in a letter to me. We are great correspondents, you know; I think I may say that I am the only fellow from our school days whom his lordship favors in that way. Perhaps you saw Mr. Esterbroke at High Goldenoakes?"

"Yes," said Tomazina, with tolerable coolness, "we did see Mr. Esterbroke there once."

"Tomazina has met Mr. Esterbroke's famous *amour*, the beauteous Miss Doronne," said Rose Elizabeth.

"Ah!" said Mr. Ashleigh. "And what is she like? Lord Esterbroke says she is quite a gal, though she is as poor as a mouse on the moors."

"Indeed, she is very beautiful," said Tomazina. "She has completely won Mr. Esterbroke's heart, and I think we may be sure he will persist in his affection for her until she marries either him or someone else."

"That is good to hear," said Mr. Hugh Ashleigh bluntly. "But now tell us, Miss Comstock, was there no fellow—I almost said *rival*—who gave you particular attention?"

Rose Elizabeth answered for her. "There was indeed. Tell them about Mr. Burck, Tomazina."

She was reluctant to subject even Mr. Burck to the tender mercies of the Ashleigh brothers; but once they had caught wind of the story, they would not leave her alone until they had heard it, and besides, she saw she must in all civility give them some version of it. Once she had begun, impulse carried her along, and scruple grew weak; and in the end she kept the Ashleigh brothers laughing heartily for a good quarter-hour with a spirited retelling of Mr. Burck's courtship of her. It was, for all its spontaneity, carefully edited, however: she said nothing of the episode in which Mr. Burck had bruised her arm.

"You have had a narrow escape from matrimony, I see," said Mr. Ashleigh when she was done.

"Oh, very narrow, I assure you," said Tomazina. "As narrow as the door of a tithing barn."

"Any man who would secure you, then," said Mr. Hugh Ashleigh, "must be sure to close the barn door and leave no room for a filly to leap past him."

She thought this an ominous statement, but she only smiled politely and turned the talk to other matters.

❁ ❁ ❁

The Ashleigh brothers were more forward than she had ever seen them. Perhaps it was a year's worth of treating Rose Elizabeth as a thing with no will of her own that had convinced Mr. Ashleigh that his sister-in-law could be bent in the same way; and perhaps Mr. Hugh Ashleigh followed his example. Encountered together they were worse than when met with alone; they supported one another, they each intensified the pressure the other brought to bear; and they did this, Tomazina saw, mostly by falling in with whatever presumption the other was first to make. Over dinner they attacked her resolution to return to Gloucestershire determinedly, and if they finally ceased their assault, it was only by failing to perceive or even to imagine that they had not persuaded her to give it up.

After dinner the gentlemen insisted that the party all visit Ransome Field, which Tomazina had never seen. They would take tea and dessert there; a boy was sent ahead to warn the housekeeper, the barouche landau was prepared and brought up, and the four of them took the very few minutes' drive that was required to move from the excessive splendor of Priedpie Hall to the more modest splendor of Ransome Field.

Tomazina could not help being impressed by the place. The manager, a Scotsman, kept it absolutely neat as a needle case. While driving in over the long, tree-lined drive, they saw this man chastising a boy trimming grass by the way, presumably because he had neglected a few stalks. Mr. Hugh Ashleigh called a halt; Mr. MacGowan bowed to Tomazina as she was introduced, with a true Scotsman's bow—a faint inclination of his body and head, sober but proud; and then he urged them to bring to his attention anything they found defective in the appearance of the estate. His attitude toward the grounds with which he was charged reminded Tomazina of her father's own fanatical insistence on the orderliness of Pilgrim's Rest. One could only wonder at the cause of the terrible fear that the mere thought of disorder evoked in him.

The house itself was all prettiness. It was older than the new construction at Priedpie Hall, and so kept its Tudor charm; but inside it had all been redone—the oak panels were blonde and gleaming, the floors rang with a clean Italian marble, the furniture was modish without being flimsy. The view from every room was pleasing. The south looked out on a beautiful pond lined with stone, set into a garden of profuse but ordered growth; the western view included the rising ground toward Priedpie Hall, as well as a stark covert of majestic firs; the eastern prospect was the extensive acreage of the estate, now in spring crops; and the north gave out on slightly rolling pasturage.

Mr. Hugh Ashleigh was manifestly in a state of bliss in showing this to Tomazina. His brother openly laughed at him for it. There could be no doubt about it: Mr. Hugh Ashleigh hoped to bring Tomazina here as his wife. He was as excited as a little boy showing his new toys to a friend. He must have her see the conservatory; he was disappointed, for her sake, when he discovered that the oranges were not ripe on the tree there; he must show her the suite of rooms reserved for the master and mistress of the house—eminently comfortable; he must make her sit down before the hearth in the main parlor, though the fire was unlit, and he must have her imagine what it would be like to while away a winter's day here; and so on, throughout the house, from the below-stairs pantries to the guest chambers to the very attics.

Tomazina told herself that she was very happy, for Vita's sake, that Mr. Hugh Ashleigh was so wealthy; but the truth was that she herself found his attention very flattering, especially when considered in combination with the amenable features of his house. When one has been rejected, the undisguised admiration of a hitherto unattractive suitor inevitably becomes more interesting. She did not, however, even for a minute go so far as to think that if Mr. Esterbroke married Miss Doronne, she might resort to making her own home here. Mr. Hugh Ashleigh might be infatuated with her, and that was all very pleasant in an academic way. But it was not possible to fall in love with him while she was in love with Samson Esterbroke, or even at any time after having loved Samson Esterbroke. Instead her assumption, made in an access of defeatism and self-pity, was that sooner or later Mr.

Hugh Ashleigh would turn his attentions to Vita, and that she herself might in the end come to live at the house of one or the other of the Ashleighs as a long-term guest.

And Mr. Hugh Ashleigh very quickly perceived that the most attractive feature of Ransome Field lay not in the virtues of its proprietor, or in its amenities or improvements, but in its proximity to Rose Elizabeth. That western view was the one over which Tomazina lingered the longest. She inquired how far it was between the houses; she was pleased that the Ashleighs had succeeded in buying up the intervening land and rejoining the two estates; she asked whether the path between them lay over dry ground. Unfortunately for the master of Ransome Field, he had no way to know that she had Vita in mind in this conversation as much as herself.

When this inspection was over, and tea had been taken, and the barouche landau was called for the drive back to Priedpie Hall, Mr. Hugh Ashleigh approached Tomazina and said, "Miss Comstock, I cannot help but be sure that you found all at Ransome Hall to meet your approval."

"You and your brother, sir," said Tomazina in a direct though pleasant tone, "have a way of *telling* a lady what she thinks, rather than *asking* her."

He was all confusion and apology. "I did not mean it that way," he said. "It is only that if you see anything of which you do not approve, you need only tell me, and I shall have it rectified at once."

"The only thing I do not approve, sir," she said, still trying to speak mildly, "is your assumption that my opinion is of any consequence here. I am very pleased, for my sister's sake, to see that her brother's home is so beautiful and so comfortable; and I am glad that if, after my return to Gloucestershire, she should write and tell me that she has visited you here on a day, I shall know how to imagine her doing so."

He was dismayed at this response; and she had the satisfaction of having so nonplussed him that she could escape to the carriage with the final word.

Chapter 40

The father waketh for the daughter, when no man knoweth;
and the care for her taketh away sleep: when she is young, lest
she pass away the flower of her age; and being married, lest she
should be hated:

In her virginity, lest she should be defiled and gotten with child in
her father's house; and having an husband, lest she should misbe-
have herself; and when she is married, lest she should be barren.

Keep a sure watch over a shameless daughter, lest she make thee
a laughingstock to thine enemies, and a byword in the city, and a
reproach among the people, and make thee ashamed before the
multitude.

—Ecclesiasticus 42:9–11

*T*he same party of four went to Broadbridge the next
morning. The day was cool and the sun was hidden in
a doubtful mist; but Mr. Ashleigh was certain that it would
appear—and it did, at times, fitfully; and certainly there was
no rain. Tomazina had to admit to herself that she enjoyed
the ride. The breeze of passage was relatively mild, and the
views of the fields at every turning of the road, damp though
they were, were impressive, though they made Tomazina
long for the Cotswolds.

It was about noon when they drove into the village.
Here the two gentlemen suddenly declared they had business with the hatter, Mr. Exton, who was known throughout
the county for his excellent goods. From the way the topic
arose, it was clear to Tomazina that Mr. Hugh Ashleigh had
not had the least thought of stopping at Mr. Exton's until his brother mentioned it, and Mr. Ashleigh himself had
not had the least thought of doing so until he happened to

notice the hatmaker's sign. Tomazina found this delay of a piece with the rest of their self-assurance—they might more politely have put off their shopping until their return from Hartswound, but they were doubtless planning to be invited to stay for dinner and thus return too late for that. Their insistence on the delay was particularly annoying because she was in need of a Jericho by that point in the day.

"Do come in, Miss Comstock," Mr. Hugh Ashleigh urged her when the carriage had pulled up before the store.

"Yes, do come in," repeated Mr. Ashleigh. "Rose Elizabeth is coming in—are you not, my dear?"

"Of course," said Rose Elizabeth gamely.

Tomazina followed them down out of the carriage and into the shop, reviewing her memory for the presence of the nearest privy of which she could discreetly make use. The inn was her usual recourse when in the village, but it was about two hundred yards away, not a distance to which she could wander off without making awkward explanations.

The men went to the counter at once and became immersed in a conversation with the obsequious Mr. Exton, who seemed to want to show them every hat in the shop. Tomazina remained at the front of the store with Rose Elizabeth; and after they had taken a brief look at Mr. Exton's offering for women and found nothing of interest, she took advantage of the entrance of another customer to slip back out onto the street through the open door.

She was standing there, further considering her options, when Rose Elizabeth joined her. "Mazie, you are forever running out of shops before one is quite done!" she said.

"I suppose it is a bad habit of mine," admitted Tomazina. "But I need a Jericho rather badly, and the nearest one is at the inn."

"Use Mr. Exton's," said Rose Elizabeth. "I have done the same before. Go round the side of the building—there is a gate at the back. It is not so very nasty, as these things go.

I shall make your excuses if the gentlemen come out before you return."

Between sisters there is no need to express thanks for these little thoughtfulnesses; Tomazina set out directly, used the privy, and even found a bucket of clean water in the back-yard with which she could give her hands at least a quick sort of wash. She was just finishing this chore when the sound of several familiar voices arrested her. She turned about and looked over the hedge, and her eyes were scarcely able to believe what they saw any more than her ears had believed what they heard.

Between the hatter's and the next building, which was Mrs. Wright's stationery store, there was a gap in the stone shop fronts, which were elsewhere on the street set very close together. A very narrow lane ran through this break; the lane was, in fact, exactly what had allowed Tomazina to make her detour so readily. It was no more than a hundred feet long, leading to only two houses: the hovel of one Mrs. Mugwamps, an ancient seamstress now severely arthritic and living on the parish; and the somewhat more well-kept-up home of Dame Beck, a widow who let rooms.

Down this lane were now approaching three individuals, who were indeed, as her ears and eyes had told her, all well known to Tomazina. But their familiarity was the largest part of the puzzle; for that one of them should be there at all, and that the three of them should be there together, was thoroughly unexpected and incongruous. The first two were her sisters Ursula and Vita; and the third was none other than Mr. Chesterfield Burck.

The latter was speaking in his usual officious tone— speaking to Vita, who was giving him that appraising look and approving simper that Tomazina knew to be her usual reaction to any potential husband. Ursula was slightly in advance of the other two; it was clear that she thought it thoroughly improper that Vita should be speaking with a stranger; and more than that, Tomazina guessed that Ursula would have instantly left Mr. Burck behind if she had not felt a compunction about abandoning her sister. Not only had she distanced herself from Mr. Burck, but she had fully turned her back to him, even though it meant she had to carry her body at an angle to her line of travel as she went down the lane; she had drawn herself up, and was frowning, and her color showed her embarrassment and disapproval.

"And so, you see," Mr. Burck was saying, "this fellow Hanscom has grossly misrepresented my actions toward your sister. There was nothing that happened between us that was not perfectly proper, the behavior of a gentleman toward a lady. You can understand, I am sure, that the situation grieves me most deeply. I am taking action against him at law, naturally; but under these circumstances, I have found it very difficult to meet with your sister herself and conclude those negotiations we had so promisingly begun."

Tomazina was in such a state of astonishment that for once she was speechless; she could only stare over the hedge in wonder. As Mr. Burck came to this point in his explanations—or rather his lies, as Tomazina would have called them—both he and Vita slowed their pace and then came to a halt, perhaps because they were reaching the end of the lane and the beginning of the public road, and they wanted to prolong their conversation out of the public eye. Ursula walked on another few yards before she realized the others had stopped; and, half-turning toward her sister, she said in a tone of terse reproach: "Vita! Do come along!"

Vita ignored her and smiled the more on Mr. Burck. "But if I understand you correctly, sir," she said, "you paid your addresses to my sister and were refused. Why pursue someone so unwilling? There are many fish in the sea, as they say. Find a lady who smiles on you." And to this suggestion she added her most pleasant smile. "I assure you," she went on, "my sister has not the least intention of marrying *anyone,* so far as I have been able to tell. She toys with gentlemen, certainly;

but aside from a couple of men who are safely beyond her reach, she has never taken a fancy to anyone."

"Vita!" Ursula hissed again, in an agony of shame, "How can you *say* such a thing?"

"Yes!" cried Tomazina all of a sudden, now in a fine fury. "How can you *say* such a thing, Vita?"

She felt very deeply betrayed, for the imputation of toying with the affections of others was a grave one in her time, or at least it was among her own set; and though she had seen evidence of cattiness from time to time in Vita, this went beyond the catty into the absolutely shrewish.

Now it was the turn of the others to look over the hedge at her in astonishment; and Vita, before she could even begin to feel ashamed, cried, "Tomazina! What are you doing in Mr. Exton's yard?"

Tomazina went at once to the gate, flung it open, and stalked through it. At the sight of her dudgeon, Vita began to look a little cowed.

"And what are *you* doing speaking to a strange gentleman in the lane?" cried Tomazina. "And *you,* sir—how *dare* you accost my sisters in this manner? Is it not enough that you have made yourself a pariah in Gloucestershire? Must you pursue me to Hampshire and insult me and my family here?

"Insult you!" rejoined Mr. Burck, in a tone that showed that he himself felt highly insulted by the implication.

"Yes, insult me—with your unwanted attentions. No woman could feel anything but insulted by the interest of such a man as you.—I say, get you gone from here, Mr. Burck, or you shall learn the cost of approaching decent young women in the street. My father is justice of the peace here, and he will teach you the meaning of it!"

"But the gentleman has done nothing wrong," protested Vita bitterly.

"Nay, Sister," said Tomazina, "that is not the line of argument you ought to take. For if he is innocent of wrongdoing, that makes your error in this all the greater. Shall we tell

Papa that *you* accosted Mr. Burck? Is that what you would have us say?—Come along!"

At this command, both Vita and Ursula practically jumped forward in guilty obedience. Tomazina led on toward the street, and they followed without so much as another whimper of objection. Mr. Burck walked briskly after them, exclaiming, "Miss Comstock! You defame me to these young ladies! And you cannot simply run away from me—we have business to settle, you and I, and postponing it will be of no purpose—" And more of the sort; until Tomazina finally turned on him and cried in bitter vexation: "Sir! I warn you, this is my home, and I have protection here just as I do in Gloucestershire! If you do not wish to be taught a lesson that will cling to your name to the end of your life, you shall give over pursuing me!"

Perhaps it was the blaze of her anger more than her threat itself that halted him in his tracks—she could never be sure; but halt he did, gaping at her as if she had suddenly turned into a Fury. She took immediate advantage of his consternation to lead her sisters around the corner of the building out of his sight.

Rose Elizabeth, who was still waiting alone by the carriage, was somewhat surprised to behold Tomazina produce her sisters—apparently from Mr. Exton's privy—and she missed the look of outrage on Tomazina's face in her innocent pleasure at seeing the others again. Tomazina cut off her effusion by saying to Vita, "Up! Up into the barouche! We shall all drive to Hartswound together. It will be a bit crowded, but I do not suppose *you* will mind *that!*"

Vita looked both wounded at this cut and more than a little pleased as she realized this was Mr. Ashleigh's barouche and that Mr. Hugh Ashleigh was most likely one of the party. She gave up the thought of Mr. Burck quite readily and climbed up into the barouche before any of them.

The peremptory force of Tomazina's order to the others was so great that even Rose Elizabeth felt compelled to obey it; and so all four of them entered the barouche and sat there for a long moment of silence—Rose Elizabeth both surprised and awed, Tomazina brooding and disgusted, Vita angry and regretful and yet eager to see Mr. Hugh Ashleigh again, and Ursula grateful to Tomazina, mortified at Vita's behavior, and hoping she would not suffer from it. This latter emotion made her the first to break the ominous silence.

"Dearest Tommie," she said pleadingly, "I hope you do not think I would ever speak to that odious man!"

"Of course not," said Tomazina, doing her best to use a soothing tone.

"What man?" asked Rose Elizabeth. "What, that fellow who is peering around the corner there?"

"Do not look at him!" ordered Tomazina. Rose Elizabeth hastily obeyed.

"I do not see what right *you* have—" began Vita sulkily.

"Oh, Vita!" said Tomazina, in a whisper so loaded with disappointment and hurt that even Vita must be silenced by it. "How could you do such a thing, say such a thing? To tell a stranger that I toy with gentlemen's feelings? Do you know what that might do to my reputation? And if mine is harmed, so is yours. And even to speak to a strange gentleman at all, on any subject! Papa will be *very* upset."

"I see no reason why he should be," said Vita, rallying now. "We were only coming out of Mrs. Mugwamp's house and happened to meet the gentleman in the lane."

"In that obscure lane? In Broadbridge, when he lives in Gloucestershire?"

"Well, we had no idea where he lives! Not at first. He only asked the way to Hartswound Park; and so of course we told him that we lived there."

"*You* told him," said Ursula. "I only said good day to him and was for leaving him to ask someone else."

"And once he found that out," continued Vita, "he of course told us his story. And I must say that I was not at all surprised to discover that he had been rejected by my sister!

It seems you travel the world breaking men's hearts and turning down perfectly good situations. Why, he has between seven and eight thousand pounds a year!"

"He *told* you that?" said Tomazina, in something between amazement and further anger.

"Well, of course he did."

"You have talked to the man in the lane for two minutes and he has already told you his income?"

"It was more like fifteen minutes," said Ursula, ready to tell the whole truth, as long as none of the fault were charged to her. "I was trying to get Vita away the whole time, but she would not listen."

"I was listening to the gentleman—quite properly, for he is quite a proper gentleman, and I think Papa will be glad to meet him."

"Papa will have him put in the stocks!" cried Tomazina.

"And it was *not* fifteen minutes; it was more like five," said Vita. "He told us all about how he had paid his addresses to you, and how you had—after the way of some ladies—given him a *preliminary* declination, though he was sure it was only a show."

Ursula snorted, rolling her eyes. "Those were his very words," she said. "'Preliminary declination'! The minute he said that, I knew that you had given him a definite no, Tommie; and I could see why."

"And then he told us how Mr. Hanscom had spread a lying rumor about how poor Mr. Burck had insulted you."

"*Poor Mr. Burck?*" exclaimed Tomazina. "You are far too ready to give your sympathy to a scoundrel, Vita."

"There is more than one gentleman who has my sympathy for the way my sister has treated him," said Vita darkly.

"If there is any man I have mistreated, name him!" demanded Tomazina.

Vita saw she was not on sound footing here and changed her line of reproach. "And why should I not sympathize with Mr. Burck," she said, "when he has been slandered so grievously by your Mr. Hanscom?"

"Oh, you are *bad!*" cried Tomazina; and in those days, the word was an indictment of great force. "You are thoroughly bad, Vita! Can you possibly credit the word of a stranger against Mr. Francis Hanscom? Who is a man of absolute probity, approved by none other than Mr. Edmund Percy?"

Vita rolled her eyes. "Oh, let us not bring Edmund into this! I shall not escape a whipping if I am held up to Edmund!"

"Very well," replied Tomazina, with considerable heat, "let us leave Edmund out of it. Let us just say instead that you have the word of your own sister that Mr. Burck is a scoundrel, a princox, and a fool. Why does that not suffice you?"

"Well, how was I to know that?" asked Vita. "I never heard you say anything about him. You never mentioned him in your letters home."

"How was I to know that I ought to warn my sisters in Hampshire against him? How was I to know that his effrontery was great enough to reach that far? But I dare say Papa will find a way to send him packing."

"I doubt that. This is England, Tomazina, and as you are so fond of pointing out, we are free here. Mr. Burck has done nothing wrong, and Papa has no grounds for driving him away. If a gentleman chooses to rent rooms from Dame Beck, what business is it of Papa's?"

"He has taken rooms at Dame Beck's?" said Tomazina. Her ability to be astonished was now becoming exhausted.

"Well, of course. *For some reason* he insists on pressing his suit with you. Now, *that* might go far to convincing me that he is a fool. But if he is to do that, he needs to be somewhere where he can visit you and speak to you."

"Visit me! Do you know that he has come within an inch of being horsewhipped for his behavior to me?" Then she added, thinking of Samson's reaction to the bruise on her arm: "To say nothing of much worse."

"Well, how could I know any of this?" protested Vita, glad that she had a good grip on at least that one sensible objection.

"You never would have needed to know it, if you had behaved properly, and walked on without falling into conversation with a stranger in a private lane."

"Oh, bother, Tomazina! You are just jealous—you are always jealous. You are afraid someone will take away your toy, even though you yourself are tired of playing with it."

"Vita!" said Rose Elizabeth in considerable horror.

"Vita!" said Ursula in similar dismay.

"Vita!" said Tomazina, deeply hurt.

"Do not *Vita* me, all of you," said Vita stubbornly. "It is long past time for someone to tell the truth to the world about the way Tomazina behaves."

This was such a bad thing for any Comstock sister to say that the others were silenced by the sheer enormity of it. Even Vita looked uncomfortable at having gone so far in her spite.

"I am sorry to have to say it," she added. "But it is the truth."

"Not a word of it is the truth," said Rose Elizabeth.

"Not a word!" repeated Ursula.

"Oh, you just defend Tomazina because she is your favorite," Vita told Rose Elizabeth bitterly.

"Since when have you become so *very* bad?" wondered Rose Elizabeth in genuine amazement.

"She will be all right," said Ursula, frightened at the idea that Vita might really be morally lost. "She just needs a house of her own, that is all."

"We all know that," said Tomazina. "But that does not give her license to traduce the rest of us.—Vita, you are far too much concerned about locating the *theater* in which the domestic dramas of your future life will be staged, and far too little concerned about rightly choosing the *dramatis personae* who will play in them."

At the moment the door of the shop opened.

"Hush!" said Tomazina. "Here come the Ashleighs. Not a word of this."

The Ashleigh brothers made a point of expressing their pleasure at finding four ladies in the barouche landau instead of two. Mr. Ashleigh boarded and sat beside Rose Elizabeth, who had been seated with Ursula on the rear of the two benches. Mr. Hugh Ashleigh mounted on the step and surveyed the arrangement, which would have put him between Tomazina and Vita on the forward bench, which faced the rearward.

"It will be a little crowded in the carriage with six of us," he said. "Why do you and I not walk the rest of the way to Hartswound, Miss Comstock? I know how much you like exercise, and I myself can never have enough of it."

"I think I would like to walk too," said Vita.

"There is really plenty of room for all of us," said Tomazina. "If you would not be comfortable sitting between me and Vita, sir, I will be glad to accommodate you." And so saying, she shifted herself to the opposite bench, crowding herself in between Rose Elizabeth and Ursula. This left Mr. Hugh Ashleigh and Vita to sit together.

"I did not mean to discommode you, Miss Comstock, truly," said Mr. Hugh Ashleigh.

"I am sure you did not, sir; and you have not."

"Then please do me the favor of sitting where you were."

"I could not think of it, sir. You said it seemed crowded to you."

"Can you not see," said Mr. Hugh Ashleigh, with the winning smile of a boy caught in a trick but determined to brazen it through, "that I was only using the circumstance as an excuse to have a private walk with a young lady?"

"And now, sir, you have neither a walk with her nor a place beside her. Is there not a fable about a dog who lost the bone he was carrying while trying to seize on a better?"

"She has got you, Hugh," said Mr. Lucas Ashleigh, grinning.

Mr. Hugh Ashleigh laughed in a very charming and winning manner and sat himself down next to Vita. He smiled at her and said, "Well, I have not done so very badly by the exchange, have I, Miss Vita? Besides, Miss Comstock, under this arrangement, I face you and can see you better. And to see you is—"

"—to know I have got the better of you," Tomazina finished for him.

"Mazie!" protested Rose Elizabeth.

"Your sister can be provoking indeed," agreed Mr. Hugh Ashleigh, smiling still. "But that is precisely why I admire her so, as I was just about to say."

This skirmish being played out, the coachman was given his orders, and off they rolled. But Tomazina found they were not entirely free of Mr. Burck yet. The carriage must drive by the opening of the lane that led to Dame Beck's; and as it passed, Vita and Ursula and Rose Elizabeth could not help peering down it. Apparently Mr. Burck was still standing in the way; for Tomazina saw, to her dismay, that Vita made a little motion of her hand in acknowledgement to him.

This was not lost on the Ashleigh brothers, who looked where the ladies were looking. Mr. Hugh Ashleigh asked, in a voice expressing some dislike, "Who is that gentleman?"

There was a conspicuous silence from the four sisters.

"I say," said Mr. Hugh Ashleigh, "who is that fellow, Miss Vita, that you should wave to him like that?"

"I did not exactly *wave* to him," said Vita.

"Well, it was something like that. You looked at him and you put up your hand and you moved it about, *so*. Is that not waving at someone?"

"I *suppose* one could say that; but I would rather describe it as *acknowledging* him."

"And why do you do that?"

"I feel sorry for him, that is all."

"Well, who is he?"

Vita darted a defiant look at Tomazina, and then told Mr. Hugh Ashleigh, "It is one of Tomazina's suitors from Gloucestershire. He has followed her to Hampshire."

"Oh ho!" said the Ashleigh brothers, almost in unison.

"This is not the famous Mr. Burck, is it, Miss Comstock?" asked Mr. Hugh Ashleigh.

"I am afraid it is," said Tomazina.

Both of the Ashleighs burst into laughter, much puzzling Vita; and even Rose Elizabeth could not help laughing as she recalled the humorous account Tomazina had given of the man. Tomazina now smiled too; and she hoped that Mr. Burck would hear this merriment and know that he was the cause.

"We ought to go back and have a better look at the fellow," said Mr. Ashleigh.

"We shall do nothing of the kind, sir," said Tomazina.

"Oh, but really! It would be great fun," said Mr. Ashleigh, though clearly he was only teasing.

"We shall continue on to Hartswound directly, and in the meantime I hope Mr. Burck will go back to Gloucestershire," said Tomazina.

Mr. Hugh Ashleigh grinned at her. "There is only one good way to protect yourself against unwanted suitors, you know," he said.

"And that is to marry them off to my sisters," retorted Tomazina impulsively.

Mr. Hugh Ashleigh laughed very becomingly at this, as at a good piece of wit. "You will not marry any of them off to Mr. Burck, I am sure," said he.

"And why not?" asked Vita.

Mr. Hugh Ashleigh looked at her humorously. "Why, I am told that he has long since been wedded," he said.

"Mr. Burck?" said Vita, both incredulous and gullible at the same time. "Already wedded? What do you mean, sir?"

"I mean he has been wedded *to his mirror*," Mr. Hugh Ashleigh said.

"And his three valets were the bridesmaids," added Mr. Ashleigh.

"And no impediment could be found; for he had never loved anyone else," said Mr. Hugh Ashleigh.

He and his brother had a good laugh at these jests.

"You must not believe anything Tomazina tells you," said Vita then.

"Oh, Miss Vita," said Mr. Hugh Ashleigh, "I am very much inclined to believe everything your sister has said about Mr. Burck. Her wit in the telling was all too persuasive."

"And she has told you she refused him?"

"Yes, and we are all glad of that."

"But Mr. Burck seems to think her rejection just a show, and says that if he persists, she will eventually accept him."

"Vita," said Tomazina, "I would prefer you did not discuss my private business in these or any terms."

"And do you think Mr. Burck is correct?" Mr. Hugh Ashleigh asked Vita, looking at Tomazina teasingly.

"Oh, I think one can never tell what Tomazina is going to do," said Vita. "Sometimes I think she will never marry; and then I think that she might say yes to any man in an instant, if she fears someone else might catch him instead of her."

"So if she says no to a man today, she might say yes to him tomorrow?" said Mr. Hugh Ashleigh, in the same teasing tone, and again looking provokingly at Tomazina.

"Absolutely," said Vita.

Mischief maker! thought Tomazina, looking on Vita with disgust.

Though it required considerable conversational dexterity, she managed to change the subject, and they continued on to Hartswound and to the next episode in the uproar of which Mr. Burck was the cause.

❀ ❀ ❀

The Ashleighs of course came into the house with the sisters, and the hubbub of conversation raised by the six younger people eventually drew the master of the house from his den. By then Mrs. Comstock, pale and unsure of herself, was sitting with the family in the library, wondering if she should order tea. She was deeply tormented by this question, for she felt she ought to do something hospitable, though even her limited social sense told her it was an odd hour to offer tea to anyone. The young people, meanwhile, rattled on without any need of her at all; only Tomazina was subdued, feeling that she needed to speak to her father, but hoping against all probability that the Ashleighs would be polite enough to leave the house before she brought on the inevitable storm.

When Mr. Comstock entered, she rose and went to him at once. She stood by with unusual patience while he paid his respects to the Ashleighs and the common greetings and conversation about the weather were gone through; and then she said to him, "Papa, I have something rather urgent that I need to discuss with you in private."

"There is no need to take Mr. Comstock aside, Miss Comstock," said Mr. Ashleigh. "We all know about Mr. Burck."

"Who is Mr. Burck?" asked Mr. Comstock.

"You do not know him, sir," said Tomazina. "We need to speak in private so that I can acquaint you with him."

"Do not be alarmed, Mr. Comstock," said Mr. Ashleigh grandly, "I have heard all about it, and Miss Comstock is beyond reproach."

Notwithstanding this officious reassurance, or perhaps because of it, Mr. Comstock took one look at Tomazina that said, *What trouble have you got into now?* Then he seemed to think better of his instant condemnation. "I had best hear my daughter out," he said to the gentlemen. "You will excuse me, please."

As he turned to lead the way back into his study, Vita made as if she would follow them, and indeed her impulse to defend herself must have been strong; but her wish to stay with Mr. Hugh Ashleigh was even stronger, so she settled back into her seat—which she had made sure should be right next to his—and looked determined to brass out later any accusations Tomazina might bring against her *in absentia.*

Once in the study, Mr. Comstock went to the chair of his desk; Tomazina closed the door behind them and stood before him. They were in their old attitudes: the miscreant and the judge. Perhaps it was the familiarity of their respective positions that made him look up at her with a spasm of old worry in his expression.

"Mr. Burck, sir," she said, plunging in directly, "is a man I met in Gloucestershire, at the house of Lord Esterbroke."

"Lord Esterbroke," he repeated. She saw at once that she had made an error in even mentioning the name of Esterbroke, which her father must of course connect Samson and his painful lecture to her on that score.

"Mr. Burck paid his addresses to me," she went on, "and I refused him."

Mr. Comstock raised his eyebrows. "Really!" he said, a little reproachfully. "You wrote nothing of this in your letters home."

"It did not seem right to make his declarations the matter of a letter that might well be carried into the sitting rooms of Broadbridge by my sisters, sir."

"Yes, I see. That was thoughtful of you, my dear; well done. But you might have written me privately. It seems something that a father ought to know."

"Well, Papa, I never had any objection to telling you; I only looked for the right opportunity. And now has come not only the opportunity, but the necessity. So let me tell you all about him."

"Very well. I suppose you ought to begin by telling me what it was that failed to recommend him to you. You know that it has been the subject of my every prayer—"

"Yes, Papa, to see us all well married—I know that. But if you knew Mr. Burck, you would not even dream for a moment that he might ever marry one of your daughters. Indeed, sir, it would be like the Nephilim marrying the daughters of men."

"Is he a giant, then?" said Mr. Comstock wryly, still inclined to doubt her discretion.

"He is a monstrosity, sir—a moral monstrosity. He is like the men in the last days whom St. Paul talks about. He loves only money and appearance. He is *a lover of his own self, covetous, a boaster, without natural affection, a trucebreaker, a false accuser, incontinent, fierce, a despiser of those that are good.*"

"These are heavy charges indeed, Tomazina," said Mr. Comstock, who, besides being inclined to see his daughters as histrionic, was particularly suspicious when they appropriated the Bible to make a point. "Can you justify them?"

"I can indeed, sir. As for *loving himself,* he keeps three valets in constant attendance upon him."

She might easily have stopped there; for that vanity alone was enough to damn the man in Mr. Comstock's eyes; but she continued on with a certain bitter relish, itemizing on her fingers the points from the list in Second Timothy.

"He showed himself *covetous* in his disappointment at learning what my settlement was to be. He *boasts* of his own prudence *ad nauseam.* He is utterly *without natural affection,* and indeed openly despises it, and describes the right marriage as a matter of a man and wife merely presenting the proper show of mutual congeniality to the world. Indeed, he told me that if we were to marry, he did not expect to love me or wish me to love him. He *falsely accused* Mr. Hanscom of interfering in an unwanted way between him and me. And as for his *incontinence,* witness his having insinuated himself into Mr. Hanscom's house repeatedly, where he conducted himself in such a way that that good man was compelled to post guards at the gates of his estate. In testimony to his *fierceness,* he once seized my arm and wrung it till it was black and blue."

"He *assaulted* you?" cried Mr. Comstock.

"He did indeed, sir," said Tomazina. Then she continued with her list. "And he *despised* my dear, estimable Mr. Hanscom merely for the good act of protecting me. And yet even *that* is not the worst of him. He made promises of the most despicable behavior as if he thought he were boasting of virtue. You know how the saint tells us, sir, that *if any provide not for his own, and specially for those of his own house, he hath denied the faith, and is worse than an infidel.* Well, this Mr. Burck made it clear that in the event of a marriage between us, he would refuse to care for my mother and sisters should they ever require it."

The effect of this last statement on Mr. Comstock was even greater than she had expected. He almost looked as if he might be sick with his anger and disgust.

"My dear," he said to her, "you did well to refuse him. *He hath denied the faith.* Let him go to damnation, if that is what he prefers."

"But that is still not the worst of it, sir; for this same Mr. Burck has come to Hampshire—has followed me deliberately to Hampshire, sir, expecting to evade the strict protection Mr. Hanscom afforded me. He has taken lodgings at Dame Beck's in the village—the inn was too dear for him, I suppose."

"Here in Broadbridge! He is here in Broadbridge! Whatever can he be thinking?"

"That is not far to seek, sir. You must see exactly what is at stake: He has been ostracized from the Hanscoms' circle in Gloucestershire. He must either sell out of the house he has bought there and move elsewhere—probably at a loss, which he probably dreads more than the shedding of his own blood—or he must elbow his way onward through the scandal he has brought on himself and reassert his position in society. He can only do that if he marries the woman whom he has allegedly mistreated. Then his discourtesy to her will be said to be merely some lovers' misunderstanding."

Never had her father reacted to any complaint of hers with such gratifying outrage. "To have such a man for a son!" he exclaimed. "How could it be endured? Indeed, though I never thought I would say it, I should rather have no son at all than such a relation! But at least we know that you shall never yield to his importunities. The Lord be praised that you have that much wisdom, my child."

Tomazina smarted a little under this backhanded compliment, but pressed on. "*I shall not yield to his proposals, certainly, Papa;* but when I discovered him in the village just now, who should I find in close conversation with him but Vita. Ursula had the propriety and good sense to try to get away from him as quickly as possible; but Vita is so desperate for a household of her own that I think she well might be susceptible to his attentions. She was beginning to make eyes at him and simper and carry on as you know she does in the presence of any single man who possesses a roof. He was all too glad to boast of his means, which are considerable; and I think that at first glance she would not find the situation he offers an unattractive one. He is superficially polite, he is good-looking in his way, he is scrupulously neat in his appearance—he is *the man who has come into our assembly with a gold ring, in goodly apparel.* For most young women, he seems a very eligible man. He is only looking for an obedient woman who is well-favored; and Vita can be quite agreeable when she has a reason to. If he cannot have me, he might very well settle for one of my sisters. That would be the next best thing to repair his fortunes in Gloucestershire. Indeed, sir, he has already turned Vita against me—though that did not take much work, heaven knows!—and she will not leave over mocking me about him, even in the presence of Mr. Ashleigh and his brother."

"Is this so?" cried Mr. Comstock, rising to his feet.

"It is so, sir. And that is why I have come to you to warn you of his presence, and to ask you to exert your influence to exclude him from Broadbridge. *For of this sort are they which creep into houses and lead captive silly women.*"

The concluding Bible verse was quite effective: Mr. Comstock stood for a moment motionless with horror. Then he said, "Go bring your sister here at once."

Tomazina curtsied and went to the library. There was enough solemnity in her manner that the conversation died when she entered.

"Father wishes to speak with you, Vita," she said.

Vita instantly flushed darkly with vexation and started up from her chair.

"Oh ho, you are in for it now, Miss Vita," said Mr. Ashleigh. "What terrible crime have you committed?"

"It is that she waved at Mr. Burck, I expect," said Mr. Hugh Ashleigh, who was always a little quicker than his brother. And rolling his eyes in a droll manner, he added, "And that is indeed a crime worth punishing." Tomazina did not miss the look that passed between him and Vita. It was as if he had said, *If you are serious about me, Miss, you had better mind your P's and Q's.* Vita, for her part, looked almost guilty.

Whatever momentary reproach she might feel, Vita would not be led into her father's presence; she insisted on going first. By that little act of discourtesy she meant to tell Tomazina that she would not take orders from her. In the hallway between the library and the office she stopped and turned on Tomazina.

"This simply *must* stop, Tomazina!" she said. "You cannot have them all, or keep me from having at least one!"

"You are welcome to any husband you like," said Tomazina, "only not Mr. Burck, whom I would not wish on anyone.—Father is waiting."

With a scowl, Vita continued on her way.

"You wished to speak to me, Papa?" she asked, when Tomazina had closed the door behind them.

"My dear, I want to make clear to you that this Mr. Burck is not an appropriate member of our society. I hope to see him depart Broadbridge within the hour; but if he does not, I wish you to know that you are not to speak with him ever again."

"It is not fair!" protested Vita immediately. "Just because Tomazina does not want to marry, am I forbidden to cultivate my own chances? First she comes back home and takes over Mr. Hugh Ashleigh; and then she works on you to forbid me from talking to anyone else!"

"There is no need to put that kind of construction on this, Vita. Mr. Burck is, by Tomazina's very credible account, not a suitable match for any of my daughters."

"Why should *she* be the judge of whom *I* should marry?"

"*She* is not, but *I* am. And I say you shall not speak to him, let alone marry him. Am I understood?"

"Oh," groaned Vita in vexation, "really, Papa, I do not care in the least for Tomazina's Mr. Burck! It is just that I am so—foiled! That is the only word for it."

"Nonsense, my girl. You must not blame Tomazina. Remember what we read in St. John: *He that saith he is in the light, and hateth his brother, is in darkness.* Besides, she has been away for a twelvemonth, and you have made no progress."

This was a true and rational observation, but unfortunately it was not likely to make Vita feel better; and in fact she began to weep.

"Do not be silly, Vita," said Mr. Comstock, vexed to see her cry. "Go compose yourself, and sit with your sisters again."

Vita turned away, and giving Tomazina one last bitter glance, went out of the room.

When she had closed the door behind her, Mr. Comstock said to Tomazina, "I will go to the village and speak to this Mr. Burck."

"Shall I go with you, sir? You will not know him by sight."

"I shall find him easily enough; he will be the only stranger about the place."

"Very well, sir. Shall I ask for the gig to be brought up?"

"Yes, thank you; and have me sent for when it is ready. I shall be here, in prayer. I am not in the mood for company."

"Yes, sir."

When she had her hand on the doorknob he spoke to her again. "Tomazina," he said.

"Sir?"

"You have grown up since you went away."

She was moved by the respect in his tone.

"Thank you, sir," she said. "No praise I could hear from anyone would please me more. I have been very foolish all my life, I know—I have always known that; and I dare say I am still very foolish, and always will be. But I do feel that I have made some little progress in my absence."

Her father regarded her in silence for a long moment; and then he said, "Yes; there is something about you. I could not put my finger on it.—And to what do you ascribe this little accession to wisdom?"

"To the company of Mr. and Mrs. Hanscom, sir, and . . . other circumstances."

"Ah, the Hanscoms are wise, then, and your mother and I are not?"

"I did not mean that, sir. It is only that they have a way of bringing to fruition the good sense you and Mama inculcated in me."

This was a little too deft a compliment for him readily to accept; he only looked at her calmly and said, "Perhaps I should send all my daughters for a season in Gloucestershire."

"It would not please them, Papa," she said with a smile.

"No, I dare say it would not. And your mother and I would be out of our minds with worry, as we have sometimes been over you."

"I hope, then, sir, that you see that your worry was not necessary."

He was silent again, looking at her.

"I am not entirely convinced," he said. "Did anything else happen in Gloucestershire that you have not told us? Here is one suitor we never heard of, one who mistreated you so severely that he caused Mr. Hanscom to close his gates against him. Were there others?"

"No, sir. I assure you, I had no other suitors."

Again the silence, the considering before speech.

"I should tell you," he said, "that I have it on Mr. Ashleigh's authority that Mr. Esterbroke has been several times in Gloucestershire since Christmas."

"On Mr. Ashleigh's authority? What has Mr. Ashleigh to do with Mr. Esterbroke?"

"Mr. Ashleigh corresponds with Lord Esterbroke, I understand."

Suddenly she understood the strategem. Mr. Ashleigh had warned her father about Samson in order to encourage Mr. Comstock to recall her to Hampshire.

"Indeed," Mr. Comstock went on, "Vita claims that the very reason you went to Gloucestershire was to see Mr. Esterbroke without my interference. She claims that the whole of the cause of your sickness last spring was that you were heartbroken over him."

Tomazina flared up a little at this news of Vita's meddling. "Vita misunderstands me in every possible way, sir," she said. "I was not in love with him, whatever she may say."

"But it is true that Mr. Esterbroke was in Gloucestershire?"

"It is true, sir. But I did not go to Gloucestershire in that expectation; indeed, I expected him to be in London, and I believe he expected the same."

"But he found a reason to be in Gloucestershire," said her father dryly.

She ignored the implication and answered the literal fact of his remark. "He did, sir; he received several commissions there," she said. She managed now to look him more steadily in the eye. "I want you to know, sir, that I did not seek him out when he returned. He is a friend of the Hanscoms, and of their friends, and I could not refuse to talk to him when he appeared in their society."

"Oh, I agree you could not! And I am sure that out of pure courtesy, you did not cut him. I am sure that when you were in his company, you quite forced yourself to speak pleasantly to him."

This was as far toward pure sarcasm as her father had ever gone in his reproaches of her, and she found his rebuke deeply galling.

"I assure you, Papa, that Mr. Esterbroke is as determined on marrying Miss Doronne as he ever was—you may recall this Miss Doronne, sir; I have spoken of her before, and I mentioned her once or twice in my letters home. In conversation with me not a week ago, he restated his intentions concerning her."

He eyed her mournfully; and then said, "Then he is more of a fool than I thought he was."

"Indeed, sir," she said, falling into his trap, and flaring up quite visibly, and letting the hurt leak out of that great reservoir of pain in her heart, "he has shown himself very foolish in that respect." Then she added, too hastily, "Not that I think him a fool—not in the least; only that she has deceived him—or that he deceives himself over her, because she leads him on most unconscionably."

"Any man who would prefer such a creature to you, my dear, must be some sort of a fool."

"Of course, I think so too, sir! I say to myself, 'How could he?' But in the end I do believe that he is only played upon, sir—you must not call him foolish—he is not that, he is most certainly not. He is—"

And suddenly she broke off, realizing that she had, in her impulsive response, betrayed the strength of her own feelings, and that her father had been testing her all along. She colored violently; she could not look him in the eye.

"My dear," he said sadly, "God has given you a conscience that reports itself in the color of your face. I have told you many times over the years that there is no point in your attempting to conceal your feelings from me or from anyone. Thank God it is true of all you girls, from Ursula to Rose Elizabeth: you are too honest and too good and too innocent to even *think* a lie without blushing." And at this she blushed the more.

He was silent for a minute, considering.

"You like our Mr. Esterbroke far too much, that is clear. You say you did not go to Gloucestershire in pursuit of him. I will believe you on that score. But once there, you were thrown into his company; and I suspect that without a father present to hold you to your promises about the man, you found excuses for spending time with him, for speaking with him in that same manner you used here at Hartswound last spring. In short, you indulged your feelings; you did not keep a rein on them; and you grew to like him more."

"But what I say about Miss Doronne is true, Papa," she said, rather desperately.

"Oh, I am sure it is. And that is all the more reason for you to avoid him. It is too much of a temptation to any man to be favored by a young woman as captivating as you, my dear. You may find yourself taken advantage of. Mr. Esterbroke, worthy though he may be, may find himself overtaken by the sinful, carnal nature that has been common to us all since our fall in Father Adam."

"Even if I or he were so weak as to incline to that error, the Hanscoms will guard against any such thing, sir, as scrupulously as you would."

"And yet you say the Hanscoms like him? They invite him to their house?"

"Yes, sir," she confessed.

"Then the peril remains."

She gathered her wits to do away with this concern. "I shall admit, sir," she said, "that I liked him—nay, that I like him still; that I like him more than I ought, in the circumstances. I shall admit that it is as you say, and that the situation in Gloucestershire afforded excuses to my scruples that in my weakness I seized upon. But that is all quite over with, Papa. I shall not see him, in all probability, for many years."

"That would be wise," he said.

The thought of not seeing Samson at all, let alone for years, was so dreary that even though she herself had raised the idea, she could not endure it; she pushed it out of her mind.

"What you ought to have done, when you found you could not avoid him," continued Mr. Comstock, "was to come home at once. And I do not think you should go back there, if you cannot escape his society at the Hanscoms."

"Oh, Papa, if you only knew!" she said. "Again, I admit all you say—that I have . . . liked Mr. Esterbroke all too well. But not to go back to the Hanscoms—you would kill me, Papa, as surely as Jephthah killed his daughter.—Look at me! Look at me, Papa! Am I not healed—am I not healthy, in body and mind? This is the work of the Hanscoms and Gloucestershire. I would sicken again if I did not go back. It is true that Mr. Esterbroke may be there, but a little anxiety about that is a small price to be paid, is it not, in exchange for my health and happiness?"

"And why can you not be happy here?" he demanded in a hurt tone.

The question gave her pause. Certainly the cause of her going to Gloucestershire—her infatuation with Edmund—was now moot. But even if she could not have Samson, she wanted to be back at Hanley Wold. She wanted to live her life out under that sky if she could, and in the company of the Hanscoms. It would be too hurtful to say this to her father in these terms, however; so she chose another way to say it.

"I cannot be happy here, Papa, because . . . I cannot explain it, but *God is there*. When I am in the Cotswolds, I . . . I feel His presence, as I do not feel it here. I cannot tell you why that is. Perhaps it is only because I have the . . . the room about me, the quiet, the clarity. For me, Hanley Wold is . . . like the convents of old. Yes, I am the same foolish Tomazina—though I have gained some little wisdom—but in that presence I am . . . I am *useful* and kind and loving and not petty. Maybe it is being apart from Vita, I do not know; she has been so quarrelsome since we came to Hartswound Park.—No, I will not blame her for it—that is only more pettiness. There is just some calm and quiet there, in Gloucestershire. When I am in Hampshire, it is as if the Lord says, *What doest thou here?* And I know I ought to be doing the Lord's work elsewhere. There my life makes sense to me. Even the littlest things I can do for others have great meaning."

He said nothing in reply. A minute went by as he looked at her; maybe another minute.

"Well, we shall see," he said quietly then.

She seized upon this ambivalent statement as a plausible dismissal, and after a final curtsy, she fled from his presence on the excuse of calling for the gig.

Chapter 41

Love and scandal are the best sweeteners of tea.

—Fielding

Another unwanted outcome of the Ashleighs' visit—besides the attentions of Mr. Hugh Ashleigh—was that Tomazina did not go to Mariah's that day; she feared that Rose Elizabeth would feel abandoned. Her cousins had not been at home when the Hanscoms had brought Tomazina through Broadbridge two days ago; she had left a hasty note for Mariah at the rectory, promising to visit as soon as she could. All she could do now was to dispatch another letter begging off and promising to be down first thing in the morning—by which was meant, in polite terms, eleven o'clock—and steel herself to endure dinner with the Ashleighs at Hartswound Park-house.

Her father came back from his visit to the village in a state of irritation; and though Tomazina did not have the opportunity to speak to him about what had happened, she could guess well enough: Mr. Burck had been as haughty and obstinate to Mr. Comstock as he had always been to Mr. Hanscom. Mr. Comstock went into his office at once and wrote a letter, which he then sent by messenger to Mr. Eaton, the village solicitor who handled his affairs—a letter that would have very strange consequences, as it would prove. For the present, however, Tomazina could only await the outcome.

When it was time for the Ashleighs to depart, they offered two proposals—either they would return to visit Tomazina on the morrow, or she would come to them; but she insisted she must make her own visits in the village, and she would not be brought to agree to include them. "There is no point in taking gentlemen with me when I visit my cousin," she said bluntly. "She will only want to hug and kiss me, and she would not be able to do that to her heart's content with two gentlemen hovering over us." They still claimed that they would return to Broadbridge and join her; but she doubted that Mr. Ashleigh was very keen on visiting Mariah; and in the event, she did not see them the next day.

The walk to the rectory that morning fortified her spirits. Having solid ground pass beneath one's feet lends solidity to vaporous thoughts; and though she did not have many of those unrestricted vistas of the sky she had come to love in Gloucestershire, she encountered enough of nature to soothe her.

She felt very strongly, however, that she was only a visitor to this part of the world; and especially so when she walked the road between the end of the drive at Hartswound Park and the rectory. It was strange, coming back after so long an absence, and seeing how people had changed; and how, perhaps as symbol of those human changes, how their human dwellings had changed—some becoming more dilapidated, some being barely kept up, some putting out ells or new dormers. And the gardens, too, were a symbol; to her, returning at approximately the same time she had left a year before, the changes in plan and bloom and maintenance were striking. Where were Mrs. Gussett's hollyhocks? Why did Mrs. St. John not weed and cultivate her strawberries, which now so desperately needed it? And Tomazina was sure there had been a yew in the corner of the churchyard; it must have blown down over the winter.

Even the serving girl who opened the door at the rectory was someone new there. A new voice, too, echoed from the parlor—the happy chirruping of a literally new baby, accompanied by the pleased voices of two parents.

A little pang went through Tomazina at the sound; she did not stay for the servant to announce her, but hastened through the hall to the door of the room; and there she looked in on a scene that filled her with a mixture of awe and happiness and longing and a little innocuous envy, all in one indistinguishable impulse of affection.

Mariah had just risen from the sofa, having heard the knock at the front door; and she was giving over a baby girl, not ten months old, into the hands of a nursemaid. Behind her, leaning quietly against the window, as was a habit of his—Tomazina only now recognized that posture as a habit, seeing it again after so many months—was Edmund, who was looking on with a smile.

"Here she is as last!" cried Mariah softly. She stepped urgently across the room, holding up her arms in welcome; and Tomazina, surprised at the power of the emotion she herself felt, met her halfway with an answering cry of "Cousin!" They hugged, kissed, and then still held each other for a long moment.

It all came back to her in a rush—Mariah's daunting womanhood. There was still that sexual fragrance about her, though Tomazina caught a new addition to it—the hint of baby and milk.

Mariah held her away from her and surveyed her. "Look at you!" she said. "Oh, Edmund, look at Tomazina!"

"I see," said Edmund quietly.

She looked at them while they looked at her.

Mariah was radiant with a double vitality: not just of womanhood, but of motherhood as well. Her color was a perfect, glowing pink, like the inside of a shell; her dark eyes were lustrous, quiet, and deep. She had finally adopted the new style of long, loose curls, which showed off the beauty of her hair as no other fashion could have, and her morning dress was cut away from her throat to reveal the soft cleavage between her breasts. If Tomazina's daemon was hunger, Mariah's was contentment. She looked a veritable goddess of maternity. Tomazina could only think how ludicrous, pathetic, laughable it was that she herself had ever set herself up as the rival of this woman.

As for Edmund—it is true that the sight of him gave her heart a little fillip. But that was far from the wrenching she used to feel; and she smiled happily at him, seeing him happy, for he was obviously was so. To her eyes there was something transcendent about him; she thought him like a pilgrim or a hero who has stepped in out of the storm and stands by the fire, knowing that he may be called away alone again into life's difficulties, but not fearful or resentful of that necessity, only enjoying his respite while it lasts.

Perhaps it was in that moment that Tomazina truly and finally gave him up into the love and care of her cousin.

"But let me see the baby!" she said then, turning to the little girl.

"Yes, yes, yes," said Mariah, instantly forgetting everything else. "Here she is—little Janetta." She took her back from the nursemaid and held her on one arm, facing Tomazina. "You must meet your Auntie Tomazina," she said to the baby. "You remember all I have told you about your Auntie, do you not?—Oh, Tomazina, wait until you hear her talk. She is such a rattle!—Now, who is this, Janetta? Who is this new auntie of yours? This is Auntie Ursula's sister—in the picture on the wall—this is my own cousin from Hartswound—do you remember what I told you about Auntie Tomazina?"

"'Zina!" the baby said. Or at least, she uttered a sound that could, with a considerable dose of imagination, be understood to be that word, or that part of a word.

Immediately the three adults in the room—four, with the nursemaid—were in ecstasies of approval.

She was indeed a beautiful little girl, favoring her mother perhaps more than her father. She had dark eyes, plump, milk-fed cheeks, and a surprising quantity of very dark hair; and not only did all these things require being exclaimed over, but her arms and hands and legs and feet as well, right out to her fingers and toes—all in their proper location and number—needed to be individually appraised and praised; and Tomazina went through all the spontaneous effusions of baby admiration without feeling that there was anything the least unoriginal in her performance. It was soon proven that the child did, as Mariah had claimed, have an enormous vocabulary, even if the comprehension of it proceeded largely on faith and resembled an aural version of the decipherment of some long-forgotten script; but Tomazina's estimate of Baby Janetta's intelligence was increased rather than diminished by the difficulty of understanding her sweet little utterances. When the little girl was at length coaxed into her arms, she held her blissfully and petted her and spoke cooingly to her; and during that happy interval, Edmund in particular looked on in complete agreement with the assertion he inferred from that cooing, which was simply that this girl was, like her mother before her, the most beautiful creature of her age and sex in the entire world.

And this baby worship went on for—if it can be believed, and of course it must be by those who have engaged in it—a full hour. In the course of which time the nursemaid had to leave to attend to some duties upstairs, and Edmund had to leave briefly to attend to a visitor at the front door, so for a moment just the three of them remained—Tomazina, Mariah, and the baby. At this point, Janetta began to fuss before her nap, and Mariah settled down on the sofa to feed the girl.

"What is it like?" asked Tomazina wonderingly, as the baby sucked hungrily at Mariah's nipple.

"Oh . . . it is wonderful, all of it. One does feel cross sometimes here and there; but that is only bodily weakness, and is soon done away with by the spirit."

"I *do* want a baby," said Tomazina longingly.

"Of course you do, dear. And you shall have one, and more than one."

The absolute certainty with which this promise was uttered made Tomazina beam in gratitude.

"How I have missed you, Mariah!" she said.

"And I you, Cuz."

"But I have missed you more, dear; I have missed you more than you could ever miss me, having Edmund as you do. I miss having a friend who . . ."

And she broke off suddenly.

She wanted to say that she missed having a friend who understood what a longing for sex was, who was not afraid of the hungers that God had given to be rightly satisfied in marriage. Mariah's arms, her parlor, her house, was a refuge for those of her kind who were not daunted by those hungers.

"You miss having a friend who understands?" said Mariah, finishing her sentence for her.

"Yes," said Tomazina. She would have said more, but at that moment Edmund returned to the room. He sat down next to Mariah, and she shifted herself so that she was leaning against him. He put one arm around her, and she put her head down on his shoulder. Over the next few minutes, the baby gradually fell asleep against her breast.

"So you are happy at Hanley Wold," Edmund said to Tomazina.

"I am, indeed I am. I love the Hanscoms dearly—they are so good to me. And Gloucestershire itself agrees with me. Oh, Edmund, I think I may live there for the rest of my life."

"It is obvious from your appearance that you are thriving there."

"Blooming, indeed," added Mariah. "But we shall miss you if you live there, dear."

"No, you shall not; you shall visit me there, and I you here. It is not so very far, you know.—The Cotswolds, Mariah! I cannot have enough of them. I am altogether a traitor to the county of my birth and raising. They are the closest I shall ever get to heaven. The fields—the hills—the coombs—the sheep—"

"We have no sheep in Hampshire?" laughed Edmund.

"Ah, but the Gloucestershire sheep are more handsome," said Tomazina, smiling.

"But the fields cannot be more handsome," said Mariah. "Edmund took fifty bushels of grain from every acre of our glebe last year. We have not told his brother yet. Christopher will be more jealous of him for that than he ever was of Edmund's being briefly heir of Brackensom, especially after the terrible start to the season we have had."

"Fifty bushels! What, only fifty!" said Tomazina. "And that trivial *gleaning* is to cause this inordinate jealousy of brother for brother? Why, in Gloucestershire they think a field of no account if they get fewer than a *thousand* bushels per acre from it!"

They laughed softly at her fancy; but then Edmund, growing more sober, said, "We shall not get fifty bushels per acre this year, I can tell you. I have several times wondered if we shall have fifty from the whole glebe. Which is too bad, too bad, for we shall need every speck of grain to feed the hungry. The times are hard, though there is plenty of wealth about to cure them."

Despite the seriousness of this new topic, Tomazina would not yet let go of her previous theme. "Well, whatever the poverty of the fields here," she said, "I cannot tell you what a great relief it is to me to be in your company again. Edmund, I was just starting to tell Mariah how I feel that you two and the Hanscoms are the only people in the world who understand me. Even Rose Elizabeth, my dear Rose Elizabeth, whom I have loved better than anyone all my life—even she has become somewhat of a stranger to me."

"That cannot be so," said Mariah.

"It is her marriage," said Tomazina.

"Ah," said Edmund. Tomazina had the feeling that somehow he knew exactly what the problem was; and Mariah, too, looked very understanding and concerned.

"Perhaps you should have a talk with her sometime, Mariah," said Tomazina. "You might do her a great deal of good. But do not tell her that I mentioned it."

"I shall be the soul of discretion, dear."

There was a long moment of contented silence in the room. Then Mariah said, "And you?" She seemed to be asking for some particular piece of information, and Tomazina was not sure what it could be.

"And I?" repeated Tomazina.

"Do you have any news for us?"

"News?"

"Do not tease Tomazina," Edmund told Mariah.

Mariah smiled, but continued, in the same vague strain, by saying "News about . . . *things;* you know."

Tomazina looked her puzzlement. "I am afraid I do not know what you mean, dear," she said.

"What I mean is," said Mariah, smiling as she committed herself, "are you willing to admit yet that you are in love with Samson Esterbroke?"

Tomazina was taken aback. She felt she had been caught red-handed; she could only smile wryly and say, "As I was saying, Mariah, I have always felt that you two and the Hanscoms were the only people who understood me."

"I think you might find that some of your sisters were in possession of your secret fairly early, too," said Mariah.

"They knew it before I did—they knew it perhaps before it was really true. But it is not *good* news."

"Not good news?" Mariah said. "And why is that?"

"Because he is in love with someone else," said Tomazina.

Edmund and Mariah laughed softly. "No, he is not," said Mariah. "He only thinks he is. He is in love with you, dear."

"Did he ever tell you so?" asked Tomazina instantly.

"No, of course he did not. He is still as you were, not so long ago; he loves and does not know he loves. How could he tell us he loves you if he does not know it? He could only tell us the way you told us—with looks, and smiles, and happiness; and with a collapse back into his grave manners the moment you had gone from his sight. You may not know it, dear, but he is grim as a tomb when you are not near. It can be quite difficult to coax him out of his shell then. But let

Miss Comstock's foot even be heard in the hall and a bliss comes over his face."

"I never saw such a transformation from reserve to affability in all my life," said Edmund. "You are air to him, Tomazina. He cannot breathe unless you are there."

"Well, then, he is determined to suffocate himself. He has made it very clear to me that he is devoted to that . . . poisonous little *chit*, Isabella Doronne.—Oh, forgive me, Edmund for putting it so uncharitably, but if you had met her, you would not think I am exaggerating by much.—I tell you, Samson is mad! He is utterly mad! It is like watching someone you love pour spirits over himself and take up a candle to set himself on fire, all the while saying, 'This is all I require to make me happy.'"

Edmund nodded, but a little more grimly now.

"Where is he now?" asked Mariah.

"I do not know. I believe he was in Gloucestershire when we left, but he was going to return to London."

"Should we invite him to visit?" asked Mariah.

"No," said Tomazina firmly. "He will not want to see me."

"Of course he will want to see you, dear."

"No, he will not. To tell you the truth, we . . . came to a kind of agreement before we parted."

"An *agreement*? Of what kind? What do you mean?"

"It was all very painful, but as I just said, he made it *absolutely clear* that he means to stick to his plan of marrying Miss Doronne."

A respectful and knowledgeable silence greeted this remark; Tomazina could see that her friends, having been given this particular emphasis, were now filling in some of the blanks in her very elliptical account. But neither of them would guess, she was sure, the full extent of her boldness and the damage it had done.

"Ah," said Mariah. "Well, that just means that he must be given more time to know himself—to recognize his own feelings. And all the better if you can be put in his way to remind him of them.—The Hanscoms said you would go back to Gloucestershire with them. Is that still so?"

"Yes, they are to pick me up on their way back through from Brackensom. We were thinking this would be in two or three weeks, or a month at most. Of course, Papa is already trying to stop me from leaving again."

"Well, that is only natural. But it is obvious how you have thrived in Gloucestershire; in the end he will not stop you."

"But he is worried about Mr. Esterbroke."

"He does not like him?"

"He thinks *well enough of* him, but he says he is not *well enough off.*"

"Well, that can be mended," said Mariah. "We have only to bring Mr. Esterbroke to the point that he sees he *must* be married to you, and he himself will do whatever is required to make it happen."

"Take a living somewhere, do you mean?"

"Yes."

"But they are not so easy to find, these days; all the officers will be wanting to find themselves a little rectory—preferably with good shooting attached."

"But Mr. Esterbroke is exceptional; he will get a living if he wants one."

"But I would not *want* him to go into the church," said Tomazina.

Mariah looked surprised. "Why not, dear? It would be perfect for him—and for you."

"Well, of course it would—and I would be grateful if we could do it. But he *must* continue to paint. It would kill him to stop, and it would kill me as well, to see him forced to stop."

"He can easily be rector on Sundays and set up his easel on Monday afternoon," said Mariah. "Others have done it before him."

"Yes, but it is not the same as being an R.A. and a painter in his own right."

"Well, that is true," admitted Mariah.

Then it struck Tomazina suddenly that this fantasy was all very pleasant, but had little to do with the reality of Samson's refusal of her.

"The fact is," she said then, "that in a month, or at least long before I see him again, whenever that may be, he may have been accepted by Miss Doronne. And once he has been accepted, there is no going back. If you are right—if he does love me—then he may not even know it until he is engaged or married. And then it will be too late."

This conversation—the topic of which she could willingly have dwelt on for days, no matter that the pleasure it brought was so bitter—was interrupted by the sound of the front door opening, followed by a canine panting, a rush of feet in the hall, and a protesting but indulgent peal of laughter from a familiar voice. Then, without any ceremony, Miss Brownton burst into the room with Sir Toby—or rather, Sir Toby came first; for the instant Miss Brownton had turned the knob and he could push his nose past the jamb, he butted his way in. He made a quick dash around the room to reconnoiter and greet everyone, threatening the contents of the tables with his thrashing tail in passing; but when he discovered Tomazina, he halted before her, seating himself and wiggling in ecstasy and craning his head up to be patted. For a minute, between Miss Brownton's effusion at finding Tomazina returned, and the dog's welcome, there was a little domestic chaos in the parlor. Then, at a few calm words from Edmund, the dog was dispatched to a corner to lie down. He performed this duty with an alacrity and steadfast obedience that was only slightly marred by a propensity to squirm closer to Tomazina when he thought no one was looking.

Sir Toby was a puppy no longer. He had become a full-grown hound; and though the Percies of Surrey were not fanatical breeders of hunting dogs, they did dabble in that sideline in a somewhat opportunistic way, taking good pups when other families offered them, and working on a little bloodline for their own estate. The result of this hobby breeding was a very idiosyncratic beast: Sir Toby had a much broader chest and shoulders than were usually seen in foxhounds; he had heavy paws, a coat so short that it had the appearance of having been newly shorn, a whip of a tail, and great, dark eyes that might have seemed somewhat stupid in a human but were very quick and sensitive in a dog. Though he was mostly white and tan, his back was decorated with a black saddle, which was matched by a similar patch in miniature over the bridge of his nose, which in turn Miss Brownton liked to say was a saddle for the fairies to ride. If it had not been for this coloring, Tomazina might almost have failed to recognize him as the same puppy who had been chasing about the village with Miss Brownton a year ago; but that and his obvious recognition of her prevented even the least doubt on that score.

Miss Brownton's greeting to her was both heart-warming and pathetic. She seemed almost to want to hug Tomazina, and yet the mere thought of it also repulsed her. After the dog had been settled in his corner, she hung back, clapping her hands together softly, and saying, "Miss Tomazina! Miss Tomazina! This is wonderful! We have missed you ever so much! And Toby has missed you—look at him, the wiggle!"

Tomazina herself longed to hug Miss Brownton; she rose from the sofa impulsively, but then stopped, poised for a moment as if she would dare it, and finally only curtsied, saying, "I am *so* pleased to see you again, Miss Brownton"; which safe and distant salutation Miss Brownton returned, beaming and blushing with shy happiness.

"Your mother is still well, I hope?" added Tomazina. "Mariah wrote that she was."

"Oh, yes, Mama is quite well, thank you; everybody is quite well here in Broadbridge, I can reassure you about that. We have had only Mr. Cadgwell die since you were gone, and Edmund said some beautiful things, and I forgot all about him till this moment, though I see his gravestone every day, as Toby is quite curious about it, since it is new. Mrs. Marmeluke had a baby, and Tommy Elphinstone was killed in some horrid war somewhere—but probably you know more about those things than I do, Miss Tomazina."

"You ought to call Tomazina 'Miss Comstock' now, dear," said Mariah.

"Of course! The Miss Comstock who was before has been married; but you know that, because you were still here then. Were you not? Of course you were; I remember you fainted when Miss Comstock—I mean . . . what is her name now?"

"Mrs. Ashleigh," said Mariah.

"Yes, Mrs. Ashleigh. She is Mr. Lucas Ashleigh's wife now, your beautiful sister with all that splendid golden hair! And I do remember how Mr. Ashleigh used to bother us so, Mariah and me, and he used to want to walk by himself with Mariah, and gave me looks as if I ought to go home, and I always wanted to, but Mariah would ask me to stay. And *your* sister is married to him now—I do not approve of it—marriage, you know—but who asks for my approval? I am no one to decide anything for anyone. But still I am glad that Mariah married Edmund instead of Mr. Ashleigh."

"Dear!" said Mariah warningly.

"Oh, do not mind me, Miss Tomazina.—I mean, Miss Comstock.—I do wish people would not complicate things by getting married and changing their names. And not only do their names change, but their next sisters' names. I would never remember to call Mariah 'Mrs. Percy' instead of 'Miss Esquith de Foye,' even if it were required *by law*. And think of me, thrown in prison! All for a name!—Yes, you are Miss Comstock now, I do recall that. But you know, I find that with every day, Sir Toby becomes less and less of a knight, because I keep forgetting to call him 'Sir'; and Mama and Mariah have always taught me to observe people's titles properly, so it feels as if I am wronging him by calling him just 'Toby.'"

Tomazina, expecting a long disquisition, sat down on the sofa again; and she said, "I am sure Sir Toby does not mind such familiarity from you, Miss Brownton."

"I suppose not—that is what people say. They tell me he is only a dog; but to me that phrase, 'only a dog'—it is very silly. It is like saying that someone is 'only an angel'—only in every conceivable way sheer perfection. I wish *I* could be a dog!"

Tomazina could not help smiling at this fancy. "You must be careful what you wish for, Miss Brownton," she said; and Mariah and Edmund laughed.

"Well, if I do become a dog, think of the tricks I shall know!" enthused Miss Brownton. "Even more than Sir Toby. Do you want to see his tricks? We must show you his tricks, so that you will know how well behaved he has become—he is not always quite so naughty as he was just now, rushing about like that—it was only because you are here, and he was excited, because he remembers you and likes you.—I shall show you his tricks."

And with that determination, she compelled earnest Sir Toby to perform a series of maneuvers such as sitting, speaking, shaking hands, rolling over, following her up and down the room on heel, and fetching. "And the most important trick of all," she added after this demonstration, "is not to jump up and get ladies' dresses all muddy. It is Edmund who has taught him all that—I have not the wit for it; though I did teach him to beg for cake very handsomely—watch!" She broke a large crumb from a some food standing on the side table and offered it to the dog, who proved that he did indeed know very much what he was about in that regard.

When this show was concluded, Miss Brownton turned to Tomazina and said, very abruptly: "And how is Mr. Esterbroke?"

There was a strained silence; Tomazina could not help but be even more taken aback than she had been by Mariah's introduction of the topic. Then she gathered her wits and said, "When I last saw him, which was only a week ago yesterday, he was in perfect health, and I have no reason to think he does not continue so." Her own phrase, *when I last saw him,* pierced her bitterly as she spoke it; she could not help wondering if it would be the last time she would ever see him.

"I only asked you," said Miss Brownton, "because we all used to have such fun together. I remember that well! I do not remember things very reliably, but I remember those afternoons in the summerhouse at Hartswound, when you and he would tell me stories. And of course I have the book you both made for me, and I read it every night before I go to sleep; so I think of you then. That has helped me remember, even after all this time."

"Mr. Esterbroke gave me drawing lessons when I was in Gloucestershire," said Tomazina.

"Can you now draw as well as he?"

She laughed. "No, not so well as he can. But I have greatly improved my drawing. I will show you; I shall draw you all. I am determined to keep up my drawing, though I am away from home this month—I mean, away from Hanley Wold."

And so the conversation went on. Tomazina and Mariah did attempt a return to some of the family news, but Miss Brownton continued to interrupt at length as her thoughts flew one way or the other, or went in spirals around the given topic.

Edmund was for the most part quiet, though he paid close attention to everything that was said; but it seemed to Tomazina that he was sunken in a veritable sun of happiness. She guessed or imagined that he could scarcely live a moment without comparing his happiness now to other times when this joy had seemed beyond his grasp. And she could not help daring to think from time to time that if such an unexpected revolution could take place in the lives of Mariah and Edmund, perhaps there was a hope that something similar could happen in her life and Samson's.

And yet this hope, like all her hopes for the love of Samson, was marred by one great bitter reality: and that was that by the mores of her time, she had disgraced herself. Among all the secrets she kept or told, the one she vowed would never pass her lips was the fact that she had dared to propose marriage to a man. Even Mariah, for all the generosity of her affection, would have been shocked at such a thing, and might, if she had known of it, have well agreed that Tomazina had thrown away any chance she had for happiness with Samson Esterbroke.

❋ ❋ ❋

In the early afternoon Tomazina heard Mr. Comstock's voice at the rectory door. She guessed that he had stopped by after some other errand in the village to offer her a ride home in the carriage, and went out into the hallway at once.

"Come, my girl," said Mr. Comstock. "It is beginning to rain again, and if you do not come with me, you will not have a comfortable walk home. Besides, it is growing late."

Edmund, who had followed Tomazina out when he heard who their visitor was, asked him to come into the parlor, but Mr. Comstock would not. "Thank you, sir, thank you," he said to Edmund, "and give my best regards to your wife; but we really must go home at once or we shall be late."

"Let me just say goodbye to Cousin Mariah, Papa," said Tomazina. She went back to the parlor, made her farewells to all there, and then returned to the front door, where her father was now in conversation with Edmund on some parish business.

He broke off to say, "Where is your sister?"

"My sister, Papa?" said Tomazina in surprise.

"Yes, Vita," he said, a little impatiently. "What is keeping her?"

"Vita is not here, sir," said Edmund.

Tomazina added, "She did not come with me, Papa—do you not remember?"

"She did not go with you when you left; but she went after you about two hours ago."

"But she never arrived here," said Tomazina.

"She has not been here all day, sir," said Edmund.

Mr. Comstock was at first almost incredulous; but his disbelief rapidly gave way to alarm. "She said she would follow the path through the park and come straight here," he said.

"She must have gone into the village after all," said Edmund. "She has been delayed there, that is all."

"Let us go look for her," said Tomazina.

"If she should come here in the meantime, I will seek you out in the village, or bring her up to Hartswound myself," said Edmund.

Mr. Comstock, now manifesting considerable anxiety, readily agreed to this course of action; and he barely remembered to bid goodbye to Edmund before he went back to the carriage. He helped Tomazina to enter it and then ordered the driver to go at all good speed toward the village. "You look out on the your side," he told Tomazina, "and I shall look out mine. She cannot be much off the main road."

Fortunately—and unfortunately—it did not take any great effort to find Vita there. Tomazina saw her first: she was standing by the side of the road in the shelter of the great beech tree next to the milliner's shop, in conversation with Mr. Burck. Or rather not conversing *with* him, but listening *to* him—hearing, no doubt, about all the wonders of his person and his good taste; and even as Tomazina caught sight of her, she could see Vita's head nodding in agreement.

"There she is, Father," she said.

He came to her side and she yielded her place to him, though she chose a place that would allow her to peer out the glass.

"With Mr. Burck!" he exclaimed. "Talking to Mr. Burck!"

"Perhaps she could not escape him," said Tomazina.

"She ought never to have come into the village to be accosted by him," said Mr. Comstock.

Mr. Comstock rapped on the carriage roof and the driver drew up beside Vita; who, as she saw she had been caught *in flagrante delicto,* crimsoned to the ears.

Mr. Comstock flung open the door, but did not deign to descend; he only glared at her for a long moment in silence from where he sat. She opened her mouth to offer an excuse, but then quailed, perhaps because any possible explanation would have been either further destructive to his opinion of her or downright deceitful.

"Into the carriage, Vita," he said. She obeyed contritely, and took a seat on the far side of the carriage, quite out of sight of Mr. Burck.

That gentleman now struck a pose Tomazina knew too well: one arm half-akimbo, and the other thrust out before him and resting on the head of his cane, which was canted at a jaunty angle. It was a posture that was intended to declare his self-possession, but suggested rather to Tomazina the existence of a deeper uncertainty and confusion beneath the show.

"Mr. Burck," said Mr. Comstock then, "I requested your departure from our village only yesterday."

Mr. Burck replied, in a defensive tone, "That is so; and I do not recognize your right to do so today any more than I did yesterday."

"Then let me be a little more explicit than I have been heretofore. I have heard of your treatment of my daughter, and I shall not allow you any further communication with her or with any of her sisters. Anyone who could treat a lady so is *not a gentleman.* That is the kindest way to convey my opinion of you."

Mr. Burck began huffing as if he were about to protest this characterization, but Mr. Comstock continued. "I am the justice of the peace in this neighborhood, Mr. Burck. You will find it unpleasant to deal with me. There is a potential charge of assault hanging over you—think on that.

"Assault!" cried Mr. Burck.

"Assault, sir."

"But that is—" Mr. Burck began to protest.

Mr. Comstock, somewhat to Tomazina's surprise, raised his voice and spoke over him.

"I ask you to go back to Gloucestershire or wherever it is you came from," he said. "If you linger here, you will only find yourself doing further damage to your reputation. You cannot save this situation, sir. You had best leave it alone and start your wooings over again elsewhere, and in a more civilized manner."

Then he rapped on the ceiling of the carriage. The driver, as if relishing the opportunity to be rude with impunity to someone of Mr. Burck's grandeur, started away at once, leaving Mr. Burck sputtering protests.

Tomazina felt considerable surprise and even some pride in her father; he was generally very self-effacing in the presence of the wealthy and well-dressed. But she reflected a little sadly that his manner would have been quite different if Mr. Burck had possessed even the most lowly form of purchased knighthood.

She was further surprised when Mr. Comstock opened the window and directed the driver to go not straight home but to Dame Beck's house. That worthy lady, who always sat by her window, periodically glancing over the quiet lane for anything of interest, came out of the house at once at the appearance of the squire, pressing close to the door of the carriage near-sightedly, curtsying and fawning, and quite heedless of the falling mist.

"Good morning to you, Mr. Comstock," she said obsequiously. "And to your lovely daughters, I am sure. Do tell me how someone as humble as I can serve you, sir."

"Good morning, Mrs. Beck," said Mr. Comstock. "I understand that you have staying here with you a certain Mr. Burck?"

"Indeed we do, sir," said Mrs. Beck, perhaps conjecturing that one of the Comstock daughters might be, or might soon be, affianced to her guest. "A gentleman, sir. Very splendid fellow, sir! He is in the village on some business at present; I am not sure what."

"His business is not the business of a gentleman, Mrs. Beck. If you will oblige me, you will turn him out and let him to go elsewhere to cause trouble."

"I never liked him, sir," said Mrs. Beck. "He gives himself very grand airs and complains about everything. And his three valets, sir, as he calls his pompous rascal servants, sit in my kitchen all day, eating my larder out and troubling the girl. I shall see to it that he shall find his bags waiting for him on the doorstep when he comes back, sir."

Mr. Comstock put his hand to his pocket, and Mrs. Beck, with the instinct of one who had long lived by catering to her social betters, came to the side of the carriage immediately. Mr. Comstock handed her down a generous allotment of coin, saying, "This is for the loss of Mr. Burck's custom. You have greatly obliged me, Mrs. Beck; I shall not forget it."

"It is my honor and pleasure, sir, to be of service to you," said Mrs. Beck. She curtsied deeply, and Mr. Comstock, with a final nod to her, called for the driver to move on.

The occupants of the carriage said nothing the entire way home. Tomazina's feelings alternated between pity for Vita, gratitude to her father, and relief that for once she was not the one who was in trouble. When the carriage pulled up before the steps of the house, Mr. Comstock turned to Vita and said, "You will please come with me."

"Yes, sir," said Vita in a faint voice.

Mr. Comstock turned to Tomazina. "And I wish you to be present, too, Tomazina."

"Yes, sir," said Tomazina.

They went into the house like a judge, accused, and accuser who were all proceeding, by some curious circumstance, at the same time and by the same door into the courts of law. Mrs. Comstock and Ursula were in the library when they entered, and sensed at once that something was wrong. Mr. Comstock dismissed the servant in the room and closed the door. He took a chair in a position facing Vita, who knew better than to even attempt to sit down; she stood with her eyes downcast and the crimson steadily mounting into her cheeks. Tomazina went to a chair that was out of her sister's line of vision, hoping to avoid adding to her irritation.

"Do you have any explanation to make?" asked Mr. Comstock.

Clearly Vita had no excuse; she fell back immediately on her old lament: "It is not fair, Papa!" She raised her eyes to his now and began to weep in shame and vexation.

"Not fair? Not fair that you have been warned to stay away from this despicable Mr. Burck? That you deliberately disobeyed me?"

"I did not disobey you *deliberately,* sir—not exactly de-liberately. It was only that after I set out from the house, it seemed so tiresome to walk through the park; and I thought it would do no harm to walk by the road—I thought you could not object to that."

"And somehow when you came to the end of the drive, you went left toward the village, instead of right toward the rectory? How was that not deliberate?"

"Well, I was thinking of something I bespoke from Mrs. Dutton."

"But when the man accosted you, you did not turn away from him and refuse to listen."

"But Papa! He has eight thousand pounds a year, and two very nice houses—he told me all about them."

"I am sure he did! He is preying on you, my dear. It would not take a man of his ilk long to discover what to say to interest a young lady of your inclination. He must merely speak of a pleasant fireside, good sound chambers, a clean kitchen, and a well-kept dairy, and you would be ready to marry him; and the mention of good attics to boot would clinch the deal."

This was harsh; and the most painful part of its force was its truth. Vita wept in earnest now.

"But you have always wanted us to marry well, Papa!" she protested.

To Tomazina's dismay, he turned to her now and snapped his fingers. "Proverbs 16:19," he said.

She knew exactly what he wanted; and though she regretted thus participating in the chastisement of her sister, she had to respond: "*Better it is to be of an humble spirit with the lowly, than to divide the spoil with the proud.*"

"There," said Mr. Comstock, nodding with an air of finality, as if with that quotation he had just exploded Vita's every possible protest. "And I might add, *There is a way that seemeth right to a* woman, *but the end thereof are the ways of death.*—Perhaps you have not heard the whole story. You may not have heard how this man has importuned your sister; how he manhandled her; how he would have broken the close of a gentleman's estate in order to get access to her to compel her to marry him. But even if you were not apprised of this, did it not escape you that he seems to be able to transfer his intentions rather rapidly? Does this not alarm you? Do you not see him for what he is?"

"No," said Vita uncertainly, through his tears. "What is he, Father, that I should not be pleased at his attentions?"

"He is a *collector.* He wants a pretty face to adorn his dinner table. Is this any basis for the joining of a man and woman in the bonds of marriage, which we in our church believe to be most solemn and holy? You cannot think so."

"But Papa," protested Vita, "I have *lost* Mr. Custance. I can make no progress at all with Mr. Hugh Ashleigh. You cannot expect me to be content to wait until *Tomazina* is married. I shall die an old maid if I do that! I must take whom I can get; and if he is odious, so be it! At least I shall have my own house, and eight thousand pounds a year!"

Here, to the great astonishment of them all, Ursula spoke up. "And you must admit, Papa," she said, "that we can meet *no one* so long as we are buried here in Broadbridge. We must get out; we must travel; we must go to London, or Bath at least. You see the evil of expecting young men to come to us. We are forgotten! We are unknown!"

"London!" exclaimed Mr. Comstock in amazement. "I would sooner send you to India! To Botany Bay!"

"That would be an improvement over staying here," said Ursula, beginning to look teary-eyed herself.

"Staying *here?*" repeated Mr. Comstock. "You speak of it as if this were a prison. Is Hartswound not one of the finest houses in all of England? Is that such a terrible cross to bear?"

"It is a good house in itself, but it is not as if it does *us* any good," said Ursula.

"Not do us any good?" repeated Mr. Comstock in dismay. "Did the Lord not provide it specifically for the purpose of raising our state in this county and finding you all husbands? Is this not an answer to a prayer fervently raised to God by your mother and me throughout your girlhood?"

Once Mr. Comstock had brought God into the argument on his side, there was nothing Ursula or Vita could say against him; they did not share in Tomazina's ability to spit forth biblical proof-texts.

He continued, pressing his point. "Did you not have a ball here—at Hartswound—last winter? And much against my own scruples, I might point out. Did you not go to—I do not know how many dances last winter with your cousin, and the winter before? Did your mother and I not dutifully accept every invitation to dinner that might bring you into good company?" He turned now to Vita and said: "And you would throw away all this effort on your behalf by conversing with a despicable mock-gentleman like Mr. Burck? There is no better way to ruin your chances among people of good standing." He paused a moment, softening under the effect of Vita's weeping, and said, in a milder tone, "Now, look—we have made very good connections in this society. Mr. Percy is of very good family. There is considerable good will still attaching to Mrs. Percy, not only because of her own virtue and beauty, but because of her own ancient blood and house. She is our cousin, and has generously accepted us, though we took this very house away from her; and in doing so, she has set the example for all the good folk of the country round. Mrs. Alton, too, is an admirable lady, and she favors us, as does Mrs. Brownton, who is widely known and loved as a humble and good and most Christian lady. The Ashleighs have paid us every attention, to the point of engaging in an alliance of marriage with us. We are well-embarked—one of you is married already, and we have not been in this house two years. Be patient, Vita, dear. Give the Lord time to work in your behalf. Bend your knee and bend your prayers in His direction; give yourself into His keeping, and all will go well."

Again he had entered into an unassailable argument, and Vita could make no attempt to refute it. But she had not the inner strength and humility of character to express her contrition effectively, as Tomazina would have done, so she only sniffled, and wiped her eyes, and wrung her hands, and somehow through all this conveyed the impression that she was really sorry only for her present embarrassment, and not for what she had done. However, she did manage to say, "I am sorry, Papa. I shall try to be more patient. I promise you I shall never disobey you again about Mr. Burck. It was very wicked of me, very wicked—though I did not mean it—but it is not fair: Tomazina gets every chance—all the chances—and she throws them all away. She goes to Brackensom and she goes to Gloucestershire. She has even been through Bath, Papa! One of these days she will send us a letter from London, or Paris, without so much as asking your leave for going there. And Ursula and I must stay here."

"I shall hear no more about it," said Mr. Comstock.

Vita held her peace; she sensed, perhaps, that she had scored as many points as she could.

"Let this be the last we speak of this," said Mr. Comstock.

"Mr. Burck has been turned out of Mrs. Beck's. If he dares to shift to the inn, I shall have him thrown out of that place as well. There will be no place for him to stay in Broadbridge. He can stay in Ambledon if he wishes, but at least that will be more inconvenient to his purposes. Until we are quite sure he has left us alone, you are not to go into the village by yourselves, you or Ursula. Is that understood?"

"Yes, Papa," said Vita.

"And you understand that, too, Ursula?" Mr. Comstock asked.

"Yes, sir," said Ursula.

"And I know I need not speak to Tomazina on this point," said Mr. Comstock. "That is an end of it. Let us change for dinner. You girls go ahead. I wish to speak with your mother about this privately."

The three sisters went out of the room as they were told and ascended the stairs without a word to one another. Vita was still, despite her show of contrition, resentful against Tomazina, as she demonstrated in her bearing toward her. Ursula, by contrast, paused to give Tomazina a kiss before they parted to go to their separate rooms.

"Tommie," she said then, "promise me that if you ever do marry away, you will invite me to visit you at your house."

"Of course I shall, dear," said Tomazina.

"Though I suppose Vita is right," said Ursula, with a little of Tomazina's own bluntness. "At the rate you are going, you will never be wed."

And with this unintended thrust at her sister's heart, she went away to dress for dinner.

❁ ❁ ❁

On the day after the second brouhaha about Mr. Burck, the house was considerably quieter. Vita and Ursula sat with their mother in the upstairs parlor, evincing a hopelessness so oppressive that Tomazina eventually had to escape from it. She took some drawing paper to the library and sat at a table there, sketching a view of the room and the portion of the garden visible through the Venetian doors, and drifting from time to time into daydreams of Samson. The drawing, while it was actually in progress, was going very well: the room was shady, and the light outside was bright, and the effect of inner coolness and outer warmth was visually very interesting.

Mr. Comstock had gone out on some business; when he returned he passed through the library on his way to his study. Tomazina rose respectfully and he paused to speak with her.

"I visited Mr. Eaton just now," he said, evincing not only displeasure, but even distaste. "It seems that we shall have to observe more caution in the comings and goings of all you girls until Mr. Burck leaves Broadbridge."

"Then he is still here?"

"He is indeed, and apparently he intends to stay."

"But where is he lodging?"

Her father gave her a look that told his frustration with the situation. "You will scarce believe me when I tell you. He is staying at the Eatons'."

"No! At Mr. Eaton's own house?"

"Yes. I am shocked at the fellow. I discovered Mr. Burck shirking about the village and went directly to Mr. Eaton to discuss our next recourse. He seemed oddly resistant to my complaint, so I again explained the entire history of the man, and how he had treated you; and Eaton sat there with complete effrontery and said that he had been to see Mr. Burck on receipt of my letter the other day and had heard his side of the story."

"And believed it?" guessed Tomazina.

"Apparently he prefers to believe it. He maintains Mr. Burck's right as a free Englishman to go where he pleases, when he pleases, and says that I exceeded my authority in having him ejected from Dame Beck's."

"This is treachery indeed! And did I not hear that the Eatons came to the ball here last winter? And how many times have they dined at Hartswound?"

"A good half-dozen, I should say. But his treachery is one thing; that he should take such a viper into his midst is still more amazing. And with all his daughters!"

Tomazina suddenly had a new perspective on the situation, and she looked at her father to see if he had had a similar insight; but he only remained as he was, frowning and perplexed.

"Papa," she said, "I think we may understand Mr. Eaton a little better if we remember those daughters."

He looked at her in surprise, not comprehending her for a moment; and then understanding arrived. "Do you think that is it?" he said.

"I do think so."

There was a rumor, a very faint one, but a rumor nonetheless, that Mr. Eaton's eldest daughter Cornelia had gotten into trouble with a certain officer. It had all been hushed up. Tomazina had asked Mariah about it, but for some reason not even Mariah, who had a weakness for good gossip, could be brought to talk on the subject. In itself, however, the extremity of the compassion for Miss Eaton that Mariah often evinced made Tomazina suspicious. If there ever had been such an incident, Mr. Eaton must feel that his family had been tainted, and that the only possibility of a marriage for any of his daughters must lie in some stranger to the area who had not heard the whispers.

Miss Cornelia Eaton was, in the days before the Comstock sisters had come to Broadbridge, the acknowledged beauty of the village—after Miss de Foye; a qualifier that had produced more than a little envy and dislike on the part of the inferior. Mrs. Alton had told Tomazina an entertaining story about trying to marry Edmund off to Miss Eaton at one point. "Fortunately," she had concluded, "Edmund saw right away that Miss Eaton, for all her corn-colored hair, her languid blue eyes, and her luscious *embonpoint*, was too impenetrably stupid to be a desirable partner. Her greatest ambition in the world is to lounge on a divan and eat chocolates. She has lately found even dancing to be a bit strenuous." Edmund had, it seemed, been saved from any further expectations in that quarter mainly by Miss Eaton's sudden engagement to her mysterious officer.

Tomazina herself had never managed to get very far towards a friendship with Miss Eaton. She had found the young woman to be of that sort who creates a sensation among men when she initially appears in a room, and provokes a certain awe in women; until she speaks. And then, almost immediately, the men desert her for the billiard tables and the card games, and the women raise their eyebrows smugly at one another and set about seeing if they can provoke her into some especially bald expression of her stupidity. Within twenty minutes, she has been utterly abandoned, except for her mother and sisters, and sits more alone and disliked than ever would have been her fate if she had been unpresumptuously homely. It is an odd phenomenon, somewhat like the cool revulsion animals in a pen suddenly display when they sense that one of their companions is deathly sick. To Tomazina's every attempt at starting a topic, Miss Cornelia Eaton would reply with something silly, arrogant, and self-centered. She made Miss Doronne look brilliant by comparison; for Cornelia Eaton was barely clever enough to be grasping or to pursue what she wanted. She expected Fortune to come to her, never realizing that that goddess can only be enticed within arms' length with great effort, and even then is only rarely caught, and by one greasy forelock.

Not even against such a stupid young woman, however, could Tomazina wish the success of the cold matrimonial calculations of Mr. Burck. But she thought Miss Eaton safe from them; for if he had once aspired to her own hand, how could he possibly settle for Miss Eaton's?

And so we set ourselves up to be insulted when we see what kind of fools our rejected partners choose when they cannot have us.

❁ ❁ ❁

On the following Monday, a week after her return from Gloucestershire, Tomazina went to give back the nightgown she had taken from Mariah's room at Brackensom over a year before. She had hidden it among her things when she returned from that journey, and having only now rediscovered it, had penitently mended it and washed it with her own hands.

In order to heighten the plausibility of her show of nonchalance in the whole matter, she took Ursula with her, and stopped into the rectory after visiting elsewhere. Of course she still must to explain to Mariah how the nightgown had come into her possession, with some necessary amplification of some parts of the story, and omission of others; but she got through this exercise with minimal blushing. And of that Mariah said, "Cuz, only you would feel the least chagrin at having temporarily forgotten to complete an act you had undertaken out of pure, spontaneous kindness of heart." Tomazina let this analysis of her embarrassment stand without correction.

This conversation had just taken place and the three young women were sitting together, pleased with this agreeable emotional appetizer, and looking forward to discussing for the thousandth time the wonders of the *baby* (who was napping, oblivious to their eagerness to praise her, in a little cradle by the sofa), when the serving girl entered the room to announce Miss Cornelia Eaton. This was quite surprising, and out of curiosity, if for no other reason, Mariah must admit to being at home; and so Miss Eaton was shown in.

Miss Eaton had that supercilious bearing that impresses one not so much with its pride as its sheer dullness. She could not be credibly proud; the attempt at hauteur must make her seem merely more silly. The Comstock sisters had learned all about true pride from their cousin Mariah; this pretence of superiority in Miss Eaton was, by contrast, at best only puzzling. What did she mean, entering with her head high in that way, and taking in Mariah with that air of—was it triumph?—and then observing Tomazina, with a faint brightening of her expression, as if the presence of another rival only made her sense of success all that much more complete? Of Ursula she took absolutely no more notice than she did of the chairs and tables.

"Good morning, Miss Eaton," said Mariah. "How kind of you to stop in and see us."

Miss Eaton did not vouchsafe a reply. She had stopped on the edge of the carpet in the little parlor and now turned her face this way and that, but without seeming to see anything—like an automaton. It was almost as though she had been asked to show her face from several angles.

"Good morning," added Tomazina, more by way of testing Miss Eaton to see how rude she might be than out of any impulse to politeness. Ursula, too, added her greeting; and Miss Eaton persisted in her silence. She did, however, sit down, facing more toward her hostess than anyone else, but obliquely even to her.

"You must forgive me for not offering you tea," said Mariah. "Sally has only just now cleared away the breakfast things."

Miss Eaton seemed to signify, by her complete lack of a response, that this omission was of no matter.

"And how are you this morning?" asked Mariah. Apparently in this she hit upon an approvable topic.

"Very well," said Miss Eaton, with emphasis.

After a silence: "And your family?"

"Very well." With less emphasis.

"Your brother James and his wife?"

"Very well." No emphasis at all this time.

"And has he finished his reading in the law?"

Miss Eaton's momentary silence seemed to protest this unfair requirement of a new form of answer. "Not yet," she said.

"Ah. It must be difficult for them. But both young Mr. Eaton and Miss Morgana Caits always were favorites in Broadbridge. I am sure their families and friends will support them in every way until he has established himself in practice with your father. And I have heard that Mrs. Caits was able to be quite generous to her daughter when she married."

"Yes," said Miss Eaton.

There was another silence, much longer this time.

"Perhaps we ought to have some tea after all," said Mariah.

Miss Eaton seemed not to hear this suggestion; but some automatic mechanism seemed to have finally clicked within her, and she began to talk at last.

"You will not have heard our news," she said. Tomazina realized now that this was the reason Miss Eaton had entered with such a triumphal air—she had some news that she expected her rivals should all know by now; and only her realization that they did not yet know it had loosed the gates of her speech.

Mariah was uncertain how to answer Miss Eaton's accusation of their ignorance, and looked briefly at Tomazina, who looked back at her with a comprehension only just dawning.

"No, most likely we have not heard it," said Mariah.

"I have accepted the addresses of a gentleman who has been staying with us since Thursday—Mr. Burck."

Mariah was surprised into a betrayal of several conflicting feelings, the foremost of which seemed to be a kind of anguished pity; but these emotions went no further in expression than her face.

"Ah!" she said. "Then ought we to congratulate you? Yes—of course—we ought to congratulate you."

"I believe you do not know Mr. Burck, Mrs. Percy."

"No—I have not made his acquaintance. I believe he has been staying in town for . . . for several days now, is it not?"

"Yes; he has been staying with my family since Thursday," Miss Eaton repeatedly pointlessly, or perhaps to emphasize the rapidity of her conquest. "It was thus that I met him."

Miss Eaton's gaze took in Tomazina for a moment. She must have interpreted the pallor of horror on Tomazina's face for something like chagrin.

"He came to Broadbridge for an altogether different purpose," Miss Eaton said. "But having once come, and sat at meals with us, and sat with us in the evening, he changed his plans."

"How . . . how very fortunate for you," said Mariah. "And of course, for him. He is lucky to have won your favor, Miss Eaton."

"Indeed," said Tomazina with impulsive bluntness, "you are much too good for him, Miss Eaton."

Miss Eaton gave her another flickering glance, as if to assess the damage she was doing.

"Mr. Burck is very wealthy," she said, to no one in particular.

There was a very long silence, which Mariah finally seemed to feel she must break. "That is very useful," she said.

"Eight thousand pounds a year; a house in London and another in Gloucestershire; and a very fine coach and four, which you may have seen about the village."

"Very useful," said Mariah. Having hit upon this inoffensive phrase, she seemed willing to employ it as often as necessary.

"Mr. Burck is talking of giving up the house in Gloucestershire, however; he is talking about Kent, which I shall not at all mind."

"Kent is beautiful, of course," said Mariah.

"We are to be married here in Broadbridge."

"Of course. How very pleasant that will be."

"Mr. Burck wants to be married in London. He says it is very fashionable these days. But Papa and Mama will insist upon my marrying from home."

"How very useful and pleasant," said Mariah, uncharacteristically caught at wits' end for a reply.

"Mr. Burck has given me this very handsome ring," said Miss Eaton, as she began to draw off one glove. "He went to Winchester on purpose to buy it." With a surprising amount of effort, she bared one plump little hand and raised it to show the ring to them. The gold stood out darkly on the pearly evanescence of her flesh. Mariah made appreciative noises. "You will want to look at it more closely," said Miss Eaton.

"Oh, absolutely," said Mariah. "I do indeed." She made no attempt to go to Miss Eaton, however, and Miss Eaton made no effort to come to her. As for Tomazina, she was not about to make an effort to view anything given by Mr. Burck. Ursula, seeing that no one else was moving, felt it was incumbent upon her to do these honors; she rose from her chair and went to admire the ring.

"How very tasteful!" she said cleverly. Tomazina had told her how Mr. Burck prided himself on his good taste.

"Oh, I assure you, Mr. Burck has the best of taste," said Miss Eaton. "In clothing, in jewelry, in everything."

"And certainly in his choice of a bride," said Mariah, with uncharacteristic hypocrisy. Tomazina was a little puzzled at her cousin's behavior; this was going beyond mere neighborly affability.

"Oh, yes," said Miss Eaton languidly. "Certainly in his choice of a bride." And she looked deliberately at Tomazina as she said this.

Tomazina opened her mouth to say something violently tart about how the ring and the bride were doubtless both great bargains; but even as she began to speak, Mariah gave her a look of grieving appeal that arrested her.

"You were going to say something, Miss Comstock?" asked Miss Eaton smugly.

"I was going to say . . . that the ring is lovely and well becomes you. I might even compare you, as Mr. Burck's future bride, to the splendor and . . . value of that ring. I wish you the very greatest happiness in your marriage, Miss Eaton. It is a splendid match for you both. I knew Mr. Burck, as I am sure you know, when I was in Gloucestershire this spring; but we never . . . agreed."

Miss Eaton did not answer this comment. It was unlikely that she had the wit to know how to make a response. She looked away from all of them; she seemed a little angry, as if Tomazina had diminished her triumph by not being piqued.

"It is a very splendid match," said Mariah with sudden enthusiasm. "It is beyond splendid. Just think! Eight thousand pounds a year!"

"It is wonderful," said Ursula helpfully; and finding Mariah's example to be impressive, added, "Such an income will be very useful!"

"And a carriage and four!" Mariah went on. "How I envy you, Miss Eaton! And houses in London and Kent! To think that we grew up together in this little village, and you will be going off to live in a grand house, while I shall stay behind!"

All these sentiments were so utterly false that both Tomazina and Ursula looked at Mariah in wonder.

"Yes," said Miss Eaton in a tone that contrived to be both pointed and languid.

There was then complete silence. Neither side had the faintest idea how to further converse with the other. Mariah did eventually make valiant attempts at small talk, unassisted by anyone but Ursula; but in the middle of a conversation about the weather, Miss Eaton rose to go. Her purpose had been accomplished.

"I think I shall go home," she said. "The sun comes into the parlor about this time, and it is perfect spot for a nap. I love little naps." She looked at Tomazina and added, "They help one keep one's looks, you know."

What is that *supposed to mean?* wondered Tomazina. *Am I to have lost Mr. Burck because I have lost my looks? You poor, stupid thing!*

Mariah was effusive in her farewells and good wishes.

"I suppose Mr. Burck will be by soon to see Mr. Percy about the arrangements," said Miss Eaton. "For the wedding, you know." It was the only farewell she would make; she glided out of the room without attempting to close the door behind her, and in a moment they heard her exit at the front.

Tomazina rose from her seat, crossed the room to close the door against the servants' hearing, and said: "How I wish *another lady* I know were so lazy and stupid! She would not so easily impose on *a certain someone* if she were!"

"Whom do you mean, Tommie?" asked Ursula in amazement.

"Oh—no one you know, dear," said Tomazina, catching herself belatedly.

"Do not speak of poor Miss Eaton that way," said Mariah sadly.

"'Poor Miss Eaton'! I do not understand you, Mariah. She has never treated you with anything like the courtesy you deserve. And since when are you one to be reconciled to a lady's marriage to an idiot by the amount of money he brings with him?"

"It is a good match for her," said Mariah.

"It is a miserable match for anyone!" exclaimed Tomazina. "What *is* it, Mariah? You have always given Miss Eaton the benefit of some mysterious goodness that none of the rest of us can see; or else you pity her for something beyond her sheer stupidity."

"Come sit beside me, and I shall tell you," said Mariah in a quiet voice.

Tomazina, baffled, did as she was told.

"And Ursula, dear," said Mariah, "you must promise never to breathe a word of this to anyone."

"Of course," said Ursula, with all the eagerness of the youngest sibling who is finally being allowed to partake of adult mysteries.

Mariah took Tomazina's hand somewhat absently and held it while she spoke. "It is just that Miss Eaton and I were both . . . ill-treated by the same man. At the same time, no less. I think Miss Eaton knows nothing of this—knows nothing of the fact that I shared the same degradation she did. But *I* know it—I know it of myself and I know it of her. So I am glad that she has made this match. Mr. Burck is a wretched fool, I am sure, and he is not likely to be very kind to her, if what you say of him is true—and I have no reason to doubt what you say. But at least it is a match. She will be able to live well all the years of her life. I have been concerned about her. I think she would have been a great burden to others if she had never married—she is not one to endear herself to those who would be supporting her. She is too lazy, as you say, and no one likes to be with such a person. She would likely have wound up living with her brother James and dear Morgana Caits that was; and though I can scarcely think of anyone who would have borne with her better than Morgana, still it would have been difficult for them all."

Suddenly Tomazina had a vision of herself, living as spinster aunt with Rose Elizabeth. When she thought of Rose Elizabeth, and any children her sister might have, she did not mind it as much; but when she thought of the necessity of watching in silence how Mr. Ashleigh treated Rose Elizabeth, she felt sick at heart. And the further idea that her presence—as a witness to how Mr. Ashleigh behaved—might thereby be a burden to Rose Elizabeth made her suddenly begin to worry about her future.

"I am sorry I spoke disparagingly of her," she said. "I should have trusted you to have good reasons, Mariah. You always do. God bless you; and may God make me a better Christian—since I seem to be doing a very poor job of it myself."

"Well," said Ursula stoutly, "I, for one, mean to get married—if there is any possible way. I for one do not intend to wind up a maiden aunt on someone else's charges. I could not endure it; and I *do* want so to get out and see the world. I do not think Mr. Burck is much of a catch; but when you consider how few eligible men come through Broadbridge, I think Miss Eaton has done very well for herself. If only I could get away—go to some watering-place—to Bath, if no farther. I am sure I could meet someone suitable."

"We shall have to see to it that you do," said Mariah comfortingly.

"Oh, Papa will never allow it," said Ursula unhappily. "I might as well have stayed at Pilgrim's Rest for all the good coming to Broadbridge has done my future."

And so might I have done, thought Tomazina. She was surprised to find that this bitter reality was still operative in her life, even after she had put her infatuation with Edmund behind her.

Chapter 42

Have you not heard it said full oft
A woman's nay doth stand for naught?

—Shakespeare

For all Miss Eaton's smug triumph in the announcement of her forthcoming union with Mr. Burck, her engagement was to all appearances very short lived. The fiancé insisted on a wedding in a high (but not too high) style in London; the fiancée's parents somewhat incautiously insisted on a wedding in Broadbridge; and suddenly Mr. Burck was gone in a huff. Miss Eaton was said to be utterly shocked and overcome, or devastated, as we would say today; which state she evidenced by sleeping nearly all the time, or at least by keeping to her bed or couch and pretending to. She did, however, rise for fairly healthy meals, at which she glared at her parents as one betrayed. Mariah heard all this through her usual invisible sources of information, and relayed it to Tomazina, though without her usual zest.

"Ah," said Tomazina sarcastically, "Mr. Burck is too much a perfectionist! It is not enough that he has Miss Eaton for a bride; he must have a London wedding."

In any case, Mr. Burck seemed finally to have departed from Tomazina's life. That was good; but his exit by means of a brief betrothal to someone infinitely less intelligent than herself was, however poetically just, strangely disconcerting.

She felt in this, and in other respects of her return to Hampshire, as if she had come into a foreign country, in which the values and customs of the natives were inexplicable to her, and often diametrically opposed to her own. It was just a feeling; if she confronted it rationally, it proved fugitive and would not stay in custody long enough to be interrogated and forced to confess its untruth. But still she felt it—as if she did not belong; as if she were a supernumerary gear in the clock of human relations; as if life would go on here in its inexorable way, including Tomazina Comstock if she allowed it to do so, but perfectly content to proceed without her if she did not. She felt at times as if her parents' and sisters' lives were led with a strange indifference to hers, as if her family did not know who she was, as if they could not see her in their midst. Likewise Mr. Burck, who had in Gloucestershire seemed to think she was an indispensable part of his future, had found—and within a matter of days of his landing on the shores of Hampshire—that she was not so very needful at all.

Even her new relationships with her cousins contributed to the sense she now had that the place to which she had returned was not the place she had left. The exalted opinion she had had of Edmund and Mariah had shrunken to a more realistic appraisal. She had always observed that there were some people in the world (a very few) who treated Edmund as an ordinary rector, and Mariah as no more than an ordinary rector's wife; and even some who said mean things behind their backs, as if Mr. and Mrs. Percy were in any way within the sphere of mundane gossip. In the past, Tomazina had been able only to stare at this behavior in incomprehension. To her in those times, the language that was to be used in describing her cousins must consist solely of nouns of eminence and of superlative adjectives. But now, though she continued to think this meanness mistaken and repulsive, she could see how some people might misunderstand her cousins. It was true that her own assessment of Edmund and Mariah, being now more realistic, had gained the blessing of being more comfortable. She did not look at Edmund with pain; she returned Mariah's affection quite naturally. But this alteration left her feeling paradoxically alienated.

And the strangest thing of all was that she sometimes felt alienated from herself here. She had *been someone* in

Gloucestershire—someone better and more alive and interesting—but was she still that same person? She felt more narrow now; and as a more narrow person, perhaps she deserved only a narrow and limited future—a future without a sky, a future in which the blissful blue of promise was blocked from her sight. She cycled through the various modes of her hurt again, sometimes in the compass of a day, sometimes within the compass of an hour: she felt her anguish over the loss of Samson more than she perceived her enduring love for him; she felt her rejectedness more than her forgiveness of him; she felt a kind of petty vengeance carrying her along, and she vowed to show him that she was not unwanted in this world. She became, in fact, a little like Miss Eaton, insofar as her rejection by one man might make her willing to accept another, howsoever bad he might be.

And this was a dangerous set of feelings to indulge, because there was in fact another man standing by to take advantage of them—someone considerably more attractive than Mr. Burck; someone already a part of her life and her larger family circle; someone who, before she had left the confines of Pilgrim's Rest, might well have been a very interesting suitor to her.

She soon realized that she need only give Mr. Hugh Ashleigh one smile at just the right time to provoke a declaration from him. She was certain of this. It would not be hard to communicate her approval, if she ever felt it. If necessary, she could say one word to Rose Elizabeth; Rose Elizabeth would speak to Mr. Ashleigh; and Mr. Ashleigh would tell his brother. And Mr. Hugh Ashleigh would be riding over from Ransome Field within a quarter of an hour of hearing the news. She could be mistress of Ransome Field within a matter of weeks. She might yet bear a child before even Rose Elizabeth; and the bearing of a child was a desideratum that had been growing on her more and more lately, as it generally will when young women start seeing others their age beginning to have babies.

Furthermore, if she lived at Ransome Field, she might make sure of her companionship with her sister for their rest of their lives; and considering her disappointing experience with men, this was something that seemed increasingly important to her. If all eligible men were to prove fools, should she not reserve for herself the company of good women?

And now, in these first weeks of June, Hugh Ashleigh sought to please her as he never had before. He was kind and quietly attentive in every way; his adoration of her was obvious and unremitting. Vita could make eyes at him all through dinner, and he did not even perceive her. More than that, he did that thing that appeals to a woman more than any other: he tried to make himself a better person for her sake. He read some history and spoke intelligently about the war with the French; he discussed the faults and virtues of Admiral Nelson with some sense. He attended the church in Broadbridge, actually listened to Edmund's sermon, and spoke about it with her afterward. He avoided the excesses of male activity common in his time—he drank less, he preferred to attend her rather than to play cards—and for whatever reason, it seemed he smelled less of tobacco and horse sweat than he had previously. When he could not sit near her, he watched her; when he could not speak with her, he spoke with kindness and consideration to others. He quite won over her father and mother, who were very pleased with his comportment toward them. Rose Elizabeth, too, said that he was particularly sweet to her in these days, and even Ursula related something about his unconsciously gallant treatment of her.

Thus began a little war in Tomazina's heart. It is a war that has been waged often enough where women dwell; and as in the case of all wars, the makers of it were men. On one side was Samson, and on the other, Mr. Hugh Ashleigh. She wanted Samson implicitly, and she had to try hard to imagine ever wanting Mr. Hugh Ashleigh. But a marriage, and particularly in those times, was not necessarily a matter of love, but a matter of practicality. Samson had walked away from her affection; Hugh Ashleigh avidly offered her his. Samson had little, and his living was uncertain; Hugh Ashleigh possessed a wealth that was already large and, by all accounts, growing by leaps. Samson was elsewhere, doing she knew not what, and the place where he would live his life was uncertain to her; Hugh Ashleigh was here, now, and settled in proximity to Rose Elizabeth. If she went on waiting for Samson, she might die as she had come to dread—virginal; if she took Hugh Ashleigh, she would know a man, in the biblical sense; and she would bear babies, she would raise children of her own.

She was at this time only four-and-twenty years of age. Perhaps that seems youthful now; but to people of that era, it did not. Fewer people then lived to great age. And besides, four-and-twenty led on to five-and-twenty soon enough, and five-and-twenty somehow led on very rapidly to thirty; and by thirty, a woman of that era was acknowledged a spinster. And the young feel a pressure of time that is in some ways even more intense than that felt by the elderly. They want to get on with life—they have waited long enough, under the control of their parents, and they want to start doing and being, they want to be actors in their own personal drama.

In Tomazina's case there was the added pressure of her sexuality. She did on occasion look at Mr. Hugh Ashleigh and think what it would be like to make love with him; and so great was her craving for the act, and so isolated was her lust from her love, that she could actually imagine this scene and not be utterly repulsed by it. He was very good looking—in some objective sense, perhaps, he was better looking than Samson, and though she never once thought him so, she was aware that others did, and that judgment did not harm him in her eyes. Some people are, after all, insane in what they will do and endure to have the company of a good-looking spouse; and though the cause of this is one of the great mysteries of the human mind, it operates in us all to some extent.

But how came it, the romantics cry, that Tomazina was able to repress, even for a moment, her longing to be known, truly known, in the personal sense, by whatever man she would marry? With Samson she had the potential for a shared life of the soul; with Mr. Hugh Ashleigh, she had no possibility of such a life.

She understood that in general we never know all of someone, and are never wholly known by any other. Our personalities are, at least in respect to the way in which they are known, as if compartmentalized, divided by rigid, watertight bulkheads. For example, of all the people in the world who knew Tomazina, she would have pointed to Rose Elizabeth as most privy to her heart; and yet the knowledge Rose Elizabeth had of her was acutely limited. Her sister knew nothing, absolutely nothing, of Tomazina's intense preoccupation with sexual matters. Tomazina could, perhaps, have talked about this preoccupation with Mariah, but there too, she could readily see that another aspect of her personality—that is, her impulsiveness—would remain forever closed and unimaginable to her cousin. Mariah would never, never, have deliberately disclosed her heart to a man unasked, as Tomazina had done. Sooner would she have perished of longing, or killed herself, than endure such a shame.

With this insight, Tomazina began to grasp a further pattern of human behavior: that when we are young, sometimes we open our hearts and disclose our secrets to others who have no desire to know them; whereas, as we grow older, we become more cautious. And so it is that later marriages are often at least superficially happier. In them we know how to tell and show only so much and no more; we never force our spouses to look into the dark and unimaginable parts of us that they do not want to see. Make no mistake: these parts may be good as well as bad. A man who has, in the long absences of his atheistical wife on business, inadvertently become a believer in some religion—for there are many ways in which a man may stray when his wife neglects him, and not all infidelities involve adultery—such a man will be careful not to let his wife know about his new passion; he will have plausible excuses for his pious reading, he will pray quite literally in his closet if he must. Or perhaps his new interests are neither good nor bad, but simply trivial—he becomes obsessed with some actress he has seen in a film, or he builds model trains, or he begins writing a very bad detective novel. Or he might, like Tomazina, have learned in his wife's absence how to live in his imagination as never before. If our loved ones truly knew all our desires, they would be shocked and disgusted and pained beyond their enduring; but with age we finally become wise enough to spare them this. We let those who love us dwell in their illusions about us; and meanwhile we live in the vault and fortress of our thoughts, secure in the fact that our life there, no matter how wild and unrestrained, whether in vice or in virtue, can never be known. So it is in marriages where secrets cannot be shared.

Tomazina, young though she was, realized that if she was to marry Mr. Hugh Ashleigh, it would have to be on these terms. She had perhaps a premature grasp of the importance of this concealment because she had been practicing it to some extent all her life. Her own sketchbook and that of Samson, for instance, were kept scrupulously locked and hidden; they were brought out only for her lonely orgies of sense and imagination after the household had retired to bed. What she did in those hours, and even more, what she dreamed then of doing with a man, were beyond the grasp of anyone else in the house, beyond the imagination of anyone in her entire acquaintance, with the exception only of Samson and possibly of her cousins. By day she was again as she had always been: scrupulously polite, if somewhat hasty in the expressions of her thought at times; affectionate and respectful towards her parents and her sisters; unaffectedly thoughtful and kind to her inferiors, properly deferential toward her superiors in society and in age; she was, as people had always said of her before this difficult time, a lively, pretty, engaging *girl,* albeit impulsive. Only a few people—her cousins and the Hanscoms and also Mrs. Alton—had ever suspected that there were deeper forces at work in her, powerful and confused and unsettled and joyful and sad forces; and even those few who guessed at it were never given license to speak with her about her deeper self. As for Mr. Hugh Ashleigh, he never suspected the existence of any such thing. He was incapable of imagining that a person might have such depths; and if he had ever glimpsed her secrets, he would have dismissed them as female silliness. The incomprehensible is often actually invisible; or to put the same thing another way, what we do not understand in another, we often refuse to see. Tomazina guessed that she could live within the veil of his ignorance without Mr. Hugh Ashleigh's ever discerning that his wife was someone other than a mere surface. Why not? She had lived undiscerned by her family and friends all her life. Why should a husband be any different? Why should she *ask* a husband to be any different? Perhaps that was asking more than God ever granted.

❁ ❁ ❁

When the proposal came, about two weeks after her return to Hampshire, it was cleverly managed. In retrospect Tomazina could see that the Ashleigh brothers had been looking for this opportunity almost since her arrival but had been thwarted by circumstances.

It was a very fair, if cool, Monday morning; they appeared in the drive in the barouche landau and sent Rose Elizabeth inside to invite the Comstock sisters for a ride and a picnic. Mr. Comstock, as the Ashleighs certainly knew, had left the house early, on his way to Winchester. They could not have known that Mrs. Comstock was indisposed and wished only to stay alone in a dark room all day; in that respect they were only lucky.

The invitation put Vita and Ursula in an extremity of delight, and they ran about the house chattering together as they got ready. Tomazina, although tempted by the outing, declined, perhaps on some premonition of its purpose that actually led her to fall into the very trap she was trying to avoid. Rose Elizabeth tried particularly hard to persuade her, but she would not listen; she went on sitting on the sofa in the library, working on a sketch from her imagination. It was turning out particularly nicely; and she was thinking how she would like—someday and somehow—to show it to Samson. A ride in a crowded barouche landau could not compete with this bittersweet pleasure.

She expected more pressure to be applied to her, and was relieved when the party went away with great gaiety and left her to her own thoughts. She heard the account from Ursula later: how the carriage had not gone two hundred feet down the drive when Mr. Hugh Ashleigh had called a halt, declaring he could not bear to leave Miss Comstock indoors alone on such a lovely day, and that he would go back to try to persuade her himself. In the meantime they should go on, at least to the end of the drive, and return for him later. Vita was very much distressed at this plan, but he listened to no objections. He opened the door of the barouche landau, jumped down to the ground, and strode away without so much as a single look back, and his brother called for the carriage to move on, "as if it had been a settled thing that Mr. Hugh Ashleigh should do so from the moment they left home," added Ursula wonderingly.

Tomazina, sitting in the library still, paid no attention when she heard the front door open; she thought it was some footman about his tasks. Nor did the sound of steps making directly for the library arrest her. It was only when the library door was closed behind the man that she looked up in surprise and saw Mr. Hugh Ashleigh.

"Sir," she said.

He bowed.

"Have you not left yet? I thought I heard the carriage depart."

He smiled diffidently and came toward her. She was a little alarmed at his look, but he came on so rapidly that she did not have time to collect her thoughts and rise. He came very close to her, very close; and before she knew it, he had fallen on one knee before her and seized her hands. The sketching easel in her lap slipped to one side and nearly fell to the floor, but she managed to get her left hand free—he would not release both—and stopped its slide. He immediately took her hand again and held it tightly. It was absurd: in her right hand she was still clutching a pencil.

"Miss Comstock," he said; and then he looked into her face, which must have shown both surprise and displeasure—and words failed him.

There was a long moment of consternation. She pulled her hands free, put aside the pencil, and made an attempt to rise; but he was kneeling so directly in front of her, with his body literally pressing against her legs, that she was unable to do so; and besides, he seized her hands yet again and used them to hold her down.

"Miss Comstock," he said again, "I am on my knees before you." This seemed to be part of some speech, previously composed but now only half-remembered, to which he was resorting under the duress of the moment.

"That is only a half-truth, sir," she said tartly. "You are on one knee."

He promptly put the other knee beneath him as well; and pressing more tightly against her, and apparently abandoning any hope of recalling or delivering his set speech, he said, "Miss Comstock, do not deny me. You know what I want; I want you to marry me. You *know* we could be completely—that we could be *jolly* happy together."

"Please let me go, Mr. Ashleigh," she said coolly.

"I shall not let you go until I have your consent," he said with a certain smugness, as if he had offered an incontrovertible argument.

"I had previously understood this suppliant position to be intended to indicate humility; but now I find that its purpose is to effect the imprisonment of the object of a gentleman's addresses. Please let me go, so that I can answer you in freedom, in a rational manner."

"I shall not let you," he said in a tone that was either truly *fervent,* as novelists describing such scenes customarily put it, or at least affectedly so; to Tomazina it seemed ludicrously petulant.

And in Tomazina, as she looked into Mr. Hugh Ashleigh's face, and truly considered what it would be like to be married to him, there arose at this point an unbearable, suffocating panic. She had thought him likeable; on a few occasions she had weighed the idea of somehow becoming his wife; but now that she was presented with the possibility in these forceful terms, she felt the kind of revulsion of a sick man forced to drink mercury. She felt almost as if she could have vomited in his face.

Her reaction was all the stronger because she saw his trick: he had her pinioned not only with his body and his hands, but by the necessity of her not doing anything ungenteel or unladylike. But in his certainty of using her good manners against her, she would now disappoint him. Her impulsiveness was too strong, and for once it defended her rather than harmed her. She jerked her hands away from him violently; she pulled her legs up under her, away from the confinement of his legs; she went to scramble over the back of the sofa to escape him; and as she put her weight on it, the sofa overturned with a crash. He leapt up; and she, as agile as a bird, did likewise, facing him across the sofa, which lay like a fallen defender between them.

"Madam!" he cried in amazement.

"Sir!" she retorted.

In some bewilderment he set the sofa to rights; then he looked at her, a little hurt and a little frightened. It was the only expression that could have defused her anger and embarrassment.

"I am sorry that I so alarmed you," he said, in a tone that seemed genuinely apologetic. "I . . . it was clumsily done. You may understand that . . . one has no practice in these things, and I was only doing what I . . . what I thought one ought, what I thought would be pleasing to a lady."

She truly pitied him now. She came around the sofa impulsively, and of her own accord she took his hand.

"I am very sorry, Mr. Ashleigh," she said. "I am afraid you see before you a girl who has more of the impulses of a wild cat than the proper restraint of a lady. It is only that . . . it is only that I cannot marry you."

He started to protest, but she squeezed his hand and tugged on it, simultaneously shushing him. "No, sir," she pleaded, "it is an impossibility. You are very sweet, very pleasing in every way; but a marriage between us is impossible." She was surprised, as she said these words, at how definite she now felt about this. "We have every interest in being good friends. In a sense, we are brother and sister—let us remain that way. Indeed, I have great hopes that we may actually be doubly brother and sister someday."

He looked puzzled at this oblique reference to Vita, so she did not expand upon it. Instead she went on to say, "I hope you will not hold my refusal against me, or against my family. You are much loved and honored among us."

Then he followed up his success in arousing her pity by doing perhaps the only thing he could have done to arouse her doubt of herself. In this he was either far cleverer than she gave him credit for, or perhaps more deeply affectionate than she had yet believed him. He let go of her hand; he went away from her; and from a distance of a dozen feet he turned to speak to her again.

"Miss Comstock," he said, "please do forgive my extreme clumsiness in all this. I see that I have fallen into the error of thinking that we were playing some kind of roles, you and I. I had a speech prepared, which of course, in seeing you in all your beauty, I completely forgot; and so much the better, because now I can tell you what I feel from my heart as it prompts me. And that is simply this: I am out of my mind with love for you. When I am in the room where you are, I can barely think. Sometimes it seems to me that I can barely breathe. You are so . . . so *infinitely* beautiful. I know that seems silly, but that is the only word that I have ever found to describe the quantity of your beauty. You know I am not a very bookish sort of person; and I know you value books and words very highly. But do not, I beg of you, think less highly of me for all that. I have been to university, and I did not utterly waste my time there. With your example, I honestly think I should do better and read more. It is true that perhaps I did more of the things young men do at university to while away their time than I ought to have done; and when I think of the waste I made of those opportunities to improve myself and make myself worthy of you, Miss Comstock, it makes me sick at heart. But it is not too late. It would be a worthy goal of my life to win your respect in this as well as in other matters."

He stopped suddenly. She thought he was done, but he took a deep breath and plunged on. "But even if I fail in that, Miss Comstock," he said, "I have other virtues. How I should glory in being your husband! Is that not pleasing to a woman, to know that the man she has married is more proud of her than he is of himself? I could never mistreat you. I would honor you in every way. I am a man, with the faults of a man, but also with the strength of a man. I have been both cautious and very successful in extending the wealth that came my way by inheritance. I am not far from being as wealthy as my brother. I would gladly use that wealth to care for and protect you and those you love. We would raise a family together—sons and daughters. We would enjoy the company of my brother and your sister into our old age quite happily. Are these advantages I offer nothing? I do not think so; I think they are much. I sense your disapproval of me—I suppose in this refusal you have expressed it—and I do not know why exactly you disapprove me; but it cannot be because I do not love you. I have been out of my mind for you since the moment I first walked into this room and laid eyes on you. It was as if I had been struck by lightning. I could not speak, I could not think. I could not even be polite; all I wished was to have license to gaze at you and listen to you. Never in my life have I felt such an instant passion, Miss Comstock."

At this point he paused. It was as good a place as any; and perhaps he sensed that if he had continued, he could only have done worse.

For Tomazina now did feel the tide of her certainty ebb. Samson, for all she loved him, had spurned her. Here was a man who felt about her the way she felt about Samson, or so he claimed; and something in her was thrilled to be sought by such love. Something in her considered, as well, that he might be, must be, very passionate in the marriage bed, if he craved her so very much.

A voice, a sensible voice—it was the teachings of her culture—told her that she would be an idiot to refuse him. She was confused by it. She turned away from him and went to the window, looking out blindly, feeling pain at her dilemma, but no longer knowing any clear choice.

"You hear me," he said, with a rising note in his voice. "You hear me—I see it. Your heart is not utterly resolved against me. These considerations have weight with you."

"Oh, yes, they do, sir!" she said, almost bitterly. "Do you think I cannot appreciate what you offer? I am honored."

"Then say yes," he pleaded.

But with a wisdom beyond her years, she guessed what this speech of his was worth. He believed every word of it; he intended its every stated intention. But he had not the strength to perform upon his promises. He would not read anything for her sake—reading had always bored him, and would continue to do so. She would give him a book, thinking it would be the first of many they would read together and discuss; he would keep that book on the bedside table, unread, and it would gather dust. He promised honor and attention to her; but he would spend his days in foxhunting and his evenings in drinking and smoking and playing cards with his brother. These were the things he had always done, and these were the things he would always do. She did not doubt that he and she might establish some kind of *modus vivendi*. He would bully her and order her about by day just as his brother domineered over Rose Elizabeth; on occasional nights, reeking of alcohol and smoke, he would grip her body and crawl upon her; and if she did or if she did not find her pleasure when he did, it would be her concern, not his.

She turned to face him again. "I am sorry, sir," she said. "I cannot say yes; and so I must say no."

In his turn now he evinced his own kind of panic. He took a step toward her, but restrained himself. He had already tried the physical form of compulsion, and it had failed.

"Do not say no!" he pleaded.

"I am sorry. I must."

"But Miss Comstock, why? What reason can you give?"

There was a long silence while she considered what reason she could in fact give him without insulting him so deeply that it would irremediably mar the relations between his family and hers.

"For this reason, sir," she said finally. "I find I do not love you as I hope to love the man I marry."

He was only momentarily taken aback by her frankness. Then he said, hurriedly: "But that is nothing! That is no reason *at all*. You shall love me—you shall, when we are married. I know you shall, because your heart is good, and you are a loving person. You cannot fail to love me when you see how much I love you, and how well I treat you."

She thought: *He thinks I shall love him as Rose loves his brother—because she has no choice left to her.*

"I shall not marry any man I do not love," she said.

"Oh, but that is no reason!" he protested again. He was smiling now; he showed every confidence. "Miss Comstock, you shall not say no. You shall say nothing rather than say no. I shall not accept any answer from you now. Do not answer now at all. Let it be agreed between us that you have not answered. The fact is that I must go away the day after tomorrow, to London, and then to the north, to Edinburgh. I have a very solid chance, at very little risk, to enlarge our personal fortune—yes, I say *our* personal fortune, Miss Comstock, because I mean to devote it to our life together; it is a chance I must follow up for *our* sake. Answer me when I return to Hampshire; or if you should decide that the answer is yes, write to me at once; or if you do not think that proper, ask my brother to write to me, telling me that you approve."

She replied almost before he had finished this eager speech. "No, sir," she said, "I cannot let it stand. I must decline your offer once and for all. I thank you for it, and I wish you the best in all your endeavors in life—particularly in this matter of marriage."

"Do not—do not say anything irrevocable," he said, speaking in that tone of cheerful denial that characterized the behavior of both these brothers when they were dealing with women who were not doing what they wanted.

"I am sorry; what I have already said is irrevocable."

"Nothing said on this earth is irrevocable, my dearest Miss Comstock—except a vow of marriage."

"Sir, you will only injure yourself—you will only injure those whom we both love if you persist in thinking I have said *perhaps* when in fact I have said *no, never, impossible, inconceivable.*"

"Miss Comstock, I refuse to hear you."

"That I believe!" she cried, now truly piqued. "For how can you *hear* anything, when you have steadily refused to *listen* since we first met? You do not recommend yourself to a lady, sir, by blocking your ears to her every speech."

"That is untrue—and unkind. I have studied nothing but to please you."

"And for all your study, you never noticed how impossible I was to please; you never stopped to think about why I might favor others and not you."

"Others? What others, if I may ask?"

He had caught her; she hesitated. "There are no others," she said. "I spoke in general terms only, sir."

"There is no other whom you love, then?"

She hesitated again. "There is no other whom I have any expectation to marry," she said.

Her evasion was not successful. He flushed with a little heat of anger or jealousy; but he said nothing further on this point. She later thought back with grief on that moment; for it seemed to her then that that one glimpse he had of her secret was all he required to cause her bitter woe.

"Well, then," he said, "I shall go away. The carriage is returning to pick me up.—Will you not come with me on the picnic now, in token of our continued friendship?"

This was the last thing she wanted to do, but he had managed it very cleverly; and for Rose Elizabeth's sake, she realized she ought to go with the party on the outing.

"Very well, sir," she said. "Allow me a minute to get my hat and shawl; I shall join you in the drive."

"You are very kind, Miss Comstock!" he said joyfully. "You are very kind to me, and I am grateful to you for it.— Come, let us shake hands like brother and sister, until we may greet each other as husband and wife." And coming to her, he offered his hand, and she took it, though reluctantly, not wishing to offend him. Once he had her hand, he held it.

"You are not hurt from the fall of the sofa?" he asked in a kind tone.

"No, sir; only in my dignity."

"Think nothing of that. Heap the blame on me—I deserve it for my clumsiness. I shall be back from Edinburgh in three weeks at most, Miss Comstock. Think on what I have said. I am certain that you will accept me. We have everything to gain, everything! Oh, I am certain of it. You shall see how I shall study to deserve your good opinion.—Miss Comstock, may I . . . may I give you the kiss of a brother?"

"No, sir," she said, withdrawing her hand abruptly from his and moving away. But he only laughed cheerfully and bowed.

"We shall await you outside," he said.

She went upstairs to her room, and he outside. In the upstairs hall she paused to look down through a window; there she could see the carriage, which had now returned from its mission of carrying Vita and Ursula temporarily out of earshot. Mr. Hugh Ashleigh was just crossing the forecourt toward it, and Mr. Lucas Ashleigh was descending from it and going to meet him—to hear the results of his proposal, obviously. She saw Mr. Hugh Ashleigh speaking to his brother privately; and it was clear, from the way Mr. Lucas Ashleigh clapped him on the back and grinned, that he was reporting that his efforts had been tantamount to success, though not perfectly conclusive.

And indeed, the afternoon was to be quite miserable for her, watching Mr. Hugh Ashleigh carrying on in the best of spirits, and wondering to herself—like many a woman before and since, as if it really were her fault and not his—how she always so mismanaged things that the word *no* was heard as the word *yes*.

❂ ❂ ❂

Tomazina hoped that Mr. Hugh Ashleigh would indeed not return to Hartswound for three weeks at the least; for at the end of that time she meant to be gone from Hampshire. Mrs. Hanscom had written; the plans were still in place for the Hanscoms to return to Hanley Wold via Broadbridge, whence they would fetch her home to Gloucestershire; though the period of their absence from Gloucestershire had, through importunities from the Percies, been extended for the full month of June. But Mrs. Hanscom wrote of

Tomazina's resumed stay at Hanley Wold as if it would be without end; she even hoped that Tomazina might wish to accompany them on a Christmas visit to Brackensom, as if she were the Hanscoms' own daughter, and not a guest. Over this letter Tomazina had wept tears of gratitude. Her father, she knew, would require some managing; but she looked upon that necessary persuasion as something that had been done once and could be done again.

This plan to escape further encounters with Mr. Hugh Ashleigh was marred by his reappearance on the very next day. All three Ashleighs had been invited to dinner as a kind of farewell to Mr. Hugh. The afternoon passed without causing too much strain; but when the gentlemen joined the ladies after dinner, Mr. Hugh Ashleigh managed to sit down beside Tomazina. She had been talking with Rose Elizabeth, slightly apart from the rest; and when Mr. Ashleigh entered, Rose Elizabeth went to join him at cards, and Mr. Hugh Ashleigh came directly to take her place. If Tomazina had not trusted Rose Elizabeth, she would have thought the exchange preconcerted. From the hurt looks she received from Vita, she guessed that her sister was thinking the same thing, but assigning the blame slightly differently.

At any rate, there he was, and she must make small talk somehow. They got this started after a little awkwardness, and it went on hesitantly for several minutes; and then, after the game of cards had started, and the conversation from it created a shield of noise, he drew a folded sheet of paper from the inner pocket of his coat and said, "My brother, you know, carries on a correspondence with Lord Esterbroke, whom I believe you met in Gloucestershire."

"I have indeed met him, both there and in Surrey. I must say that I cannot understand why Mr. Ashleigh corresponds with such a man."

"Why, he is a lord, after all, and not to be slighted. And he and my brother are acquainted from school, and they have naturally maintained the connection."

"Even allowing for the social obligations of correspondence—which his lordship seems unlikely to feel, in my humble opinion—I remain surprised that Lord Esterbroke has the patience to set pen to paper in any regular manner."

He at once hastened to reassure her on that score. "Oh, he does not do the actual writing himself; he is indeed far too lazy for that. His half-brother, Mr. Upton, does the honors."

"Do you mean Lord Esterbroke dictates, and Mr. Upton writes?"

"Well, I do not believe it is quite as direct as that. Mr. Upton writes more or less what he thinks Lord Esterbroke might say."

"So this correspondence with Lord Esterbroke is not really a correspondence with Lord Esterbroke at all?"

"I admit it is a little unusual. Mr. Upton writes to my brother, and my brother writes to Lord Esterbroke. But it is a good arrangement for everyone; that way my brother maintains a connection with the nobility, Mr. Upton retails all his lordship's secrets—and Lord Esterbroke, without any effort to himself, maintains a connection with certain friends whom he views as sources of revenue."

This was a much more cynical comment than she had ever heard from Mr. Hugh Ashleigh before, and she was surprised at it.

"In any case," he went on, "my brother has had one of these letters, and it might be of interest to you. It concerns our mutual acquaintance, Mr. Esterbroke. I asked my brother if I might show it to you; and he consented, though he gave me only the page on which the relevant part is written."

He held the sheet of paper out to her; and though her heart told her to snatch it up eagerly, her mind was reluctant and suspicious. There was something in Mr. Hugh Ashleigh's manner that made her think of a man loading a mousetrap with a particularly succulent piece of cheese.

"Ah," she said. "But it seems improper to read Mr. Ashleigh's correspondence. Perhaps you could summarize it."

"It is true that there is some language that a lady perhaps ought not to be exposed to; but you are not a child, and I think you know what kind of man Mr. Upton is. Why not read it yourself?"

She made a blunt counteroffer without preface: "Why do you not read it to me?"

He was equally blunt in reply, ignoring her wishes still, and continuing to hold out the paper. "Why do you not read it, Miss Comstock?" he said again. "I think it will be of interest to you."

"You can hardly wish me to read his lordship's secrets, can you?"

"Indeed I do, in this case; for they are open secrets."

Still she would not give in, though her curiosity was undergoing agonies. Seeing her continue to hesitate, he rattled the paper and said, "Why do you not simply take it and look?"

"Because, Mr. Ashleigh, the Bible says something worth remembering about *he that sendeth a message by the hand of a fool.* I fear Lord Esterbroke and Mr. Upton may run afoul of that very verse, and I would not wish you to do the same."

"Let that be on my head," he said. And he thrust the paper at her again.

The possibility of gaining some news about Samson proved more than she could resist. With great reluctance, in a kind of dread of even touching the thing, she took the folded note and opened it.

It appeared to be the second sheet of a letter, written with no sense of economy in the use of paper, which was a rather precious commodity in those days. The hand was slovenly and difficult to read, and it seemed to begin in the middle of something that had been treated on the previous page.

an ase of spades—you may imagine my disgust at that, but I soon had £5s revenge off his lrdship. Aside from that spat, thre is good news in the wind: Jos Leverin and Treworgy wounded each tother in a dual. Pucks been blackballd for his insult to Trevorish. Lady P is preggers, and they say not by P hisself, but he seems not to care, and meens to hire his Lrdships cousin Sammy to paint h' in all h' maturnal splendor. I am sure he will make h'appear a madonna, if anyone can. On that score, it seems Sammy has finlly propsed to his own donna, Miss Dorronne, and though she has given coy rsponses, as one wld expect of a ldy playing her cards skilfully, it is genrally believd he will get h' after all. They say his paintin biznis is goin on famusly, and he is in a fair way to bein wealthy in a few yeers. His lrdship is damnd lucky in the mattr, for he resently offered Sammy a rathr large wagr that she wld never have h'''', whch Sammy was fool enuph to refuse. You will say that his lrdship shld give over laying bets on yong ladies and their matrimonnial intentions, and that is good advice; but you know as well as I do that his lrdship shll be damnd and hangd and sent to hell if thre is anythng he can do to turn down the opportunity for good fun, and thre is nothng so fun as a good wagr. I ony wish I had bet agin h''''.

There was more, too, but when she saw that it had nothing to do with Samson, she stopped reading it and handed back the letter.

Despite her foreknowledge of all of this, it gave her a pang to see this interpretation of Miss Doronne's conduct. Perhaps there was something in it after all—perhaps Miss Doronne was only making a feint for some reason, and would soon accept Mr. Esterbroke in spite of her denials. This sudden fear was not mitigated by her certainty that it was the very emotion Mr. Hugh Ashleigh had meant to elicit in her by making her read this communication.

"So you see, Mr. Esterbroke has paid his addresses to this Miss Doronne," said Mr. Hugh Ashleigh.

"Indeed, I knew that, sir."

"You knew it?" he said in some surprise.

She would have enjoyed shocking Mr. Hugh Ashleigh by telling him that she had been present at the very proposal and heard it with her own ears; but of course she would not have exposed Samson to ridicule in that way. She only said: "I did know it. The account in this letter does not come as any news to me. Mr. Esterbroke always said he would, and therefore I always said he would; and he did as he said he would, and therefore I have always said he did so. I have known of it for quite some time now. No one ever believed my assertions; but this letter vindicates me."

He was puzzled; he hesitated, and then said, "So then . . . you wish Mr. Esterbroke success in this marriage?"

She turned to him fully and stared straight into his eyes. "It is my fervent hope, as a friend and admirer of Mr. Esterbroke, that he may be exquisitely happy in the marriage he makes for himself." To herself she added: *His marriage with me.* But even as she thought this, it seemed so hopeless a wish that it hurt more than helped her.

She could see that Mr. Hugh Ashleigh was still mistrustful. He sensed that something did not add up. He opened his mouth to say something more, to pry into her feelings still more deeply; but she forestalled him by rising.

"I could wish, Mr. Ashleigh, that you had spared me the perusal of that disgusting document. You expressed some doubts about whether I ought to see that letter before you forced it on me; I wish you had listened to them. Let me leave you in no further doubt now about my disapproval of your heedless determination to make me privy to the thing."

And she left him and went to sit down with her mother and father. He was very upset, but the circumstances were too little private for him to protest to her and try to wheedle a forgiveness out of her; and so she had the satisfaction, small though it was, of bidding him farewell that evening, in a tone of wounded dignity and justified dislike. Though it was pleasing to her to practice this hauteur upon him, it was probably a tactical error; for as it turned out, she only provoked him to further mischief in her pursuit.

❋ ❋ ❋

Tomazina did not speak to Rose Elizabeth about Mr. Hugh Ashleigh's offer. She meant to do so, but for some time they did not have even a few minutes alone when she could have; and by then she thought better of it. She knew it would only be a disappointment to Rose Elizabeth; and she preferred the gentler route of simply disappearing into Gloucestershire to the harshness of openly disagreeing with her sister on the wisdom of marrying into the Ashleigh family. She would have had a hard time explaining what was wrong with Mr. Hugh Ashleigh's character without casting even worse aspersions on that of Mr. Lucas Ashleigh himself.

It was a great relief to her when her suitor was gone out of Hampshire. And yet absence does have the curious effect of softening the difficult aspects of another's character. The very sense of relief is mistaken by the heart as some kind of pleasurable emotion toward the absent one; and Tomazina was, by her upbringing, one who was more prone to forgive and to make excuses for others than to cling to recollections of their worse qualities. She remembered Mr. Hugh Ashleigh's boyish admiration of her and his declaration that he was out of his mind with love for her, and out of a sense of British and Christian fair play—or perhaps only because we are inclined to forgive others for their infatuation with us—she tried to excuse his improprieties and insensitivities on those grounds.

Not that she fell in love with Mr. Hugh Ashleigh. But she did think of him occasionally; and when she did so, she tended to think slightly better of him than she had when he was present.

Lending some faint further heat to these lukewarm sentiments were bouts of utter despair over Samson, times when in her hopelessness she seemed momentarily emptied of any love for him. But she realized that this emptiness was not an absence of love, only a supreme isolation from the loved one. This sense of isolation was frightening, and under its compulsion, she did from time to time fleetingly reconsider marriage with Mr. Hugh Ashleigh, thinking how it would keep her within the social framework of family and friends and neighbors—that it would ease that perilous loneliness to some degree.

Furthermore, it struck her now very forcefully again (for she and Samson had written of this to one another last winter) that for most people, the institution of marriage had little to do with any passionate sexual and imaginative bond. For most, the sexual interaction in marriage was confined to the result of an brief impulse once every week or every few weeks or every few months or even years. There might be friendship between husband and wife at best; and if so, perhaps it was in general the best that could be hoped for. There were very few couples like Mariah and Edmund who seemed to have a marriage of true passion and spiritual intimacy. For most others—even her own parents, she understood—marriage was more like a business arrangement in which the two partners are so closely bound by mutual interest that as a result they become increasingly fond of one another over the years. At times, reflecting on this practical reality, she was certain that if she bore children with Hugh Ashleigh, she would learn to endure those things about him she now found insufferable.

In the last analysis, however, her certainty that she would put up with Mr. Hugh Ashleigh's failings actually frightened her still more than the thought of being forever isolated.

And she saw that if she were trapped into marrying him in some moment of weakness, there would be no escape for the rest of her life, not even the mode of escape Mr. Hanscom had once told her was ever available to all. For she had realized that the Epicureans and Stoics were wrong about this much, as Mrs. Hanscom had once forced Mr. Hanscom to confess. The door was not always open. The minute a woman realized she was pregnant, then she had given a hostage to life, by which she could be compelled to dwell in the land of the living all her natural days. Perhaps a Stoic—especially a male Stoic—of olden times could live in a bubble of self-centered principle that would allow him to open his veins and slip into death without concern for those others who were dependent on his love and care; but she saw that she herself could not, or at least not when she was thinking rationally. Her previous brush with suicide had come at a time when she was not thinking at all, only acting from a desperate animal instinct to escape pain. If she stayed well enough to think well, she would not be able to neglect, by departing from this earth, any child she had ever conceived on it.

The fact was that—like the foolish Moria in her own story—she was growing wiser, and in ways she had not expected. It was not a pleasant process. She looked forth from her youth, the time when the horizon of possibilities should appear broad, even infinite to young eyes, and saw how her fate looked likely to be very narrow and limited, whether she bound herself in marriage to someone like Mr. Ashleigh, or whether she remained a maiden aunt.

It was some relief to her, however, that whatever her transient confusion about marriage might be, there was no mistaking whom she truly was in love with. She loved Samson Esterbroke; she thought most of all about Samson Esterbroke. She wrote poignant little laments in her sketchbook that might typically start with complaints like this:

> Where is my love? Why does my love leave me alone? I walk by the gates of the city, and he is not there. I walk on the city walls, and my brothers mock me. I walk in the hills, and I am alone. Why does he not change his mind? Why does he not listen to his heart? Why does he not come to me?

These questions were not strictly literary; they were also literal, and she put them to herself over and over. She suffered that great suspense of the lover who feels that she must *get a message* to the beloved, or even more, that she must find the beloved and confront him; but she knew that for her, the opportunity for messages and confrontations was over. The impulse to write him, to go to him—these were an ache without an anodyne.

As often happened when she was brooding on things, a stray verse from the Bible recurred to her in these days, like an inner monitor, warning her; and it said, in the coarse but beautiful language of the old prophets, *Thou hast also taken thy fair jewels of my gold and of my silver, which I had given thee, and madest to thyself images of men, and didst commit whoredom with them.* And she interpreted this prompting to mean that to love Samson was to love what was right, and to marry him was to dedicate the jewel of life she had been given to the right service; while to attempt to love anyone else would be to make a false image, and to wed that other would not lead to a true marriage at all, but only to a vulgar and merely physical union—in biblical terms, a whoredom.

She often thought of the Shulamite of the Song as well. Would that exalted lover ever have loved anyone else but her beloved? Her vague suspicions that the old commentators were right after all often drifted through her mind: perhaps the Shulamite truly did represent the soul as the beloved of God, or the church that was the beloved of the Son of Man. And if that were true, could she go against that symbolism? Could she, as the soul, love some other than God? Could she, as the church, love some other than Christ? Farfetched though this symbolical compunction might have seemed to others, on Tomazina Comstock it had a powerful effect.

Chapter 43

I will rise now, and go about the city in the streets, and in the
broad ways I will seek him whom my soul loveth.

—Song of Solomon 3:2

The weather had continued so poor that the hay and clover crops were quite despaired of. This would not in itself have been a tragedy; but it encouraged farmers to feed grain stocks to cattle, thereby reducing a food that was already in short supply and driving grain prices higher. Furthermore, the outlook for the other crops was very bad. Many farmers, particularly in the north, ploughed up the failing wheat crops and sowed barley as a replacement. The air was so cold that those Britons who could afford the fuel kept fires burning on their hearths through the summer, while those who could not felt their chill as a compounding misery to their hunger.

And compounding these very real indicators of hard times were certain symbols that weighed upon the national consciousness, arguing to the afflicted that the time was come to seek desperate remedies. From Windsor Castle the news had spread that the king of England had been despaired of by his medical men. His condition seemed an analogue of the British nation as a whole, as he wandered fitfully in his gilt prison, mad and blind and miserable with a mysterious and incurable ailment. His son, the Prince of Wales and future George IV, was by contrast a symbol of all that was wrong with the upper classes, sunk as he was in debt, and careless of anything but preserving his own wastrel style of life. Nor were dire omens limited to the human sphere: in April of that year, a large spot had appeared on the sun, all the more frightening because the phenomenon had not yet been explained by science. Even the least urchin in the streets knew of its existence, for the sun itself, veiled as it was by Mount Tambora's ejected dust and gas, could be viewed by the naked eye without injury.

Within this larger national and even global disaster, the little tragi-comedy of Tomazina's life continued now into a new scene. And this commenced in the last week of June, with a great but very brief battle that took place between the House of Ashleigh and the House of Comstock.

The deepest and most secret origin of this dispute was a letter from Mrs. Hanscom that had arrived the week before. The letter fixed the date of the Hanscoms' return to Gloucestershire, and thus the date of their passage through Hampshire. To Tomazina's dismay (and Vita's as well when she heard of it), she found that this return had been put off until the middle of July. It seemed likely that she would be subject to Mr. Hugh Ashleigh's attentions once again prior to her departure, for a period of a week or so. It was true that Tomazina heard from Rose Elizabeth that Mr. Hugh Ashleigh now had traveled on from London to Edinburgh, and that his business was likely to delay him there longer than he had expected; but she began to doubt her escape.

Yet this item of news was not itself the immediate cause of the upset between Priedpie Hall and Hartswound Park. That lay in another paragraph altogether; and though it flowed in the same elegant hand and was joined seamlessly to the rest of the rather full account of Baby Hereford and of how Grandfather Hereford was spoiling the boy rottener than last autumn's windfall, Tomazina had no doubt that it had been carefully considered before it was set down.

On Saturday we had a visit from Mr. Esterbroke. He is now in London again, though I should think he is the only English gentleman who is. He was rather vague about his painting business, though he did say that he has one great commission he is working on. That is easy enough to say about him—here is the difficult part: namely, that I cannot quite describe to you the impression he gave us. He looks to all outward appearances in good health—do not alarm yourself over that. But he looks as if he were—I think the only thing I can say is *spiritually injured,* as if he has suffered something terrible. He seems softened somehow, humbled. Bronwyn is sure that it is the rejection he has had from Miss Doronne that is working on him. He seems to be carrying on in a kind of dream of duty or something. The only thing that makes him smile at all is the mention of his friend, Miss Tomazina Comstock; and even then his smile is miserable in some indefinable way. When Mr. Hanscom and I spoke of the pleasant times we all had together this past year, he seemed to be afflicted with an almost unbearable pain; and so great and so obvious was his discomfort that we desisted. It is really too bad you could not come to Brackensom to meet us; then perhaps we could have Mr. Esterbroke to dinner, and you might judge for yourself what his state of mind is, and perhaps do something to cheer him. Would it help at this juncture if Mr. Hanscom wrote to your father, urging him to let you come to us again? Though if, as you say, his primary objection is the proximity of Mr. Esterbroke to us in Gloucestershire, I must say that in that case we could not in good conscience represent any journey to Brackensom as certain to be unobjectionable to him.

Tomazina's first thought was: *He cannot bear to think of me!* And then: *He thinks only of how my recklessness has ruined all chance of comfortable conversation between us. I was his only and his best friend—he could tell me everything; and now he is as alone in the world as he was when I first met him.*

This thought was so overpowering that she lay on her bed and wept for ten minutes without stopping. Then she became frightened for him; she sat up, wiped away her tears, and thought: *I must get near him somehow. I must get to Brackensom. I must see for myself that he is all right. Perhaps*

I can talk him into forgiving me for what I did, if I can only see him again. He must see me act as if nothing has happened—he must know that it was only a momentary aberration, and I shall never trouble him again—that we can and shall be friends forever without any importunity from me. We were forced apart too soon! We did not have time to heal our friendship after the blow I gave it in my recklessness. I must get to Brackensom!

It was not long, however, before she became uncertain about this plan. Was it possible that she could control herself in his presence? Could she be as she had been before, in the days when she had not known what she truly felt towards him? To pursue him, to throw herself in his way—that was the course of a Mr. Burck. She would not do that.

She was sitting quietly in a chair in her room, dry-eyed again, but in a stupor of hopelessness, when there was a tap at the door and Rose Elizabeth entered, flushed and breathless; she had run in from her carriage and headlong up the stairs. "Oh, Mazie!" she cried excitedly, shutting the door behind her, "you will never guess what is afoot!" She came to Tomazina's side and seized her hands. "We are going to London!" she said. "Mr. Ashleigh and I! Is that not exciting?"

Tomazina answered before she could even think. "Father will never let you!" she cried.

Then she looked at Rose Elizabeth, and Rose Elizabeth looked at her, and they both laughed. "I am afraid Father has relinquished all power over me," said Rose Elizabeth.

"Yes, you have a new master now," said Tomazina ironically. "But did you not go for the Season last winter?"

"No, we never did. We were meant to; but at first Mr. Ashleigh was helping Lord Burley with the hunt; or at least, he said he was, or thought he was—I was not sure that everyone else seemed to think so. And then Mr. Ashleigh was upset about the building of his sister's monument, and would not trust the architect to finish it without his direction. And then there were any number of other such things that came in the way. So we did not go, and did not go; and finally it became so late that Mr. Ashleigh said there was no point in going at all."

"But if that is the case, why go now? It is all the more late. Is not the town said to be dull in summer? And why must you go away just when I am home to see you?"

Rose Elizabeth laughed and tugged at Tomazina's hands in her excitement. "That is exactly it!" she said. "You have not heard everything yet." She paused for a moment for effect and then she said, with something like pride mingled in her excitement: "Mr. Ashleigh proposes that I should take you with me."

"To London?" said Tomazina incredulously.

"Yes, to London. To keep me company when he has business. Is it not sweet of him to think of it? And of course, he shall pay for everything, Mazie; and you shall have plenty of pocket money besides for gifts for everyone. Mr. Ashleigh has a house there, you know, and we shall be quite safe and comfortable. Papa cannot possibly object."

Tomazina sat for a long moment in silence, looking up at Rose Elizabeth, while Rose Elizabeth beamed at her and hung over her, waiting for an expression of her pleasure in this prospect. And indeed, Tomazina thought of Mrs. Hanscom's letter—thought of Samson, in London; felt again that hollow ache to see him once more.

But then she came down to earth.

"Oh, but Father *can* object," she said. "And he can not only object, he can positively forbid it."

"But he shall not—he shall not! We shall talk him into it."

"Oh, Rose, have you so quickly forgotten how he feels about London? He would sooner allow me to tour Sodom itself."

"But he shall not object if you go with me and Mr. Ashleigh."

"With you and Mr. Ashleigh? Rose, when I was at Brackensom he would not let me go with *Edmund,* who is a clergyman, and in whose morality Papa has implicit trust."

"Are you saying he does not trust Mr. Ashleigh's morals?" said Rose Elizabeth, beginning to be hurt.

Tomazina saw she had spoken too impulsively. She now in turn tugged at Rose Elizabeth's hands and said, "No, no—that is not what I meant. It is just that he would not even trust *himself* to guard us against corruption if we went to London. How will you ever persuade him?" At this point her previous question came back to her in a faint premonition. "And why now, Rose? Why does Mr. Ashleigh go to London now? It is not the Season."

"Oh, I have not the faintest idea—it is business, that is all I know. Something to do with some stocks he owns."

"And where is Mr. Hugh Ashleigh in all this? Is he to meet us in London?"

"No, I am sorry to say," said Rose Elizabeth with a little smile. "Mr. Ashleigh was lamenting that fact; but his brother is still in Scotland, as I told you; and will be so until sometime about mid-July. Nothing has changed there. It is said to be business that takes him there, but to tell you the truth, I think it has to do with purchasing shooting rights or a hunting lodge or something more to do with pleasure than business. They positively will not explain it to me, and I am sure that there is some concern between Mr. Ashleigh and his brother that *a certain lady* might not like to feel she had been slighted for that kind of thing."

Tomazina, by a great effort, kept her silence on this point. If Mr. Hugh Ashleigh was to be absent from London, she herself would not mind being there. Perhaps while Mr. Ashleigh was busy, she and Rose Elizabeth could arrange a visit to Brackensom; and perhaps things might just somehow fall out that—

And so the little push that Mrs. Hanscom had given in her letter coincided with Mr. Ashleigh's invitation, which she might otherwise have instantly rejected.

"Then I shall go with you, if there is any way we can talk Papa into it," she said. "But do not get your hopes up, Rose; I think it is an impossibility."

They went downstairs at once. When they actually came into Mr. Comstock's presence, as he sat in his office reading a book of sermons—it was perhaps an unfortunate occupation in which to interrupt him—they reversed their usual roles; for Tomazina quailed at the thought of asking him for a permission he must certainly refuse to grant, and Rose Elizabeth, fortified with the strength of her own independence from him, acted with more boldness than Tomazina had ever seen in her.

The result, however, was the same as it would have been a year ago or ten years ago. Mr. Comstock was panicked and incensed at the mere notion that his daughters should be taken anywhere near London. He ought perhaps to have been more alarmed than he was at the recent unrest in the rural areas around the city; but like many country squires of the times, he tended to believe that a stern showing of dragoons had been enough to silence this rabble, which was in any case was a fragmentary minority. But about the moral state of the capital he had no such mitigating thoughts. He not only forbade Tomazina to go, he forbade Rose Elizabeth as well, though in the same breath he admitted he had no right to do so. "I can only express my disappointment with Mr. Ashleigh," he said. "I did not marry my daughter off to a gentleman of his standing only to see him escort her to the very inmost circle of debauchery in this land—to let her be stained with its iniquity!"

"Oh, Papa!" said Rose Elizabeth, dismayed as the recollection of her father's intractability was forced upon her, "It is not so very bad."

"Not so very bad!" cried Mr. Comstock. "Do you not recall what Ezekiel says? *Woe to the bloody city, to the pot whose scum is therein!*"

"But Papa," said she again—for the frequency of a daughter's use of such diminutives increases in direct proportion to her father's opposition to her wishes—"we shall be under the best protection the entire time, and in Mr. Ashleigh's very fine house."

"Oh, it is a fine house, I am sure! But what good is the fineness of such a place, if it be situate in the precincts of hell?—Good gracious, my dear Rose, do you not realize that the *Prince* himself lives in London from time to time?"

"Oh, Papa," said Tomazina feebly, "you talk of him as though he were the Prince of Darkness instead of the Prince of Wales."

"He *is* the very prince of the moral darkness that lours over our benighted land," said Mr. Comstock.

"But *London,* Papa," she said, tapping her patriotism in an attempt to muster up a more hopeful argument. "It is our capital! It is *our city!* It is the center of our British nation! It is where the king resides! It is where Parliament holds session! It is where Nelson walked! It is—" and she paused as she caught herself mentally saying: *It is where Samson lives.*

Mr. Comstock, however, finished her sentence a different way: "It is a place where you will not find ten who are righteous!" he said. "It is filled with the children of Belial!"

"But Papa," said Tomazina, "*If thou shalt hearken unto the voice of the Lord thy God, blessed shalt thou be in the city.*"

Mr. Comstock, however, overmatched her, and retorted: "*But if thou wilt* not *hearken unto the voice of the Lord thy God,* cursed *shalt thou be in the city.*—It is not *your* virtue I doubt, my dear; it is the virtue of the metropolis around you."

"But Papa, will not the Lord protect us?"

"*Thou shalt not tempt the Lord thy God,*" said Mr. Comstock; and for good measure he threw in another verse, not particularly relevant, but which happened to occur to him at that moment: "*Gilead is a city of them that work iniquity, and is polluted with blood.*"

The two sisters expostulated further, but with decreasing hope of persuading him; and at last they had to admit defeat, and contritely leave him to fume and fret at the mere idea that one of his daughters should be exposed to the haunts of sin. They stopped together in the main hall.

"I am very sorry, Rose," said Tomazina. "But I never thought we would persuade him."

"We shall see what Mr. Ashleigh has to say about this," said Rose Elizabeth.

"Please, Rose, do not start a war between Papa and Mr. Ashleigh. It is bad enough that he is taking you there. If he makes a fuss about taking me as well, it will only create bad blood between our houses. Let us not see that happen."

"I must at any rate tell him what Papa's response was," said Rose Elizabeth. "And when I do that, there will be no stopping him. There is no controlling Mr. Ashleigh in anything he chooses to do; I have learned that already. I have no hold over him whatsoever."

Tomazina wondered if the situation might be a little different if Rose Elizabeth were able to be a little more responsive to her husband in the marriage bed. It stood to reason that a man would be more domineering when he felt he had nothing to lose; but that was only speculation on her part.

"Well," she said, "do your best not to let Mr. Ashleigh challenge Papa about this. Papa will never give in, and Mr. Ashleigh will not like having to do so. It would be better if the idea had never come up."

They left matters thus, and Rose Elizabeth went seven miles home with nothing to show for her journey.

❁ ❁ ❁

The Comstocks were just finishing breakfast the next morning when Mr. Ashleigh arrived. He had ridden over on horseback, and the vigor of his exercise added to the air of impetuosity about him when he strode into the breakfast room and asked to speak with Mr. Comstock privately. Mr. Comstock rose with barely a word, appearing irritated as well; and the two men retired to the study, while the women looked at one another in dread. Mrs. Comstock and Tomazina's younger sisters had by now heard from Mr. Comstock all about Mr. Ashleigh's mad plan to take Rose Elizabeth and Tomazina away to Babylon, and they knew enough of Mr. Ashleigh's character to guess that he would not take kindly to being gainsaid.

The gentlemen were closeted together for no more than twenty minutes. By then the ladies had removed to the library, where they had continued to wait in expectation of a major falling out between the households. But when Mr. Comstock and his son-in-law reappeared, lo, the *pater familias* was as mild and abashed as a boy, and Mr. Ashleigh was smug and beaming with triumph. The women were absolutely astonished. Mr. Ashleigh did not even give his father-in-law the opportunity of saving face by addressing Tomazina first; he went directly to her, took her hand, and said, "I have persuaded your father, Miss Comstock; you are to come to London with Mrs. Ashleigh and me."

She looked wide-eyed at her father; who could only add, "I believe it will be all right, Tomazina. Mr. Ashleigh has persuaded me that he will look after you."

Tomazina later heard the story from Rose Elizabeth. His turnabout was a consequence of her father's great flaw, an undue deference to those he considered higher than himself on the social scale. He could never quite believe himself master of Hartswound Park, heir of the rights of the de Foyes as well as of their domains; and he had knuckled under to Mr. Ashleigh in a way that would have made the de Foyes of old burn with rage and disgust. When faced with active resistance from Mr. Ashleigh, of ancient family and ancient wealth, his own will had quickly collapsed. His concerns about the moral and physical safety of his daughters were expressed only hesitantly, and were quickly met and brushed aside. They should travel to London in Mr. Ashleigh's very own coach; Mr. Ashleigh owned a very fine house in Park Lane, thank you; he himself would accompany them on their every outing in town. Mr. Ashleigh engineered the conversation in such a way that any doubts Mr. Comstock might express became attacks against Mr. Ashleigh's own pride; and *that* indomitable force Mr. Comstock could not overcome.

For the first time in her life, Tomazina was ashamed of her father, and wished she had forestalled his moral collapse by refusing to go to London in the first place. She told herself that it was only her wicked and vain hope to see Samson that had led to that.

But it was too late to go back on the plan now; and once she grew used to the idea, she was able to overcome her regrets at her father's failure. She had never in all her life expected to see London, any more than she thought of traveling to Mecca. Now she would visit its wonders, in the company of her beloved sister; and who could guess what else might happen on such a journey, and how it might affect one?

Who, indeed? Certainly not those who were to be affected by it: Tomazina Comstock, her sister, her brother-in-law—and all of Britain.

❀ ❀ ❀

It was on the fourth day of July that Tomazina, Rose Elizabeth, and Mr. Ashleigh set out from Priedpie Hall in the Ashleighs' private carriage.

It would have been impossible for Tomazina to describe what she felt in boarding that vehicle. She had been so excited the previous night that she had not slept well; but she did not feel tired or irritable now, only pleasantly agitated—*fluttery* was the word that came to her mind, as if there were a pair of wings in her chest, rustling and skirring like those of doves as they take flight. To her hope of seeing Samson again was added the ecstasies of her childhood patriotism; she felt she was being transported into a living history book, that she would see the unique stage on which the lives, the successes, the follies of the great men and women of England had been acted out—whether Elizabeth the Queen, Shakespeare, the heroes of the late war, or any of the other uncountable geniuses of the common British story. London, for those not born there, will always have the aura of a place come to life out of a storybook. Like others before her, Tomazina had seen prints of its Thames, its bridges, its towers; to be assured now that those things existed in literal fact was to be like seeing a land in a fiction suddenly made real. True, the revisiting of the locus of these histories remained only an ancillary cause of her excitement; but to her it seemed not petty at all, but quite proper, that her own personal story, her search for her beloved in the city, should in her mind take precedence over even the relived greatness of those others; for had not they all been pursuing their own individual destinies when they made their mark on the life of the great commonweal? And so would she do—seek her own life story out of all the stories that had been told, and were being told, and would be told in that metropolis. And in so doing, she thought, she would add her mite to the larger story of England.

She was not the only one transported by anticipation. Mr. Ashleigh was for some reason in a very fine mood. He was chatty, affable, even funny at times. He was affectionate to Rose Elizabeth, holding her hand for much of the journey, and even at times flirting with her in a very teasing, boyish, and pleasant way. Not even in the days of their courting had he been so kind and considerate. Rose Elizabeth was completely overcome by his behavior. At an inn where they stopped on the way, when she and Tomazina were alone, she whispered, "I cannot understand what has gotten into Mr. Ashleigh!"

"He is certainly charming today, I must say," said Tomazina.

"If this is the way he behaves in London, I shall beg him that we may live there all year," said Rose Elizabeth.

"It is odd, truly odd. I wonder if there is something afoot, some surprise for you. He seems very pleased with himself, as well as more generally with you and with the journey itself."

Rose Elizabeth smiled, apparently at the thought that in some unknown way she had pleased her husband. They were then interrupted by a maid bustling into the room, so she said no more.

As it happened, Tomazina reboarded the carriage before the others, unobserved by the servants, and thus came to overhear the conversation of the coachman and footman as they awaited Mr. and Mrs. Ashleigh's return. "The master's in a rare mood today," said the coachman. He was a fairly elderly man, Dakes by name, somewhat coarse in speech and appearance, but a highly skilled driver of horses.

"That he is. It makes me wonder what he has up his sleeve," said the footman, who was younger, and had seemed to Tomazina on other occasions to be wary of his master's variable temperament.

"Oh, naw, would you not be in a merry mood if you had such a buxom, pretty wife as he do? And sweet-tempered; not like your missus or mine, eh?"

"That would put a man in a fair way to be in love with the whole world," agreed the footman.

"Especially if she had a pretty sister to boot—eh?" said Mr. Dakes.

And the two servants laughed to themselves.

Given her own excitement, it was not difficult for Tomazina herself to be caught up in Mr. Ashleigh's rare merriment. She put aside her suspicions of his sudden affability and was happy for her sister's sake. Besides, every mile they traveled closer to London was a mile closer she went to Samson; and though she could not have any rational hope of seeing him, or of having the opportunity to mend the great tear she had made in their friendship, merely to walk the same ground as he did, merely to see the sun shining at the same time from the same angle, set in her mouth a cake of happiness that was better by far than the bitter bread she had been eating since that last sight of him at Hanley Wold.

The boundary, so to speak, between the country and London was in those days rather abrupt. One moment they were rattling down a fine road between summer fields, and the next they were amid crowded houses—not by any means fine houses; but even these yielded soon enough to a district of great wealth. Mr. Ashleigh commented that the town was deserted, their visit being very much out of season—but to Tomazina the place seemed swarming with life.

Indeed, she was not disappointed. To her country mind, London was vast, dirty, noisy, foggy, confusing; and yet that only made it perfect. As she looked out of the carriage at the tumult of the town, a stray line from the Book of Nahum came to her: *The chariots shall rage in the streets, they shall justle one against another in the broad ways: they shall seem like torches, they shall run like the lightnings.* And so they did—and how perfect that was, how satisfying that all of London seemed on the very verge of a brawl. If she had had to live here, she would have been frightened of it; but as a visitor, she found it all the more satisfying the more alien it appeared.

They reached the house in Park Lane late in the day. It was a handsome town house, not extravagantly grand, but perfectly appointed. The ground floor consisted of a modest dining room on the left, a handsome parlor on the right, and a larger sitting room at the back with a view over Park Street, which ran behind the house on the side away from the park. Tomazina's room was on the first storey, across the open stairwell from the room that was to be Rose Elizabeth's dressing room; the master bedroom and Mr. Ashleigh's dressing room were at the back of the floor, looking out on the garden behind the house. The house went upward for another storey and a garret—she did not see them, but she understood there were other guest rooms and servants' quarters. Below stairs were the kitchen, the larder, the laundry, and the offices. It was all very compact—very different from the sprawling extravagance of Priedpie Hall. Tomazina was a little surprised that Mr. Ashleigh did not expect more of his city house. It was almost as if entering the city made him more rational as well as more likeable.

They dined at home that first evening. The food was not the best; it did not compare, in freshness, with what Tomazina was accustomed to; but Mr. Ashleigh seemed not to mind. He drank too much, but he did not turn short-tempered, as Tomazina had seen him do on some other occasions in the previous month. He did his best to ply both of the Comstock sisters with wine as well; and though the wine was very good, Tomazina's last encounter with drunkenness was still too recent in her memory for her to be tempted by more than a mouthful.

Rose Elizabeth, however, was not so cautious. Her husband had never been so pleasing; she was pleased with him not only for her own but for her sister's sake; and in such a frame of mind, she would do anything to please him in return, to reward him, as it were, for his pleasant behavior. So she drank as she was bid; and it was not long before Tomazina discerned the same signs of inebriation that must have been evident in her that night at Skycastle Lodge. Rose Elizabeth's face became flushed; her eyes shone with doting fondness as she looked at her husband, at the same time they grew dull with the confusion of the drink; she laughed more than she ought; she swayed a little in her seat, and leaned on the table as she spoke; and when she and Tomazina rose to withdraw, Tomazina had to help her from the room as Mrs. Hanscom had helped her.

"You have had too much wine, Rose Elizabeth," she told her when they were alone in the drawing room.

"I expect I have," said Rose Elizabeth. "But doing so once will not hurt me. And you saw how Mr. Ashleigh asked it of me; and he is being so very amiable that I cannot deny him anything."

Tomazina wanted to call for tea, as had been done in her case; but Rose Elizabeth would have none of it. "The master would be insulted if he saw we had called for tea before he had come into the room," she said. "He is only having a smoke and a little port; he will be here in a moment."

"Oh, Rose Elizabeth," Tomazina said, trying to inject some conscience into her, "you will have a fierce headache tomorrow, and you will spoil our seeing the town."

"Not at all," said Rose Elizabeth.

The evening was short. They were all weary with travel, and in the case of Rose Elizabeth there was little she could do besides go to bed. Tomazina parted from the others in the upstairs hall, carrying with her their drunkenly effusive wishes for a good night's sleep.

Sleep was not something she quickly found, however. She had left her sketchbooks at home, safely locked away, not daring to bring them to London with her; and she missed the comfort they afforded her and the stimulation they provided. She lay awake for quite some time, thinking of Samson; thinking how close he might be to her; thinking she might see him, if only by chance, on the morrow. At one point early in her wakefulness she thought she heard a distant cry, like that of a woman in pleasure, but it was very faint, and she was not sure where it came from, whether from within the house or from without; but after that, there were only city sounds—the clatter of late-returning carriages on the cobblestones of the street outside, the chiming of the hours, conversations half-heard through the partly opened window.

When she went down to breakfast, she found only Mr. Ashleigh there. He was a little worse for his consultation with the wine bottle, but despite a somewhat worn appearance, his mood had, if anything, soared still higher. Indeed, she thought she had never seen him more ebullient; and he wore as well a particularly self-satisfied air, as of one who has at last accomplished a great feat that has long eluded him. "Mrs. Ashleigh is going to take her breakfast in bed," he said. "She has a little headache—she is not used to wine, you know, though I am working on that. I think with a little food in her, she will be quite ready to go out on our adventures today."

"May I go see her?" asked Tomazina.

"Of course, my dear sister. Do not be so absurd as to ask my permission for such a thing. I would never do anything to keep Mrs. Ashleigh apart from the sister she loves so well. In fact, I would do all I can to keep you two together." And he smiled broadly, so that she could not help knowing exactly what he meant.

She went up to see Rose Elizabeth as soon as she had finished breakfast. She found her sister sitting up in a magnificent bed in a lavishly furnished room; a fine, warm sunlight, rare enough in London, but doubly rare in this cold summer, was spilling through the open windows, and a city breeze was bringing in the scent of some windowbox flowers mingled with the less fragrant odors of the gutters. The moment Tomazina entered the room, Rose Elizabeth smiled, and colored, and lowered her eyes, looking both pleased and embarrassed. It was an odd reaction. She set the breakfast tray to one side, and Tomazina came and sat on the bed beside her.

She put one palm on her sister's brow. "How do you feel, dear?" she asked.

"A little weak and unsteady," said Rose Elizabeth. "But otherwise not too bad, considering how foolish I was with the wine." And then she smiled and blushed again.

"You are all coy smiles today," said Tomazina in a low, teasing voice. "What is *that* all about, my dear Rose?"

"Oh, Mazie!" said Rose Elizabeth, blushing again. "I am not sure what happened—I am not sure what I should tell you. I should probably say nothing at all—it is not proper, I am sure.—But you *are* my sister. I know you would never repeat anything."

"Of course not," said Tomazina; and when Rose Elizabeth continued to remain smilingly reticent, she only smiled back, and widened her eyes expectantly, and waited.

"For some reason," Rose Elizabeth said then, speaking in a whisper, "our . . . our conjugal relations were . . . they were very different last night. I do not know what happened. I wish I did! But it was as if something came over me. It was . . . it was exquisitely pleasant, Tomazina. It makes me want to try again this very minute. I shall think about it all day, I know I shall. I feel . . . this will probably quite disgust you, but I feel . . . as if *it is still going on.*"

Tomazina could find nothing to say. She took Rose Elizabeth's hand and kissed it.

"Is that a tear?" asked Rose Elizabeth.

Tomazina laughed a little and openly wiped away the tear that had gathered at the corner of her eye.

"Yes," she said. "That is a tear. Love is feeling another's joy as if it were our own; and I do so love you, Rose, dearest Rose; and I am glad for you."

As she said this, she could not help wondering if this was truly the beginning of a change, or instead the only glimpse Rose Elizabeth would ever have of married pleasure. She feared it was likely to be the latter—the lone incident of sexual happiness in her entire life.

"Well," whispered Rose Elizabeth, "if you would listen to this *old, married woman,* you might hold out a little more hope for marriage than she offered you before."

"Indeed I shall, Rose," said Tomazina, thinking of Samson. "Indeed, I shall take your words as auspicious.— But do you really think you will feel well enough to brave the sights of the city?"

"After such an event, how could I help but feel well enough? I shall take some more tea, and then you may leave me to dress, and find me again ready for anything when we meet downstairs."

⚙ ⚙ ⚙

Rose Elizabeth did seem fresher when they went forth together to see the sights of Mayfair. They filled that first day with visits to shops—indeed, they went in and out of more shops than Tomazina had entered in her entire life to that time.

For that was Mayfair in those days. There were bookshops, clothiers, hatters, cap makers; there were tobacconists and wine merchants; goldsmiths, silversmiths, jewelers, shoe shops, hosiers, glove makers, haberdashers, drapers, watchmakers; teashops, fruiterers, coffee shops, spice shops, pastrycooks' shops; and all of the most excellent rank. There were stores that sold nothing but silks, or canes, or pelisses, or riding whips, or coats of fur, or buttons of exotic materials such as ivory and horn, or swords of silver and gold, or perfumes, or ornamental feathers, or cosmetics, or fans, or snuff boxes. There were shops that sold only furniture, or china table settings, or glassware, or silverware, or pewterware, or tinware, or mirrors, or wonderfully mysterious scientific instruments. There were shops devoted exclusively to equipping one for a career in the navy, or the church, or the law; there were shops with ladies' fashions so outlandish that they were scarcely credible; there were shops with dresses and hats and shoes so alluring that Tomazina, who had always been rather sensible about spending money on things she could find for less elsewhere, veritably itched to buy them. Mr. Ashleigh was very free with his cash, and they bought presents for all the Comstocks, to say nothing of new finery for Rose Elizabeth; and two servants followed behind to carry their purchases. When they grew weary of shopping, they sat down in a confectionery and ate ices. They saw no few studios, and entered several, and admired the paintings; and once Tomazina asked timidly after Bond Street. "It is the next street over," said Mr. Ashleigh. "We shall have to walk up it at least once before we leave." But he seemed smugly mysterious about it, and in no hurry to go there soon, so she let the subject pass.

At the end of this day Tomazina felt she had seen all London. She knew she had not; she had barely seen Westminster from a distance, and none of the Tower or the Thames since they had arrived; but she had a sense of having walked for miles and having seen all there was to see of shops in all the world. But the next day they went out and did much the same again. They breakfasted out in a charming public garden; they shopped and toured; and at night they went to Vauxhall, dined in a supper box on very good food, and saw the fireworks. This latter park was a wonderful fairy-tale world within a story-book city: there were walks and wildernesses, sculptures and statues, pavilions and mock-temples, all lit by the magic of gas lamps. Mr. Ashleigh danced with Rose Elizabeth on a dance floor there, and they all sat down briefly to listen to an opera singer in one of the concert halls.

Rose Elizabeth was in an ecstasy. Mr. Ashleigh's fine mood went on and on, fed, among other things, by the evident delight of his wife in the novelties of the city. Occasionally, too, they met friends of his bachelor days, whose very frank admiration of the match he had made for himself also increased his good spirits. More than one gentleman friend tried to attach himself to their group, but he would not allow it. "But *Ash*," one gentleman complained, "you cannot have two to yourself; it is positively *Mohammmedan*." To which Mr. Ashleigh replied that Miss Comstock was reserved for a better man; and he gave a wink to Tomazina that made Rose Elizabeth laugh.

The next day was a Sunday. They went to the church in the morning, and suffered through a very bad sermon, delivered in a high and pretentious style. It was the first moment in all their visit to London that Tomazina felt a little homesick, yearning for a homily that showed a little honest piety and humble good sense. The afternoon was spent somewhat quietly; their most strenuous undertaking was to walk in the park, where they stared at the London fashions, and the London fashionable stared at them.

At the end of that day, they spoke of the plans for the morrow. Mr. Ashleigh promised them a tour of the riverside, the Tower, and London Bridge (the ancient structure still stood at that time, though without the many houses and shops it had supported during the medieval period). "And Bond Street?" asked Tomazina. "I think we missed it in our first day's outing in Mayfair."

"We did," admitted Mr. Ashleigh in an odd tone. "Perhaps we shall take it in at the end of the afternoon tomorrow. Or perhaps we must wait a bit." And he smiled as though he had a secret.

She discovered some part of this when she came down to breakfast the next morning: Mr. Hugh Ashleigh was there. When she entered the room, he rose and bowed to her, smiling with delight; but so sorry was she to see him, and so displeased, that she managed only a token curtsy. Mr. Ashleigh himself was smiling smugly, and even Rose Elizabeth looked pleased by this turn of events.

"I had not known you were to be in London, sir," Tomazina told her suitor. "In fact, I had understood the precise opposite. I supposed you to be arranging for future shooting in Scotland."

"Shooting! Nay, I was on business, I assure you. But when I heard you were to be here, Miss Comstock, I could not stay away."

She said nothing further, but sat down in silence and began her breakfast. He came to her chair, gazing down at her as though he could barely resist seizing her and kissing her.

"You are not sorry to see me here, are you, Miss Comstock?" he asked.

She could not think of how to answer him without being either rude or untruthful; so she only repeated, "I had thought you were not to be here, sir."

This was very discouraging to him, and he went back to his chair and looked at his brother, who only grinned and rolled his eyes at him, as if to say, "You are the one who wants her, man; do not blame *me* if she is perverse."

"Well," said Mr. Hugh Ashleigh after a time, again speaking directly to Tomazina, and in a forcedly cheerful tone, "it is splendid weather, and such days have been few and far between this summer. We must take advantage of it. I hear we are to see Westminster, and the Tower, and the Bridge, so that you may tell your children all about them."

"So that I may tell the children of Mr. and Mrs. Ashleigh about them," Tomazina corrected him coolly. "I do not believe I shall have any children myself."

Mr. Ashleigh thought this jab at his brother's plans extremely funny, and had all he could do to keep from bursting into laughter. Mr. Hugh Ashleigh saw his merriment and rose to the challenge of it.

"There will be more than one Mr. and Mrs. Ashleigh who have children," he told Tomazina. "But in the meantime, we have a very pleasant outing planned."

"And we shall dine in, Tomazina," said Rose Elizabeth. "We shall have a guest tonight."

"Yes," said Mr. Ashleigh, proudly holding up a letter to show her. "Lord Esterbroke is in town and will dine with us.—Fortunately that fellow Upton is not, so we shall be spared him."

Two toadies at one table is one too many for Lord Esterbroke, apparently, she thought; but she limited her irony to the comment, "I did not know his lordship was capable of writing without Mr. Upton's assistance."

"There is not much to the note," explained Mr. Ashleigh, opening the letter now and holding it up so that she could see the contents. Two cramped and nearly illegible lines had been scratched across the sheet at a wild angle. "But it is an honor to our house to have his lordship dine here," he added.

"Indeed, sir," she said, "I think the honor rather flows in the reverse."

The pleasure Mr. Ashleigh had from this remark was well worth the price, for it had not cost her the least insincerity.

"And unfortunately I shall not be able to join you," Mr. Hugh Ashleigh said. "I have a very important dinner to attend."

"That is all right, sir," she said. "You shall not be missed, as you were not expected."

Mr. Ashleigh laughed outright; and Mr. Hugh Ashleigh, smiling grimly, said, "I say, Miss Comstock, are you not too hard upon me?"

"Not at all, sir. You were expected to be attending to business, or at the very least to your sport; so we are not surprised to find that you still prefer business. I hope your business is not faro, sir, or *jeu d'enfer,* or any of the other wickednesses we read are common in London."

"Good God, no, Miss Comstock," he protested. "I dine with some stockholders of a company that is about to pay me very handsomely for some shares I hold. It is no small matter."

"It is faro at a much higher level," said Mr. Ashleigh, finding it entertaining for the moment to side with Tomazina against his brother.

"It is a game that will allow me to buy my second son a very fine preferment someday," said Mr. Hugh Ashleigh boldly to Tomazina.

"Have you already a *second* son, sir—and I have omitted to congratulate you on the first?"

"You are very provoking, Miss Comstock," said Mr. Hugh Ashleigh, with the same grim smile. "But I shall have my revenge on you, I think."

She did not like the way he said this; for he seemed to truly mean it. And as she continued to eat breakfast, conversing with Mr. Hugh Ashleigh as little as she could, she began to think that Mr. Ashleigh, in proposing her visit to London in the first place, had intended all along that they would meet his brother here. In fact, it was likely that Mr. Hugh Ashleigh himself had proposed the plan to his brother. Rose Elizabeth had been fed misleading information about

Mr. Hugh Ashleigh's plans, which she passed along innocently to Tomazina. Her sister apparently thought Mr. Hugh Ashleigh's early return from Edinburgh all a happy change of plan; but Tomazina wondered if he had ever been so far north at all.

❖ ❖ ❖

They went out to view the sights as no more than tourists; but the Ashleigh brothers were determined to make the Comstock sisters' visit to the city memorable at all costs. A boat had been hired to take them along the river from point to point; and though the fantastic stench of the Thames, and the insane crowding of the waters, did to some extent detract from the pleasure of this novelty, the effort to amuse and entertain was appreciated. Mr. Hugh Ashleigh was so charming and affable that Tomazina did at one moment think that if he could have been trusted to be so amiable every day of his future life, or even half the days of his future life, he would be a bargain of a husband for someone.

And if the sights they saw that day were new to Tomazina and Rose Elizabeth, their reaction was nothing novel to the ancient and impassive structures they visited. Westminster and Whitehall inspired their awe and pride; the Tower was both chilling for its history and disappointing for its smallness; and London Bridge was only a noisy thoroughfare, already glimpsed from Westminster Bridge. Between viewing the Tower and walking the Bridge, however, they had a picnic in a diminutive private park that the Ashleighs had rented for the occasion. A shopman supplied an excellent luncheon of cold meat, fresh fruits, champagne, and assorted cakes and ices, enough to feed four times their number. These preparations seemed to have been the work of Mr. Hugh Ashleigh himself, sometime late the previous day. It did not escape Tomazina that this meant he had been in London at least twenty-four hours without leaving word to this effect at his brother's house. Furthermore, her suspicions about his whereabouts in the last week were increasingly confirmed by other comments about his doings that he carelessly let drop over the course of the day.

Late in the afternoon they hired two open cabs to take them back to Park Lane. Even this means of travel seemed to have been concerted, as it later appeared that the cabs had been paid in advance. Mr. Hugh Ashleigh and she must ride in one, and Mr. Ashleigh and Rose Elizabeth in the other. Tomazina thought almost constantly of Mr. Ashleigh's hint that they might walk Bond Street, but she made no mention of it. She had no desire to encounter Mr. Esterbroke in Mr. Hugh Ashleigh's company, and she was thinking that it would be much safer to revert to her previous plan—to go out to Brackensom for several days, and during that time to engineer an invitation for Mr. Esterbroke.

As they drove back toward Mayfair, Mr. Hugh Ashleigh pointed out the key landmarks to her with the gentle condescension with which a parent exhibits city sights to a child. She reversed the condescension; she acted as a parent does when a child points out commonplaces along the highway. It was ultimately quite baffling to him; but from time to time he darted her a look that seemed to promise that she would get her comeuppance soon.

They wound through the London streets in a very confusing way. She saw that for some reason they were skirting Mayfair; they turned onto Oxford Street, part of which she had walked two days ago. Then the driver, with no word from Mr. Hugh Ashleigh, turned abruptly left at a corner, leaving Oxford Street and clattering down a narrower way; and it did not need eyes as active as hers to discern the signs that told her where she was.

"Is this not Bond Street?" she asked Mr. Hugh Ashleigh.

"It is a shortcut to Park Lane," he said.

She sank back into the seat of the cab in a kind of panic. What if Samson were to see her, traveling with Mr. Hugh

Ashleigh? She looked back and saw that the cab with her sister and Mr. Ashleigh was still immediately behind theirs. Samson might not notice them there, all the same; and if he saw her alone with Mr. Hugh Ashleigh, he might not be able to draw any conclusions but the very worst. She drew her parasol about so as to hide herself from at least one side of the street, and for a moment she turned her face into it, away from the eyes of passersby. Mr. Hugh Ashleigh misunderstood her action. "You need not fear anything," he said. "Bond Street is not like St. James; ladies are not at all out of place here. In any case, you will not be offered any rudeness with me beside you."

She had never heard of this characteristic of St. James Street; but now that he said it, she took some solace from the fact that the Bond Street she could see seemed to be inhabited by both men and women—though, admittedly, more by men, the bucks and beaus of the time, very well dressed gentlemen, walking together or standing in small knots before the glittering shop fronts, conversing. But even these gentlemen, as their clothing proclaimed them to be, looked up as the cab passed and stared boldly at her; and she heard low whistles and occasional remarks of admiration after she had gone by. This kind of affront apparently was not enough to provoke Mr. Hugh Ashleigh's protectiveness; he seemed rather to enjoy having this homage paid to the lady he was accompanying.

Suddenly he turned to her and said, "There is something I would very much like you to see. Do you mind?"

"I do mind," she replied in an urgent tone. "Let us go straight home."

But he paid no attention to her; he gave a command to the driver and the cab pulled up to the curb. This was the last thing she wanted, and yet she could not deny his apparently innocent request without revealing her reluctance to be anywhere on this street at all. She took his hand, and he helped her to descend; she looked about in alarm at the passersby, fearful that Samson would be among them, but she saw only strange men, city faces, equally curious about her, but not familiar. She turned away from the street, placing her parasol over her shoulder to hide herself, and studying the shop window before her, even though it was empty, the interior of the bow frame blocked by plush velvet drapes.

Rose Elizabeth and Mr. Ashleigh joined them. "What is it?" asked Rose Elizabeth eagerly. "What are we to see here? Is this not Bond Street?"

Mr. Hugh Ashleigh did not answer, and Mr. Ashleigh, too, wore a smug and mysterious smile. Mr. Hugh Ashleigh offered his arm to Tomazina, and she took it with an increased sense of dread.

They went through the shop door that was immediately beside them. It was curious that the Ashleighs abandoned proper precedence here without a thought—the younger brother and the younger sister of these two couples going first. This alteration in their usual way of doing things in itself would have made her uneasy. She was further flustered by the sudden need to collapse her parasol, and did not read the nameplate beside the door post, though she looked for it at the last moment—an instant too late.

They stepped into a kind of waiting room, luxuriously appointed with the very best furniture of the latest French design. A little bell rang as the door was opened and closed, a signal that customers had entered. Here manners and precedence broke down even further; for Mr. Hugh Ashleigh, letting go her arm, went ahead by himself, leading the way on across this room towards a door on the far side, not only as if the ladies were not present, but as if he were the owner of the place himself. Just as he was about to pass through the inner door into whatever lay beyond, a man in a pristine white smock entered through it and blocked his progress.

"Mr. Ashleigh!" he said in a tone that expressed surprise.

"We are here to view your master's progress," said Mr. Hugh Ashleigh—rather rudely, as Tomazina thought.

"I'm sorry, sir; no visitors. Those are master's orders. He made that clear on your last visit, sir; he will write to you when all is ready."

"I do not accept those terms, man; I am here to see for myself."

"You may leave your card, sir; that is all I can tell you."

Mr. Ashleigh drew himself up in irritation. He was, as an avid sportsman, well built and vigorous, and would have been daunting to many an opponent; but this servant was a large man, and he stood squarely in the doorway, giving every indication that he would have to be knocked down before he would be overruled.

"I have a right to go in," said Mr. Hugh Ashleigh. "I am paying good money for your master's services."

"I believe, sir, you have not paid a shilling yet," said the man.

"But the point is that I have *engaged his services* with an offer of money; and therefore I have a right to enter."

"But it is my obligation to prevent you, sir; that is the service I render my master, and that is what *he* pays *me* for."

"I say, fellow, it has been more than a fortnight since I engaged him; I must see how the work progresses."

"I am sorry, Mr. Ashleigh; I have my orders, and I cannot let you in. I am especially forbidden to interrupt my master when he is engaged in that particular work; and to tell you the truth, sir, even if I had not had that order, I would be loath to do it, because it is only when the master is engaged in *that particular work* that he is at all happy."

"I care nothing for his happiness or unhappiness, man; I am here to see what I came to see; and see it I shall."

The altercation went on in this vein for another minute, Mr. Hugh Ashleigh becoming increasingly rude and sarcastic, and the man remaining cool and unmoved. He was like a stone wall; Tomazina could see, if Mr. Hugh Ashleigh could not, that he would not yield to any persuasion Mr. Hugh Ashleigh could possibly offer. And this fact gave her a palpable sense of relief. Anything Mr. Hugh Ashleigh could want so very badly must not be entirely right; in a minute more, she was sure, he must acknowledge himself defeated, and they would all leave. She and Rose Elizabeth would have to listen to the consequences of this humiliation—the Ashleigh brothers would bitterly complain about the arrogance of whoever it was who had ordered this servant to prevent their access—but that would be preferable to suffering the gaucheness of barging in where they were so clearly not wanted.

But at that juncture Mr. Hugh Ashleigh tried a new form of persuasion. He turned to Tomazina, and seeing that she was behind him and realizing that his larger frame must have blocked the servant's view of her, he stepped to one side, indicating her to the man with a gesture. And now the servant did look at her, and his dour and immoveable expression changed into one of astonishment and awe.

"Can you deny that *this* lady has a right to enter here?" Mr. Hugh Ashleigh asked.

For some inexplicable reason, this changed everything.

"I beg your pardon, madam," the man said to Tomazina, bowing. All his righteous obstinacy instantly melted into uncertainty; he was torn between his master's orders and whatever compulsion the sight of Tomazina seemed to offer. "I did not see you there," he said, in a hurried murmur of pained contrition, "I did not understand who you were. I shall have to—I suppose I shall have to—I trust my master would wish—if you would be so kind as to wait here—"

And then, still baffled and unsure, he turned about and went back into the inner room. Mr. Hugh Ashleigh looked at her triumphantly, and taking her by the arm again, led her confidently onwards after the man.

"But we are expected to wait," she protested.

"Nonsense," said Mr. Hugh Ashleigh, in his best bullying tone. And he literally pulled her forward so that she must either go with him or fall to the floor.

And as she entered this next room, she realized at last where she was. It was the last place she had ever thought Mr. Hugh Ashleigh himself would ever lead her, and that perhaps accounted for what seemed to her now to be a complete obtuseness on her part in not guessing the facts of the matter any sooner.

For indeed, the worst had happened, the very worst: what she had both dreaded and hoped for in this journey to London. The realization came upon her so suddenly that she could do nothing to forestall or avert any damage from the circumstances; she was borne along right into the midst of them before she could begin to think about fleeing.

The room they entered was very large; it seemed that the walls of several rooms had been knocked down and the interior of the building refinished to form a large and echoing space. It was a studio, albeit still sparsely filled with paintings, but a studio all the same, littered with all the accoutrements of the painting trade—easels and canvases and palettes and paints, ladders and stools and backdrops of various kinds. A few portraits hung at one side, but for the most part the walls were bare and blank, only whitewashed, reflecting the light of several huge skylights tilted toward the north. There were also some sketches posted on a long board that had been set up on the support of two easels; and though Tomazina did not at first perceive the common subject of these sketches, she saw at once, standing near the easels on a stand of its own, the portrait of her that Samson had started in Gloucestershire and had so abruptly removed before it was finished.

For this was indeed Samson Esterbroke's studio into which she was being led. She slipped her arm out of Mr. Hugh Ashleigh's grip instantly, and she paused in confusion, but she felt a hand on her back, between her shoulders—it was her brother-in-law's, behind her, and it was compelling her forward into the room. She heard a murmured exclamation from Rose Elizabeth, and she looked up, toward the far end of the room, and saw, in part at least, what her sister had just discerned.

A large—a very large—canvas was in progress there. It was so tall that the painter had had a stepladder set up to one side of it, near the top of which he was at this moment perched, applying color to the background of the picture, with his back turned to them. At first she saw nothing but him; she paid no attention to what he was painting. Her heart beat harder; she tried once more to stop, but Mr. Hugh Ashleigh took her arm again determinedly, and in her confusion at seeing Samson once more she did not resist; she barely even noticed the compulsion to which she was being subjected, any more than she observed the painting itself. Thus it was not until she had been drawn halfway down the room that she perceived exactly what it was that Samson was working on.

It was a full length portrait of herself, of Tomazina Comstock.

And finding herself . . . here, in London . . . there, in that portrait . . . was inexpressibly disorienting, like meeting a doppelganger, or a twin sibling one did not know existed.

This other Tomazina, or . . . this same person as herself . . . was dressed in antique garb, facing the viewer directly. She stood within the outline of the door of a garden, as if she had opened the door itself inward; and indeed, the garden door was visible on the left; she stood beside it. The picture frame, when the canvas was mounted in one, would form a continuation of the frame of that doorway. That enclosure was a startling effect in itself; it was as if the door was mounted in the very wall of the room, and as if the woman on the far side had thrown it open to admit the viewer. The garden beyond the woman was both familiar and foreign, and Tomazina realized that it, too, was in exotic and ancient garb; it was no English garden. Despite this context of doorway and garden beyond, the painting was incontestably a *portrait*—it had been conceived and executed fully in the purpose of rendering an image of Tomazina Comstock, and insofar as the fundamental likeness to her was concerned, it showed Tomazina nothing that she had not seen in her mirror on many a day.

But what a portrait!

Rather say not a portrait at all, but the vivid image—not of a dream, but of an instant of *déja vu*, etched on the brain in some other time, and intruding, recurring *now* on waking life in baffling reality. How had he done it? And yet *he had* done it: it was the picture he had once said he had always wished to paint—the picture of the Shulamite, the lover in the Song of Solomon. And yet it was both the Shulamite and Tomazina herself. It was her own face looking longingly forth out of that painting, her own figure in that ancient and simple robe, her own dark hair that was stirred by the movement of the fragrant air. The arms—one holding open the garden door, the other reaching forward, beckoning—were, in the words Samson had once used about hers, sweet and round; those were her breasts beneath that gossamer raiment, full, voluptuously female, *real;* the mouth, sensuous, the lips parted as if with the anticipation of a cry of love, of an open kiss—this was Tomazina's mouth. Only the skin, bronzed by the sun, was unlike hers; and only the eyes, which were of the same blue as those that looked back at her every day from her mirror, were unlike the Shulamite's. And for all the beauty of the figure and the gesture, it was the eyes to which the viewer returned again and again: the eyes half-adream with desire, both captivating and mysterious, penetrating and remote, healing and wounding, the eyes of an Eve and a Lilith, both innocent and bold, and yet also of a Queen of Sheba and a Sophia, learned and wise.

To Tomazina—steeped as she was in the Song of Solomon, and despite the long certainty she had had about the meaning of that poem, which had been shaken only slightly by reconsideration in the past year—the picture was a revelation. For here was a physical (a very physical) woman depicted in exacting detail in her mortal raiment; and yet this was not just a pictured body, but a pictured soul—a soul as she herself was inwardly a soul. And she understood suddenly, in an eyeblink of time, how it could be that something so fleshly as the Song could symbolize something so spiritual as the longing of the soul for God; and by extension, how the copulation of lover and lover, in all its ineffable intensity, could stand in for the union of human and divine. Though she was still a virgin, she had had a presaging experience of sexual delight, and it had been enough to allow her to guess at the ecstasy of the union of man and woman. And knowing that, and seeing that ecstasy and longing represented in this painting that was both herself and not herself, she understood now how in some higher sense the soul could be wedded to God. *This is a mystery,* as the apostle said; it was an epiphany; she could not have articulated how she understood now what she never could have known before. The Song was pure, in both its earthly and its spiritual sense; and the two senses overlapped and intertwined inextricably, both in the original and in this painting of its theme.

Unto the pure all things are pure; and Tomazina, for all her little sins, was certainly still in higher eyes pure. Someone else looking at that picture, someone defiled and unbelieving, would have seen it as impure instead, because of the impurity that he or she brought to that room to look with and thus to see; or as something inexplicable, because of a personal limitation of understanding. The Ashleigh brothers, certainly, did not achieve Tomazina's epiphany; nor even did Rose Elizabeth. But the picture was of such power that even those who did not understand it could sense that it had deep significance. It was not just a portrait of a beautiful Englishwoman in foreign and ancient costume. It aimed at sublimity, and it achieved the sublime. It was not, like the many portraits Rossetti and his circle were to paint in succeeding decades, an attempt at the sublime that achieved only a worshipful idealization of a particular subject; or that remained caught in the sensual, unable to free itself and soar; or that did soar but then also fell like Daedalus into the sea of romantic kitsch, which is littered with so many wrecks. Despite its being English, and of its age, and thus to some extent caught in time and place, it was also universal, as the statuary of the Greeks is universal, for all its Greek particularity, for all that its marble and bronze is frozen, soundless, in its Greek moment; or as the Girl with the Ermine or the Leda or the Mona Lisa or the Mary in the Annunciation of Leonardo are all universals, showing us so casually what seems at first to be mere loveliness but proves on a longer viewing to be a concealing shell for the high arcana of womanliness; or universals as are the descended Christ and the tormented slaves of Michelangelo; or universals as are the craggy Dutchmen of Rembrandt. It was not *illustrative,* as the vast majority of paintings are, merely saying, "This is how I, the artist, say that you, the viewer, ought to see this story." Rather it achieved an independence from its source; it was an icon in its own right, rife with meaning; and the viewer groaned beneath its beauty, feeling inadequate to the task it set, like a person being forced to awaken to dazzling day who tries to retreat and hide again in oblivion and illusion.

Those who have set their aim at sublimity and fallen short know the bitterness of that failure. And indeed, it may well be a happier and more useful kind of art, to speak of common things, the domestic comedy, than to attempt the austere and the superlative and so, through a littleness of one's powers, to accomplish nothing. Besides, often enough even those who aim at the sublime are not aware when they have failed to achieve it. But Samson Esterbroke had here taken the dare of his mortality, believing that it was better to try at the best and to fail than to confine himself to what he could easily do. He had taken the dare; he had succeeded.

This was not a painting; this was an entire poem in one image—all the longing of the Song of Solomon sketched out on canvas and illuminated with the double-dye of oils. This was not a painting; this was a song. And yet it was neither poem nor song nor painting, but all of them.

As she saw this act of art and felt its power, Tomazina stopped, finally, beyond any capability of Mr. Hugh Ashleigh to draw her further onwards. She was speechless, overwhelmed. Around her could be heard—she did not notice them then, but she remembered them later—the petty muffled exclamations of the others: Rose Elizabeth saying, "Oh, Mazie! Oh, Mazie!" over and over; and Mr. Ashleigh cycling through various dull oaths: "Good God! I say, good God! Good word! Good Lord!"; and Mr. Hugh Ashleigh murmuring, "Capital! Capital!" like a banker approving the filling up of his accounts.

Samson's assistant meanwhile had gone directly to the base of the ladder; and laying one hand on it, he now said, "Excuse me, Mr. Esterbroke, sir, but there are some visitors."

Samson did not look down from the ladder. "Mr. Tompkins," he said, "you know I told you not to admit any visitors. No visitors! Please ask them to come back next week, or better still, next month."

"But sir," protested Mr. Tompkins.

"No *buts,* Mr. Tompkins. Please do as I ask you."

"But if you'll only look, sir—"

And it seemed that only then did Samson realize that the visitors were actually in the studio. He turned about abruptly on the ladder, and his eyes . . . met hers . . . and stopped, completely arrested. The ladder, however, was not arrested; it jolted and rocked and surely would have toppled over if Mr. Tompkins had not clung to it and secured it.

"You see, sir," Mr. Tompkins said. "I had to let *that* lady in, sir."

She did not hear Mr. Tompkins making his excuses; and it seemed Samson did not either. He stared at her, and she stared at him; and all she could think was that she wished that a pit would open beneath her and she would sink out of sight for all time. This was not how she had wished to see him again—to barge into his studio in Mr. Hugh Ashleigh's company, without notice; and she was, furthermore, baffled and strangely, deeply hurt by the sight of this enormous monument to her that he was creating on canvas, beautiful though it was. It seemed a monument to his love for her; and yet she knew that he had rejected her, knew it bitterly, knew it better than any known sweetness.

Someone else was talking, but she could not put the words together. Samson, for his part, seemed to pay no attention either. He backed down the ladder unsteadily, keeping his eyes fixed on hers; and then he thrust his palette and brush unseeingly at Mr. Tompkins and came toward her.

She saw now what Mrs. Hanscom had meant by the look of suffering in his face, of spiritual injury, of something broken and humbled in him. He had been prone before to look unhappy when they first met after an interval apart; but this was different. She almost wondered if he had discovered he had some terrible illness, except that he looked physically hale. His gaze, though humble, was yet so piercing that she felt naked before it. She thought again of her shame, of how she had thrown herself at him—and beyond that, of her Blue Book—and instantly her face and throat stung with heat.

She turned abruptly away and went as if to view the long board on which the sketches had been pinned. She looked at them without seeing them for a moment, while she heard Mr. Hugh Ashleigh saying, "Capital, Esterbroke! It is coming along splendidly! I dare say you are nearly finished— what do you have, another few hours of work at most? We have come just at the right time."

Mr. Esterbroke did not answer. She darted a look back at him; he had come to a halt and was still staring at her with that strange new expression.

"I say, Esterbroke," said Mr. Hugh Ashleigh a little more loudly and forcefully, "you do not mind our letting ourselves in like this, do you? We quite insisted; you cannot blame your man. I think I have a certain right, as the commissioner of the picture, to see how it is going."

The commissioner of the picture! she thought to herself with horror. *Whatever is he about? How dare he commission a portrait of me without my consent?*

She realized, even as she thought this, that the sketches pinned to the board were those that had been taken of her in the days when Mr. Esterbroke was planning his picture of her and her sisters. In her absence, they formed his model now, along with the portrait he had done for the Hanscoms. Somehow this evidence of his deliberate, methodical undertaking of the portrait hurt her still more.

"I suppose you can claim that right," said Samson in a quiet voice; a voice so strangely altered that she turned to him at once to see the meaning of it; but he was now looking at Mr. Hugh Ashleigh. He seemed now not only humbled but *defeated.* It was inexplicable in the extreme.

"Well, when will it be finished, then?" demanded Mr. Hugh Ashleigh.

"I do not know," said Samson.

"It looks finished to me," said Mr. Ashleigh.

"It is not," said Samson. "And I alone shall say when it is complete."

"It shall be finished if I think it is," said Mr. Hugh Ashleigh, with an arrogance that made Tomazina feel sick to be even remotely associated with him.

"You have not paid me a penny," said Samson.

"I offered to do so!" said Mr. Hugh Ashleigh. "I offered you the full commission in advance. You would not take it."

"Now you know why," Samson said.

"I do not understand you, sir."

"I did so in order to be able to assert my absolute right to determine when it is finished. You cannot be said to own it if you have not paid me anything for it."

"But I *do* own it. I was the one who commissioned it; and that gives me moral rights over it," said Mr. Hugh Ashleigh.

To Tomazina, this was a mortification on mortification. It was unbearable that Mr. Hugh Ashleigh should assert any right over her even at this remove. As he said this, Samson looked at her; and there could be no doubt what he was thinking. He was thinking how she had loved him; and how, when he had rejected her, she had turned and allied herself to Mr. Hugh Ashleigh, as her next best option.

What else could he conclude? Indeed, he must have concluded it before he began this painting. What Mr. Hugh Ashleigh had done was inconceivably improper—to publicly commission a portrait of a woman who was not married to him. A man would do such a thing only in the case of some mistress or common actress (and actresses in her day were frequently understood to be prostitutes); or in the case of a woman married or engaged to him. Indeed, there could be only one conclusion anyone could draw from this public act: that she had accepted Mr. Hugh Ashleigh as her future husband. And surely Samson had drawn that conclusion: He was looking at her with the same pity she had felt for him in his infatuation for Miss Doronne; he could be thinking only what she had thought about him, that the partner she had chosen was far beneath her.

She wanted to cry out and protest against this misrepresentation—but there was a reproach that stopped her. *This is the man who rejected me,* she thought to herself, as one who twists a knife in her own wound. If she knew any single thing about Samson Esterbroke, it was that he did not want her. He had had his chance at her and turned her down. What did he care, or why should she care if he did care, about whom she married instead?

Although she had now turned abruptly away again, she could sense him approaching her. She felt it almost as if some intense source of heat were aimed at her, some great light shining upon her that would have cast its blinding rays into her eyes even if they had been closed.

"Miss Comstock," he said.

His tone gave a wrench to her heart, and she looked at him miserably, unable to speak.

"May I offer you my very best wishes and felicitations," he said.

He pities me! she thought. *He does not love me, but he pities me for agreeing to a marriage so far beneath me!*

It was unbearable. All she wanted to do was to get out of the studio; and yet at the same time all her will was directed at restraining herself from turning on her heel and getting away from him. She had to say something, and she could not think what.

"No such wishes are in order, sir," she said curtly; but she spoke so indistinctly that she herself could not hear what she was saying.

"Pardon?" he asked. The very gentleness and deference of his voice tore at her.

"I said no such wishes are in order," she repeated, her voice now seeming, in its hurtness, to be harsh and repellant.

He, too, now looked hurt. He bowed to her very humbly and said, "My apologies, Miss Comstock."

He thinks I am angry at him for his daring to offer congratulations—for his pretending to esteem my decision to marry, after he himself rejected me, she thought. And she realized that in fact he was right about her feelings, though his premise was totally mistaken. To disabuse him of the mistake he had made would have looked as if she were appealing to him once again—it was impossible to say anything in response that was not either untrue or repulsive to her own self-esteem; so she sought desperately for some more conciliatory topic.

"I trust you are in good health, sir," she said.

"I am; I am indeed. I am in perfect health," he said, looking relieved that she had relaxed her forbidding tone.

"I am very glad to hear it, sir.—I understand you were at Brackensom not so long ago."

"Yes; to visit Mrs. Percy, and of course Mr. and Mrs. Hanscom. And the new heir there; I am sure you know that he is thriving, or certainly was when I saw him."

"Yes, we are all well pleased." She was horrified to hear herself sound so cool and regal.

"And you are well?" he asked.

"I? I, sir?"

"Yes, Miss Comstock. You are well?"

She felt her resentment rising again. "I have never been better, sir." The instant she said it, she wished she had bitten her tongue off; for naturally he would connect her proud insistence on her good health with her supposed engagement.

"Ah," he said. "I am glad to hear that."

He studied her, but she refused to meet his eye. "Dare I ask," he began falteringly, "if my painting . . . if it pleases you?"

She looked up at it again, but was so overwhelmed by the emotions it stirred in her that she had to look away.

"It is . . . it is beyond my powers of speech to say how sublime it is," she said.

He was silent for a long moment. She darted a look at him; his eyes were closed, and he wore an expression of painful bliss, as if her opinion meant more to him than anything on earth.

Then, as if at an anxious prompting, he opened his eyes and he spoke to her again. "And you do not fault my depiction of you?" he asked.

"The likeness in particular, do you mean, apart from the symbol you have made of me?"

"Yes," he said.

"Well, *that* . . . *that* is . . . I can only say that it is extravagantly generous, sir."

"Not at all," he said urgently. "It is a mere shadow of the reality it attempts to depict. Until this instant it pleased me—I thought it a likeness and representation of you; but now that you are here it, it is revealed as a colossal failure. I had thought it beautiful—until its subject came into the room to be compared to it."

She was bitterly confused and upset by what he was saying. "Do you offer these compliments to—"

But she could not think why he would praise her so, unless he pitied her. She sought another topic of conversation, any other, somehow found one in pure irrelevancy, and seized on it.

"You have not seen my sister since her change of condition," she said.

He was disappointed that she had changed the topic. He turned to the others now, though he seemed to do so only perforce. "Yes," he said to Rose Elizabeth. "You have become Mrs. Ashleigh since the last time I saw you—since those wonderful, those halcyon days I spent with your family in Hampshire—I have never had the opportunity to congratulate you. Forgive me for my neglect. These changes all come so suddenly; they are gone by before we can think to communicate our feelings; they are overwhelming. And you, Mr. Ashleigh—forgive me for neglecting you, too." He went to Mr. Ashleigh now and offered his hand, which Mr. Ashleigh took with a smug, condescending air. "Congratulations on securing one of the Misses Comstock," said Samson. "That is a marriage that would make any man blessed."

Hypocrite! cried Tomazina bitterly within herself. *It is such a marriage as you yourself declined!*

"I am indeed quite blessedly happy," agreed Mr. Ashleigh, with a satisfied glance at Rose Elizabeth. "And I am soon to be happier still," he added, with a significant glance and smile at Tomazina.

With that glance she had a new epiphany, and nowhere near as exalted as Samson's portrait had achieved in her.

She saw all of sudden what they were doing—what these Ashleigh brothers had had in mind from the moment this stay in London had been planned. It was not simply to trap her into spending more time with Mr. Hugh Ashleigh; it was to bring her here, as his purported fiancée, and to make sure that Samson understood that she had been claimed; it was to drive the final wedge between Samson and her; and it was to compromise her honor yet more by making her acknowledge, by her silence in the presence of this portrait, the connection between herself and Mr. Hugh Ashleigh.

And the most painful part of it all was that it was utterly unnecessary. Samson *did not want her.* He had proven that; this nasty little ruse of the Ashleigh brothers' was not in the least required.

As she saw through the strategem of the Ashleighs'— this breathtaking piece of effrontery and manipulation—she felt in fact breath-taken, suffocated, sickened, and she could bear it no longer. She walked abruptly away from them all and went up the long studio, through the door to the waiting room, and out into the street. She felt, as she did this, as if she were walking through a series of webs, each stronger than the last, webs that bound her to Samson; and she had the terrifying thought, which came over her with the intensity of a prophetic intuition, that if she left him now, she would never again see him in her lifetime. But she had been scorned—no matter how kindly and gently; she had offered him her self and her life, and he had refused it. To her it seemed she had no choice but to be silent and to go.

I could have been his Shulamite, she thought to herself, *in flesh, in spirit, in life, and not just on canvas; but he did not want me. And yet in his imagination—he takes me as a lover! On his canvas I become his Shulamite! And beyond the plane of his canvas, outside the frame of his imagination, in his life itself, he still pursues the illusion of Isabella Doronne. Oh, Samson! You have chosen between the real and the unreal, between the demonstrated fact and the imaginary hope—and you have made the wrong choice, the choice fatal to us both.*

She came to, as it were, standing before the studio. The very day seemed to have grown dim; the sunlight was as if wan, dusty, filtered through her own disinterest in anything but this love that she had lost.

She looked about her, both carelessly and defiantly. She was suddenly puzzled, both existentially and in the most ordinary way: she did not know what to do with herself, both forevermore and in the moment. She thought of the cabs, and of boarding one of them to isolate herself at least somewhat from the passersby, but in looking about she found they had departed. Instead she went to one side of the studio door and leaned, nearly sagged, against the wall. She was surprised that tears, even sobs, wanted to rise from within her; they seemed so petty and inadequate; and holding fast to the full depth of her sorrow, she fought them back. To avoid the bold stares of the gentlemen who were promenading by her, she put up her parasol and effected half a privacy; and then she waited for what seemed an eternity before the others followed her.

Rose Elizabeth came to her at once. "There you are! We thought you were waiting for us in the foyer."

Tomazina could find no word within her to bend into an answer.

"Oh, Mazie!" said Rose Elizabeth then, "is it not the most beautiful thing you have ever seen in your life? I could not have enough of looking at it! And to think that it is *my sister*—but that is the what you have always seemed to me, dearest: the most beautiful, loving, *mysterious* girl in the world." She put her arms around Tomazina and clung to her for a moment; and though her affection almost broke Tomazina's ability to restrain her emotion, still Tomazina remained stiff and silent and unmoving, glaring at nothing.

"Yes," said Mr. Hugh Ashleigh. "It has turned out better than even I ever thought it could. The only difficulty will be getting such a great canvas home to Ransome Field in one piece." And he smiled at Tomazina in that same smug fashion.

By all the goodness of God, she thought, *you may get that portrait to Ransome Field in one piece, but I myself shall be cut to ribbons before I ever go over your threshold again!*

"Let us go back to Park Lane at once," she said then.

"Yes," said Mr. Ashleigh. "The afternoon is getting on. We shall want some time at home before Lord Esterbroke arrives; though he always can be counted upon to be late."

"That is one respect, at least, in which he is *unlike* the Devil," cried Tomazina, venting on Lord Esterbroke the anger she could not safely discharge against the Ashleighs; but the others were merely puzzled by her unaccountable spitefulness.

The departure of the cabs had apparently been against orders; it was now she learned that they had been paid in advance, as Mr. Ashleigh reproached his brother for making this error. After a great deal of shouting at passing hacks, the gentlemen secured another vehicle, this time a larger one, with facing seats. Tomazina had the relief of not having to be alone with Mr. Hugh Ashleigh again. She said nothing for the remainder of the short distance to Park Lane, only staring out the open window, fuming over the trick that had been perpetrated on her, and agonizing over the catastrophe of seeing Samson again under such conditions. The other three seemed not to notice her silence, or perhaps ascribed it to pleasant causes; they chattered on among them, enthusing about the portrait. Mr. Ashleigh was particularly happy and fond toward Rose Elizabeth, and she, as a consequence, toward him. Tomazina could think of nothing else about him but how perfidious he was, and in this moment his very fondness toward Rose Elizabeth seemed hypocritical and odious to her. What was more, she was hurt by her sister's absorption with his evident approval of her; Rose Elizabeth had not in the least perceived how angry and upset Tomazina had become.

About Mr. Hugh Ashleigh's perfidy she did her utmost not to think at all, for she was certain she would snap at him if she did. He sat beside her on the seat, half-turned to watch her, with a self-satisfied expression on his face. She had that impotent feeling to which women are sometimes prey: she wished to strike him and cause him some hurt that would wake him out of his certainty that he had mastered her; but she knew it was beyond her physical power to injure him enough to effect that awakening.

Chapter 44

It is as sport to a fool to do mischief.

—Proverbs 10:23

When they returned to the house in Park Lane, Tomazina excused herself and went at once to her bedroom. She shut the door behind her, drew off her gloves and hat and set them aside, and then paced about in the middle of the room, holding her head with both hands, reliving her encounter with Samson in excruciating chagrin and distress.

The literal fact and symbolism of it all were mixed up together; she could not sort them out; but she tried. Somehow her longing for Samson was entangled with her religious beliefs; which, though they had been watered and cultivated continuously throughout her childhood, had remained curiously dormant then; until in the last year they had burst their husk and begun to grow into something solid as oak, a knowledge and certainty that promised to tower over trouble and grief.

And the thing that forced the growth in her now, as if that living tree were bursting out of her very heart—was that picture. That picture—that amazing product of Mr. Esterbroke's imagination. As always, his imagination made her heart grow, forced it to grow—as she had once written: the roundness of him, filling the roundness of her.

What that picture said was true: She *was* the Shulamite. It was almost as if Mr. Esterbroke's wild theory were proven true, that she had lived in other lives; and in one of them— nay, in every one of them—she had been the Shulamite, the woman seeking her lover, her husband, as the symbol of her search for the God Who Had Come Down. Did not St. Paul say that—that the woman and the man were the type, the allegory, of the Christian and the Christ? And now, having seen that picture, she knew who she was—she knew what her search in this life was, both on the personal and the superpersonal plane.

And the man who had shown her that—he was blind to the personal himself. He was a blind man, a blind *painter.* The irony of it wrung her: that Samson could see *her* for what she was, but not see *himself* for what he personally was; which was her lover, her *destined* lover. He was a blind seer; and he needed her eyes to find his way in life as much as she needed his to see herself.

Or no—she jumped back in thought to where she had for a moment thought of herself as having multiple lives. She must once and for all issue the great correction: that idea of our living more than one life was craziness. She was Tomazina, and she had only one life, one mortal life, one chance to be with that one man she loved; and she had foolishly left it up to him to decide whether it should happen, and he had thrown the chance away. That was the terrible error she had made in not following her plan: by speaking too soon, she had forced him to decide, before his eyes were open, between her and his false idol.

These thoughts tumbled through her head in disarray; they were too exalted for this hour, and she came down from them, as one regains consciousness; she remembered her body and Samson's body, and her thoughts tumbled on, but on a lower plane.

If she had to sacrifice herself by losing Samson, she would accept that; she had already determined on doing that if it were necessary. But she felt still a powerful revulsion against accepting that he was lost to her. Just as she must always seek the God-Who-Had-Been-Mortal, so she would always seek that man her heart had fixed upon. She would not close the door to him; she would still seek him in her heart, still pray for him to be a part of her life. She had to have that mercy on herself, of allowing herself to love on and still in heart pursue him. If she had ever, for even a moment in time, thought seriously of stooping to marry anyone else, she saw now that it was only a temptation, a trying, a testing of her resolve. Thank God she had won through it! Though Samson might look at her in pity, thank God it was not a pity she deserved.

She had been pacing—or rather, almost reeling about—for several minutes in this confused state of combined meditation and epiphany, thinking these thoughts, or trying to think them; when a soft tap sounded at the door and Rose Elizabeth's voice said, "Tomazina? May I come in?"

She wanted to send her sister away, but she also could not bear to. "Of course," she replied.

Rose Elizabeth entered, shut the door, and stood still for a moment, looking at Tomazina with undisguised joy. Then she rushed to her sister and threw her arms around her, hugging her so tightly that they almost lost their balance together. "Oh—you naughty thing!" she cried. "Why did you not tell me?"

"Tell you what?" said Tomazina, though she already knew the answer, and dreaded it.

"That you and Mr. Hugh Ashleigh had come to an understanding!"

"Because we have *not*, Rose! Oh, Rose, do not do this to me. We have come to no *understanding* at all—as you put it." She held her sister away, but she was so ashamed that she could not look into her eyes.

Rose Elizabeth did not believe her; she only smiled at her denials. "There is no point in dissembling any longer," she said. "This whole business about the painting has made it very clear. Mr. Ashleigh is in heaven at the thought! The instant you went out of the room he congratulated Mr. Hugh Ashleigh very joyfully, and Mr. Hugh Ashleigh accepted his congratulations with great pride and happiness. You cannot pretend any longer, dear."

"Oh, Rose!" Tomazina cried again, "this is dreadful! Do not allow yourself to be imposed upon. I have never accepted Mr. Hugh Ashleigh. He made me an offer—I did not tell you that, it is true; it was all too painful to talk about. I did not even consider his proposal; I refused him."

Rose Elizabeth laughed with uncharacteristic merriness. "Oh, come now, dear," she said. "You cannot conceal this any longer. Your secret is out for all the world to see."

As Tomazina paused, mute with consternation, Rose Elizabeth regarded her with loving approbation, and the tears suddenly glistened in her eyes. "I do not claim to know how anyone else feels about it," she said, "but you have made *me* the happiest of beings. My dearest sister—at Ransome Field! Short of having you in my very house, nothing could be better! Our children shall play together—we shall see each other *every day!*" And in an ecstasy of anticipation, she hugged Tomazina close to her again and kissed her cheeks again and again, making a little happy sound as if she were eating something delicious.

This Tomazina could not endure; she forced Rose Elizabeth to stop and cried, "No! No! You mustn't! Do you not see—you are playing his game—this is exactly what he wishes you to do—to believe in this illusion he has created! Oh, Rose, I have never come to any understanding with him. I told him no in no uncertain terms, and he refused to hear me. I believe the whole purpose in bringing me to London was that I should be placed in his company in this compromising way."

She succeeded in staggering Rose Elizabeth's happiness, but only temporarily; her sister's smile faltered, but then returned. "You cannot tell me that he would commission your portrait without your consent," she said, in absolute assurance that this was a telling point.

"Rose, Rose, that is *exactly* what I *am* telling you.—Oh, can you not see how mortifying it is—mortifying to me, and presumptuous in him!"

"But I cannot believe such a thing of him," said Rose Elizabeth, growing alarmed as she saw Tomazina stick to her story.

"He is not a *bad* man," said Tomazina. "I am not saying that. But he is a silly one, and in his zeal to get what he wants, he is dragging my name in the dirt. He is creating a situation that I can only rectify by marrying him. And I shall not be coerced into doing so by such a trick! To present all the world with the appearance that he and I are affianced lovers! It is unconscionable—and yet he has done it. It is not the part of a gentleman—it is very wrong, it is detestably wrong."

"But you do not detest him?" cried Rose Elizabeth.

"At this moment I do! Rose, you must believe me, I never agreed to his commissioning that portrait. I had no idea he had done so until I walked into that studio and saw it."

"Oh, I am sure this is all some misunderstanding," said Rose Elizabeth eagerly.

"That is what you always say, Rose, when someone has done something wrong and hurt someone else. And you are sometimes right; but not this time."

Rose Elizabeth hesitated for a moment; but then she followed what was for her the path of least resistance—belief in the best in people. "Well," she said, "I am not sure how this misunderstanding about the painting came about—but can you not like him? Can you truly not like him? Can you not love him, dear? He loves you very much—it is really very touching to see his devotion to you. He is so infinitely pleased about that painting.—And Tomazina, truly it *is* the most beautiful portrait I have ever seen. I could not have believed a painter could capture you in all your loving radiance as Mr. Esterbroke has done."

At the name of Samson Esterbroke, Tomazina burst into tears and hid her face in her hands. She turned away from Rose Elizabeth and went to her bed, where she threw herself down headlong and gave herself over to sobbing.

Rose Elizabeth came after her now, uttering little cries of alarm—"Mazie! What is it? What is the matter?"—and then sat by her on the bed and tried to soothe her.

After a few minutes, Tomazina made an effort to get her feelings under control, but still hid her face from Rose Elizabeth.

"So much feeling!" said Rose Elizabeth then, wonderingly. "Dear, are you *sure* you do not love Mr. Hugh Ashleigh? Where is all this passion coming from, if not from your feelings for him?"

"I am quite sure I do not love him," said Tomazina hoarsely, sitting up abruptly and wiping her tears away, even as she wept more.

"Quite sure?"

"Quite sure, Rose."

"But perhaps someday you could love him?"

She restrained her impulse to reply with wild denials. Perhaps calmness would be more persuasive. "No, Rose," she said. "I could never love him. I am quite sure of it."

"Why so very sure?" asked Rose Elizabeth, in a pleading and endearing tone.

"I could never love him *ever*," said Tomazina, her voice sinking to an agonized whisper, "because I am not in love with him *now*."

Although her choice of words did not indicate any present commitment of her affections, Rose Elizabeth must have guessed at the meaning behind it. She was silent for a long moment, grasping at the implications of this declaration and looking intently at Tomazina, as if she would be able to divine more of what her sister meant from her expression. And when she could not, she asked in the same fraught, anxious whisper: "Are you in love with . . . someone else, then?"

Tomazina nodded, shortly and mutely.

There was a long moment of shock; and then Rose Elizabeth asked, urgently: "Oh, Mazie! Who is it?"

Tomazina debated whether she would answer. Ten seconds went by; twenty; thirty; and finally it seemed to her that she must tell her secret, whether she wanted to or not; and it burst out of her at last.

"Mr. Esterbroke," she said.

Rose Elizabeth was speechless for so long that Tomazina looked at her inquisitively, afraid that she had somehow offended her.

"Mr. Esterbroke!" cried Rose Elizabeth finally.

"Shh! Shh!" pleaded Tomazina; and Rose Elizabeth understood the urgency of this request and lowered her voice.

"But you always denied loving him when we teased you about it," said Rose.

Tomazina acknowledged this with another nod of her head.

"But how long has this been?"

"Since I went to Gloucestershire. I fell in love with him there. I think that up to then I was proof to him—fool that I was—or I told myself that I was. Or maybe I always loved him, but did not know it—I was such a fool!—Mariah says that she and Edmund always knew how I felt—and you and Vita and Ursula always teased me about it, as you say. But there, in Gloucestershire, I soared into such a state of complete ecstasy over him I cannot describe it to you."

Rose Elizabeth stared at her, open-mouthed.

"Yes," said Tomazina, with a bitter little laugh at the surprise she had caused. "It is true. And I still love him. If it would do him a bit of good, I would let the blood run from my own veins, to the last drop. Seeing him just now was—I cannot tell you. The word 'agony' does not compass it. If I had known what I was going to find in that studio, I would sooner have thrown myself under the wheels of a carriage in the street."

"Tomazina!" cried Rose Elizabeth in horror. "What is this violence of language?"

"It is only the reflection of the violence of my feelings."

To Rose Elizabeth such an intensity of emotion was unimaginable; but she said, "You always were so impulsive, Mazie! You never did anything halfway. I suppose that it only makes sense that when you fell in love, you fell in love *too much*. But does Mr. Hugh Ashleigh know how you feel about Mr. Esterbroke?"

"Oh, he has guessed it well enough. I believe that is a good part of the reason he went to Mr. Esterbroke and represented himself as my fiancé—to discourage him, because he saw him as a rival. Unfortunately, Mr. Esterbroke does not need to be discouraged."

"What do you mean?" demanded Rose Elizabeth.

"I mean that Mr. Hugh Ashleigh is wasting his time in preventing Mr. Esterbroke's attentions to me. Mr. Esterbroke is still very much in love with that ninny in Gloucestershire—God forgive me for calling her that, but that is truly what she is."

"But I still cannot believe it all. If you really loved him so, why did you never tell me? We have told one another everything, ever since we were little girls."

Tomazina wept afresh at this reproach. "Oh, dear Rose!" she said. "Maybe not everything. I have loved him too much to tell you; that is all I can say. And it all happened in Gloucestershire, and I was trying to put it behind me. And one feels so stupid, loving someone who loves someone else. It is like opening your purse to pay for something you have bought, and the money simply is not there. It is like going out for a walk on a sunny day without an umbrella, certain that it will not rain, and then a shower comes and you are absolutely cold and wet through. Oh! I do not know *what* it is like, but it is the most miserable thing I know. To love so much—always staring into the reality that you are not loved in return."

Rose Elizabeth was silent; and her silence bespoke such trouble and uncertainty that Tomazina looked inquiringly at her again.

At the prompting of that glance, Rose Elizabeth said, "Are you so sure Mr. Esterbroke does not love you?"

"Yes," said Tomazina. The shortness of her reply made it a definitive statement.

But Rose Elizabeth, after hesitating, persisted: "I only say that because he looked at you so strangely today."

"He did indeed look at me strangely; but it can only be because of the way Mr. Hugh Ashleigh has behaved in this matter. It is mortifying! Can you imagine, Rose, how awful it is to be claimed as a fiancée by someone I do not love, in the presence of one I do?"

"Oh, Mazie!" said Rose Elizabeth, tears of sympathy at once rising in her eyes. "But at least you have this consolation—Mr. Esterbroke knows nothing of how you feel about him."

At this unwitting thrust, Tomazina hid her face in her hands again and wept the more. For a minute they sat thus, she weeping and Rose Elizabeth looking on in gradually dawning realization and dismay. At length Rose Elizabeth said, in a tone of great distress, "Oh, Mazie, tell me that he does not somehow know it!"

Tomazina could not compose herself enough to answer.

"But how could he?" asked Rose Elizabeth, as if trying to convince herself.

"He knows," said Tomazina wretchedly.

"But *how?* How, Tomazina?"

"Never mind that. He knows, that is all I shall say. We have talked about it."

Rose Elizabeth blushed for her sister. "You have *talked* about it! Oh, Tomazina, you did not *make a dead set* at him, did you? You did not *throw yourself at his head?* You are impulsive, it is true—but it cannot be! How did it *ever* happen that you came to talk of it with him?"

"Do not ask—please, do not ask me that."

Rose Elizabeth considered these facts for a time in silence, while Tomazina gradually brought her weeping under some sort of control.

"What I do not understand," said Rose Elizabeth gravely then, "is why Mr. Esterbroke did not follow the course of honor and offer marriage to you."

Tomazina emitted a short, anguished laugh. "God bless you, Rose! Whoever said that a gentleman is obligated to marry every little fool who happens to fall in love with him? Especially when he has made it abundantly clear, from his very first meeting with her, that he is in love with someone else?" Then she thought of another thing, and she grew equally grave, and her seriousness gave a natural check to her weeping. "Do not think for a moment that he has been anything but exquisitely kind to me," she said.

"Thank God!" said Rose Elizabeth. "I am glad to hear that. I cannot tell you what a relief that is—though I must say that, for practical reasons, one might wish he had not been so kind after all."

"I know what you mean. He has never given me any reason to dislike him."

"Except that he persists in loving this . . . this silly young lady in Gloucestershire."

"Oh, people must be forgiven their mistaken first loves," said Tomazina.

At this remark, in spite of the late happy interlude in her marriage, Rose Elizabeth turned very pale. It was a telling moment; it revealed to Tomazina that Rose Elizabeth herself did not trust her own happiness. Tomazina seized her hand in remorse and kissed it.

"Some people have no second loves, my dear," said Rose Elizabeth in a dull tone. "They are not allowed them. And perhaps Mr. Esterbroke is such a one. His painting work is clearly very successful. I cannot doubt that he will soon persuade this lady to have him. And I must say, he has every quality one could want in a husband."

"Yes," agreed Tomazina fervently.

"Except this one thing, dear: he cannot love you. And this ought to make you consider other choices."

"It ought indeed," agreed Tomazina hopelessly.

"And what you say of him so readily, you should say of yourself: you should put your first love behind you."

Tomazina felt a twinge of her old guilt at this reminder that she had concealed from her sister her true first love, her passion for Edmund. But she ignored it and said: "I am almost ashamed to say it, but I have sometimes tried to forget Mr. Esterbroke. There have been times when I have thought about whether I could be married to Mr. Hugh Ashleigh. If he had not done this unconscionable, presuming, maddening thing—if he had not brought me in front of the man I love and paraded me about as his own possession, he might have persuaded me—who knows? But I could never forgive him this. This has revealed his character to me in an unforgettable manner."

"Do you not think it can be forgiven him, as a sign of his love for you?"

"That he has tried to trick me into matrimony?" said Tomazina scornfully.

"Trick you? Whatever do you mean, Tomazina?"

"Do you not see? By creating the expectation in everyone else that we *are* engaged, he forces me toward accepting that belief myself. By creating the illusion that we have some understanding, he enlists even my innocent sister into pleading his case. He will soon have everyone persuaded. Vita and Mother are all too ready to be convinced, though it is the last thing they want; and Ursula will probably soon be quite sure of it too. Soon enough Father will be asking me for some explanation of the rumors he has heard. People in the village will begin to congratulate me."

"But Mr. Hugh Ashleigh cannot be doing that deliberately!"

"Who knows how deliberate it is, how aware? He is doing it; and because he is not clear in his principles, his behavior is acceptable to him. That is what I could never stand—living with a man who would allow this kind of indirect coercion to make do where open and honest appeal have failed."

"Then he has really asked you?"

"Oh, yes. And I have refused him. And still he persists in pursuing me, in misrepresenting the relationship between us."

Rose Elizabeth considered the situation for a long moment. "This is dreadful," she said. "Mr. Ashleigh is completely convinced that you have accepted his brother; and Mr. Hugh Ashleigh has been doing nothing to dispel that notion. I think he believes it himself."

"He probably does—he is that single-minded, and that foolish."

"Downstairs just now Mr. Ashleigh and I were congratulating him, and he smiled and laughed and accepted our best wishes without the least hint of denial."

"Rose, listen to me—I tell you, I do believe that I was brought here to London specifically to be put in this compromising situation. I know you will never believe that—you are too free of guile yourself to imagine it in anyone else."

"Indeed, I cannot believe it of him. He cannot be so evil!"

"Dear, do you not understand? A gentleman may be a good *person* and a bad *man*. It is odd—it is terrible, it is strange, it is unfathomable—but it is true, it is the way God has ordered things. And the same is true of a lady: she may be a good *person*, but infinitely wicked and cruel as a *woman*. I do not know how to explain it. What we are as common humans may be perfectly decent and good; but in our relations with the opposite sex, we may well be fiends that torture and oppress them. Have you never seen a woman you liked and admired—who was good and kind to others, and yet bitterly mean to her husband? Have you never seen a man who was a very saint to all except to the companion of his own bed?"

Rose Elizabeth looked almost haggard. Though the description did not fit her own husband, there was apparently enough in it that paralleled her experience to cause her grief. "Yes," she said. "Yes, I know what you mean. I am sorry, dear, to find that you, too, already understand this."

They were silent together now for a minute or more.

"Then you will acknowledge that I must leave here immediately," Tomazina resumed then. "I cannot remain in this situation."

"Yes," agreed Rose Elizabeth, though not without some evident regret.

"Then you will support me when I announce that I am leaving?"

"Yes," said Rose Elizabeth, with more firmness.

"Thank you, dear. I shall go to Mr. Ashleigh at once, as soon as I have repaired what I can of my appearance.—Is Mr. Hugh Ashleigh still here?"

"No; he has gone away to dine with his associates."

"Then I shall go down as soon as I can."

Rose Elizabeth rose with reluctance. She went to the door and then turned and looked back. "There will be a scene, you know," she said. "I hate it when Mr. Ashleigh makes a scene."

"I am sorry to expose you to it, dear," said Tomazina. "Perhaps you should just go to your room and wait until it is all over."

"Never," said Rose Elizabeth. "I owe it to both of you to be there when it happens."

She made as if to go, but then turned to Tomazina again. "Oh, Tomazina," she said, "I hope you will forgive him—Mr. Ashleigh, I mean."

"Of course I shall, dearest Rose. He is your husband; and I shall always love and respect him for your sake."

Rose Elizabeth looked uncertain about this; but she said only, "Come to my dressing room when you are ready, and I shall go down with you."

❁ ❁ ❁

It was fifteen minutes before the two sisters descended the stairs to the sitting room. Mr. Ashleigh was having some wine and reading the paper; he looked up affably as they entered. "You have missed Hugh, Sister," he said to Tomazina. "He has gone off to his foolish dinner, leaving only his abject apologies for the necessity.—Will you join me in some wine, my dears?"

Tomazina approached and stopped directly before him. Rose Elizabeth accompanied her, timorously but loyally. Tomazina turned to her briefly before she began. "Do sit down, Rose Elizabeth," she said.

She thought that Rose Elizabeth would gratefully take advantage of this permission to retreat from the field of battle; but her sister said, "No, dear, I shall stand right here."

She was touched by Rose Elizabeth's support. She turned back to Mr. Ashleigh now and said, "I am afraid I must return at once to my father's house, Mr. Ashleigh."

He was so surprised that it took him a long moment to fully realize what she had said, during which he only stared at her. "What!" he said at last. "To Hampshire!"

"Yes, sir. I am afraid I must go first thing tomorrow."

"Impossible, my dear sister! Whatever can you be thinking? We have just arrived here. We shall be here for at least another week, or maybe two. I would stay two months except that I should hate to miss the shooting."

"I shall leave tomorrow," said Tomazina. Rose Elizabeth seemed almost to cringe beside her. "There is no need for you to leave; I can travel alone if need be. It is a short journey—it can be done in a day. Or perhaps I shall go directly to Brackensom and join with Mr. and Mrs. Hanscom. That might be the best course of action."

"You are mad!" cried Mr. Ashleigh. "My dear Miss Comstock, put it completely out of your head! I could not possibly allow such a thing—especially after I promised your father to watch over you."

"I appreciate the difficulty of your situation, sir; but nevertheless I must go."

"Impossible, Miss Comstock," he said, in great displeasure. "It shall not happen. I forbid it. I am *in loco parentis* here, and you shall do as I say.—Whatever has gotten into your head that you want to rush back to Hampshire?"

"The presence of Mr. Hugh Ashleigh here in London has made my situation in this house improper," she said.

"What?" he said, genuinely baffled. "Hugh? Hugh has got something to do with this madcap fantasy? Whatever are you talking about?"

"It is improper for me to be seen in public with Mr. Hugh Ashleigh in this manner, Mr. Ashleigh. I have no intention of marrying him, and I find others have fallen victim to the misunderstanding that I am in fact engaged to him."

"Do you deny it?" cried Mr. Ashleigh.

"I do. I utterly repudiate it. I shall never marry Mr. Hugh Ashleigh."

"Why, girl, you are mad! He said you were engaged—he said as much not half an hour ago, standing right where you are standing."

"He is quite mistaken then, sir. I regret his misunderstanding, but I cannot be faulted for it."

He stared; he stared. He looked in wonder at Rose Elizabeth.

"Dear," Rose Elizabeth said then, in a faint, propitiating tone, "I have found in thinking over what Mr. Hugh said, that he did not exactly say that he *was* engaged. *We* said so, but he did not."

Mr. Ashleigh still could not comprehend. He turned back to Tomazina. "But Hugh is quite in love with you!" he protested. "He offers you everything. You cannot possibly turn him down. And do you really deny that you have accepted him? I cannot believe it!"

"He knows perfectly well that I have never accepted him; that I did in fact definitively reject him on that day he proposed—that day you and he came to take us all out driving in the barouche. And I dare say you yourself know I did so; for I doubt he keeps any secrets from you."

"Do you accuse me of dishonesty, Miss Comstock?"

"No, sir. But I do fear you may be allowing the facts to be misrepresented. You could relieve me of that suspicion of you by assisting me to leave this compromising situation at once and return to Hampshire."

"Absolutely impossible!" he cried, now casting aside his newspaper and getting to his feet, the better to tower over her and intimidate her.

"I shall go tomorrow, will you or nil you."

"You shall go nowhere! You have not the least idea how to navigate about London, or where to go for the coach! You would be taken away by ruffians—robbed—murdered—worse!"

"Nevertheless, I shall go," she insisted, although her heart quailed at the practical difficulties he presented.

"You shall not!" he cried. "That is final! That is the end of all conversation on this subject!"

"If I do not see you tomorrow before I go, sir," she said, as she curtsied, "I wish you the very best in your continued stay here, and I thank you for your hospitality to me."

With that she withdrew and went back to her room. As she ascended the stairs, she could hear Mr. Ashleigh venting his vexation on Rose Elizabeth.

"What the devil has gotten into your sister?" he cried. "What *is* this all about? One minute she is to marry my brother, and the next she has jilted him. Whatever is the minx up to? And this mad talk of going back to Hampshire by herself—it is unconscionable, it is unfathomable! I shall send for Hugh at once and see if he can talk some sense into her! Good God, I would not marry so perverse a woman for all the money in the world, and she comes with only a thousand pounds! You would think from the way she carries on that she was heir to the wealth of the Indies!"

What Rose Elizabeth said to this tirade, when she had the chance to speak, Tomazina did not hear. She set about dressing for dinner, and then did some packing, though the fear of how exactly she was to go about returning home was very distracting to her.

The idea of fleeing to Brackensom now grew larger in her mind. Reconnecting with Mr. and Mrs. Hanscom would make her return to Gloucestershire all that much more probable. She would stay at Brackensom until it was time for them to leave. If they went direct to Hanley Wold, she could deliver the news of that fact to her father as a *fait accompli;* and if they chose to travel back through Hampshire, she would carry her determined plans and the Hanscoms' expectations as ammunition against his reluctance.

She was often to think back later on what might have happened if she had put that idea into effect; if she had gone to Brackensom alone and left her sister and brother-in-law in Park Row. But as matters turned out, she was not able to.

About an hour later Rose Elizabeth came to her room again. She looked a little drawn and very unhappy.

"Lord Esterbroke is come," she said. "He is downstairs. Will you not come down and sit with us before dinner?"

"Of course I shall, dear Rose," said Tomazina. "I had not realized he was here, or I would have been down before this."

Rose looked embarrassed and unhappy still; and Tomazina, suspecting that Rose Elizabeth had been charged to say something further, asked her: "Is there anything more I should know?"

"Yes," said Rose Elizabeth, with apparent reluctance. "Mr. Ashleigh has been telling his lordship about your . . . your decision to go back to Hampshire. His lordship in on his way back to Gloucestershire, and has . . . Oh, Tomazina! Mr. Ashleigh made me say this—I do not think it is at all proper, and I hope you will not do it. Lord Esterbroke has offered to go by way of Hampshire and see you home—to travel there alone with you!"

"I shall walk first," said Tomazina flatly. "There is no point in even entertaining the idea of going with Lord Esterbroke. Do you not remember, Rose? *Travel not by the way with a bold fellow, lest he become grievous unto thee: for he will do according to his own will, and thou shalt perish with him through his folly.* I would sooner take the Devil himself for company. I shall be glad to tell Mr. Ashleigh that myself, Rose."

"No—no, dear, I shall tell him," said Rose Elizabeth, clearly alarmed that there would be another scene.

"I do not see why you should pay the cost of my insistence on my departure," said Tomazina.

"It is better this way," said Rose Elizabeth. "I shall tell him and come back and report to you."

"Whatever you think best, dear."

Rose Elizabeth went away, and after a quarter of a hour she returned, looking a little more cheerful, though not entirely at ease.

"This is what has been decided," she said. "Mr. Ashleigh and I will return with you."

This change of plan was a great relief to Tomazina, but she was surprised that Mr. Ashleigh had been brought to agree to it. She could not imagine he would do so without some incentive.

"How did this ever come about?" she asked.

"Lord Esterbroke has accepted an invitation to Priedpie Hall. We shall all go together."

"We are to go with Lord Esterbroke? That is too bad; but at least Mr. Ashleigh will be there to defend us against the man. But why, Rose? Why would Mr. Ashleigh suddenly decide that he wished to leave London and entertain his lordship in Hampshire?"

"He loves to be associated with the nobility—he is quite slavish about it. He talks often about how the Ashleighs ought to have a title, and he would like at the very least to get a knighthood for himself someday. It is quite an honor to have a lord stay with us, you know."

"If I am not mistaken, this thirst for noble company has already cost Mr. Ashleigh dearly. My guess is that the bill for your hospitality will be tendered not by Mr. Ashleigh, but by Lord Esterbroke; and it will run into the tens of thousands of pounds. Mr. Ashleigh must know this?"

"I am sure he does. But we are in no danger of running out of money, even if he does throw away another ten or twenty thousand pounds on his lordship. He has told me before—it is all a down payment on a title, either for him or for our son."

"A strange way to go about getting a title! But I confess I do not understand these things. And Mr. Ashleigh is willing to throw over his journey to London and dash home again, now that he may have the company of Lord Esterbroke?"

Rose Elizabeth looked wretchedly contrite. "To tell you the truth, dear—I can see it all a little better now. I think Mr. Ashleigh only came here as you said—to put you in the way of his brother. Now that Mr. Hugh's schemes have blown up in his face, Mr. Ashleigh is all for going home again."

"Ah," said Tomazina. This was quite plausible. "After all, the Twelfth is nearly a month away, and he will not want to miss even the anticipation of shooting, the fussing with guns and dogs and keepers. He is already concerned about missing it. If I had been a clever woman, I would have said nothing about my wanting to go home; instead I would have wheedled visions of shooting into Mr. Ashleigh's head, and he would have called for his horses tonight."

Rose Elizabeth had seemed increasingly relieved as she saw that Tomazina was going to fall in with this new plan and could even jest about the situation. They were soon agreed on it, and in a few more minutes went downstairs to sit with the gentlemen before dinner.

When she entered the sitting room and came into Lord Esterbroke's company, Tomazina was instantly overwhelmed by the memory of his many detestable qualities; but as usual, consideration for her sister motivated her to conceal her feelings. Mr. Ashleigh looked at her with an exaggerated display of ironic displeasure and said, "Here is the trouble-making Miss herself."

Lord Esterbroke rose and let himself be curtsied to, all the while inspecting Tomazina in his rude way. "I hear you are the cause of my invitation to Priedpie Hall, Miss Comstock," he said.

"I am sure you yourself are the cause, my lord," said Tomazina.

"Do you see?" said Mr. Ashleigh. "She cannot open her mouth without contradicting a man."

"That is true, Mr. Ashleigh," said Tomazina. "And in affirming what you say, I prove you wrong."

Lord Esterbroke laughed. "She has got you there, Ashleigh! She is a logic-chopper, too! By God, you must admit the minx has spunk!"

"I would never deny *that*," said Mr. Ashleigh wearily. "But Miss Comstock, I put you on notice that I have sent a message to my brother, and you shall have to justify your doings to him at some point before we go."

"I shall be glad to clarify the situation for Mr. Hugh Ashleigh, sir," said Tomazina pleasantly. "And we are leaving first thing tomorrow?"

"I expect.—What say you, my lord?"

"If you mean first thing after I wake tomorrow, yes; but I warn you that I do not wake till late."

"But we do go tomorrow?" asked Tomazina.

"Oh, yes, yes," said Mr. Ashleigh condescendingly.

"It is very kind of you, sir, to change your plans," said Tomazina.

Mr. Ashleigh made a sound expressive of suspicion and irritation, but did not carry the matter further. Lord Esterbroke took over the conversation, and soon the two men were deep—or at least, as deep as the topics would allow—in the subjects of shooting, wagering, card play, and the affairs of others. They made no attempt to include the women, and so Tomazina and Rose Elizabeth sat silently by, like carpets that existed only for men to walk upon.

Dinner itself passed in very much the same way. Tomazina would have continued to be bored and disgusted with Lord Esterbroke, but her head was full of other thoughts, thoughts of Samson, and of a new inner query that was coming to the fore now that she had more opportunity to think—about the strange change in his aspect. Passing the time became almost more difficult after she and Rose Elizabeth withdrew after dinner, because then she had to give over her fixation on Samson and carry on a conversation with Rose Elizabeth.

The men did not join them until very long thereafter. His lordship was quite tipsy by then, but Mr. Ashleigh seemed to be holding his liquor unusually well. After another half-hour, his lordship went off to play cards elsewhere.

As Tomazina was following Mr. Ashleigh and Rose Elizabeth up the stairs, Mr. Ashleigh said, over his shoulder, "I hope you are content with getting us involved with his lordship, Miss Comstock."

"Content, sir? And did *I* get us involved?"

"Yes, you did; do not deny it. And I shall not be quit of him until he has stolen another twenty thousand pounds from me."

Tomazina thought: *And thus the weak blame the consequences of their failings on those who show strength.* But she said nothing.

She had not been in her room more than a minute when the maid brought word that Mr. Hugh Ashleigh had just entered the house and was hoping she would do him the honor of speaking with him.

She did not flinch from this inevitability. She went at once, following the maid downstairs to the drawing room. Here she found Mr. Hugh Ashleigh alone in the room— even the omnipresent footman had been dismissed, and the maid retreated, closing the door behind her after she had shown Tomazina in.

Mr. Hugh Ashleigh rose from his seat the moment she entered, with that expression he always had when he set eyes on her, the same kind of awestruck, innocent wonder that a boy of seven has for a beautiful woman. It had always seemed one of his most charming idiosyncrasies, but it left her quite cold now.

"My brother has sent me a note," he said. "I understand you are leaving for Hampshire tomorrow."

"That is correct, sir."

"Why this suddenness, Miss Comstock? I had counted on your being in London at least another week, or perhaps two."

"I would rather not discuss my reasons, Mr. Ashleigh.— Now, if you would excuse me, I have some packing to do."

"But Miss Comstock, you cannot go like this, without some explanation of the suddenness of your departure. I cannot help thinking that I have offended you in some way."

"Your thoughts and conclusions are your business, sir. I cannot prevent them.—Good evening." And making the most minute of brief curtsies, she turned for the door.

He caught up with her, however, and detained her by laying a hand on her arm. After one frosty look from her, he removed it, but in the meantime he managed to put himself between her and her exit.

"I have indeed offended you," he said, in a pathetic tone. "Will you not explain to me in what way?"

Part of the reason came out of her, almost against her will. "I feel badly used by you, sir," she said. "It was ungentlemanly of you to bespeak a portrait of a lady to whom you are not affianced—as if she were a common mistress."

She could read the horror in his face as he realized the tactical error he had made.

"But Miss Comstock," he said urgently, "I never intended it as any offence to you. You cannot believe that—you know my feelings for you; you know I would never—I shall have the painting destroyed instantly—I shall send to Esterbroke at once—"

"By God, sir," she cried, now truly incensed, "you would heap infamy on insult and destroy that astonishing painting, now that it has been created? I feel certain Mr. Esterbroke would deny you that avenue of further error."

He was nonplussed; and while he stood silent, she remembered herself enough to be able to say: "Mr. Ashleigh, you are my sister's brother, and I would spare you every reproach I can for the sake of the peaceful connection between our families in future. But I cannot allow you to pretend that there is any understanding between us. If I expressed myself in weak terms to you when you paid your addresses to me, I regret it now, though I do not remember any ambiguity on my part—rather the reverse. Let me make my feelings perfectly clear: I shall not marry you—I *will* not marry you—though I do not question the compliment of your offer. I wish you the utmost happiness, and I regret this . . . this misunderstanding over the painting."

"Miss Comstock," he said, moving to still more effectively block her departure, "do not say no! Whatever you do, do not say no!"

"Sir, I say *no* and *no* and *no* again. *No,* absolutely, positively, definitely, and finally."

"No, Miss Comstock!"

"*No,* Mr. Ashleigh! It is a simple word, but for some reason men seem to be deaf to it! You are not the first gentleman who has refused to hear and understand it from my lips."

He smiled at the opening her remark offered. "There is something else I would rather have from your lips," he said.

"Do not insult me, sir!" she said coldly.

"But what reason can you possibly have for refusing me? Am I not perfectly amiable to you? Do I not offer you a fine home, near the sister you love? What more could you want?"

"A husband I can love," she said bitterly.

"And why can you not love me?"

"I do not know why; I only know most emphatically that I do not."

"It is Esterbroke," he said then, with the nearest approach to a scowl she had ever seen on his face.

"Mr. Esterbroke?" she said, with a plausible affectation of surprise. "Do not be absurd, sir. Mr. Esterbroke's affections are already attached."

"And yours are not?"

"Mine have never found a safe place to fix themselves, sir."

"Then fix them on me, Miss Comstock."

"I pray you, sir, mend your ways! Otherwise it will be impossible for you and me to meet amicably in future, even for the sake of my sister and your brother."

"I want nothing more than to live in perfect amity with you," he said. "And that is why I have asked you to be mistress of Ransome Field."

"And is that why you have treated me as a mistress of another sort altogether? You have a strange way of going about your acquisition of a wife, Mr. Ashleigh—dragging her name through the mud in the hope that she will be forced to turn to you for countenance when her reputation is past all cleansing!"

He turned almost white as again he saw, despite all his willfulness and self-assurance, how the situation must seem to her. She saw her moment—she pressed past him—he yielded uncertainly—and she had her hand on the knob of the door when he cried, "Miss Comstock!"

She turned and regarded him icily. She almost pitied his distress, but she did not dare reveal her compassion, for fear it would confirm him in his blind self-confidence once again.

"*What*, sir?"

"You cannot—" he began.

"I see you have nothing new to say to me, Mr. Ashleigh. Good night, sir."

He made no further attempt to interfere; she returned to her room.

❀ ❀ ❀

She spent some agonized minutes in self-reproach, thinking of her impulsive words and wishing she had found some kinder way to make her point, for Rose Elizabeth's sake. She felt so guilty in this regard, in fact, that she resolved to go to Rose Elizabeth and apologize; and she slipped back out into the hall and started for her sister's private dressing room, where she was most likely to find her.

As she went along the top of the stairs, however, the sound of laughter from the sitting room below arrested her. It was Mr. Hugh Ashleigh's laughter, and his brother was chiming in. Apparently Mr. Ashleigh had been summoned from his dressing room after Mr. Hugh Ashleigh's failed interview with her.

She stopped almost involuntarily in surprise, and she heard, faintly but clearly, the voice of Mr. Hugh Ashleigh say: "She gave me what for in great style, I can tell you.

"I do not see why she is so damned upset about the foolish picture," said Mr. Ashleigh. "Any young lady in her right mind would take it as a compliment."

"It does not matter what you and I think," said Mr. Hugh Ashleigh in a humorous tone. "The lady has her reasons. I will only say that she is a hundred times more beautiful still when she is angry, though I would settle for the milder loveliness without hesitation."

"I agree the lady is beautiful—if you do not mind a brunette; but I still say she is absolutely too perverse to make her worth the trouble. And if you cannot get the brunette, I hope you will not stop there, but will take a tilt at her younger sister."

"Well, I am not ready to give up yet," answered Mr. Hugh Ashleigh. "But I do agree that Miss Vita would be the next course of action. She is not so pretty, nor, I think, so clever by half; but she is a very lovely girl, and tries desperately hard to please, which is something her sister does *not* do.'"

"Well, think on it, man, before you have got Miss Vita so mad at you for chasing her sister that she will have nothing to do with you."

"Yes; this pursuing a young lady who does not want me is sometimes jolly fun; but then at other times it is very tedious stuff."

"Believe me, I know what you mean! You know how I damn near broke myself on Miss de Foye. I think these two cousins have the same strain of curstness in them. It has something to do with the dark hair, no doubt. I am quite willing to believe that all dark women are by heredity curst and obstinate."

"You know," said Mr. Hugh Ashleigh, "in pursuing this Miss I have often felt rather like I was hunting a vixen without the benefit of hounds. I do not know where the damned thing has gone half the time—whether she is somewhere before me or is running gaily off in another direction, laughing at me, beyond the very hedgerow where I stand.'"

Mr. Ashleigh laughed. "Indeed," he said, "I think this vixen has gone to earth, old man. Better see if you can find the drag of the other.—When will you rejoin us in Hampshire?"

"I must remain in town another three or four days."

"Well, come back to us ready to set off for a new cover."

Mr. Hugh Ashleigh did not assent to this; and though he did laugh, it was a little uncertainly.

"And what business do you have to keep you here, anyway?" continued Mr. Ashleigh. "You might hire a carriage of your own and follow mine, you know, and you could have the wench to yourself to try your persuasions."

"Well, I should like that. I dare say she is as susceptible to the pleasures of a stolen kiss as any other maid—or even more so, if I judge rightly from that saucy look she has in her eye sometimes. It is the one thing I have not dared try. But it is this stock company of Mr. Daines Jenkins's that has me trapped here."

"Not going badly, is it?"

"Not at all—going very well, so far as I can see. I have made a good twenty thousand out of it, which I should like to see secured."

"Well, good for you. I am glad one of the Ashleigh brothers is making something to compensate for the loses endured by the other. Do not keep company with importunate and bankrupt lordlings, that is all my advice to you. It is a borrowed honor not worth the cost of the borrowing—or, I should say, the lending."

"I also intend to get that painting away from Esterbroke and bring it home," said Mr. Hugh Ashleigh.

"Well, that is something worth staying for."

"Is it not something wonderful? I am glad you agree with me about that. My plan has always been to get it to Ransome. If I could bring the whole county round to look at it, the lady would absolutely have to marry me."

"I guessed as much. But do not count on this particular lady to fall in with your plans. If you took the painting home at this point, I think it would only prove an obstacle to any further intentions you might form in regard to any other eligible lady. A woman will forgive much in the history of a lover, but she does not like to see a testimony to his past affections on twelve square yards of canvas in the drawing room—especially if the charms depicted are superior to her own."

"Canvas burns rather readily, I believe," said Mr. Hugh Ashleigh.

To his credit, Mr. Ashleigh protested. "By God, man, you could not burn something so exquisite. If it comes to that, give it to old man Comstock."

"It may be an academic question, in any case," said Mr. Hugh Ashleigh. "I may have the dickens of a time getting it away from Esterbroke. I suspect he will go on claiming it is not finished forever and ever."

"Yes; did you hear him today? He said something to Rosie about wanting to show it at the Royal Academy if he could obtain the lady's permission."

"Really? He said that? The Royal Academy?"

"Yes. It would make him an R.A., and he knows it."

"Well, so much the better. I shall tell him he must call it *Miss Tomazina Comstock, Fiancée of Mr. Hugh Ashleigh of*

Ransome Field, Hampshire.—Did you hear what *he* wants to call it?"

"I did, but I could not make head or tail of it. What was it, something biblical?"

"Yes. He wants to call it *The Shulamite.* It is the woman in the *Song of Solomon.*"

"Is it really! That does not seem entirely a proper way to refer to another fellow's wife, does it?"

"Not at all. And I am not at all sure I like the sense of possession he has about this commission."

"You should have paid for the painting up front. Then it would be yours, and you could set the bailiffs on him."

"He would not let me. He was adamant about it. And he is known for being keen to get his money up front, too— which makes this case rather suspicious."

"Oh, do not let that worry you. Let him admire Miss Comstock all he likes. He is living hand to mouth, or so his cousin says. No woman in her right mind would take him over the master of Ransome. If he has taken a shine to her, it means nothing. He is not the first painter who has become temporarily infatuated with his model. And the entire world knows that he is all but engaged to that fortune-hunter in Gloucestershire."

Mr. Hugh Ashleigh's silence was eloquent of his doubt about these reassurances.

"Well," said Mr. Ashleigh then, "if I cannot persuade you to come home with us, I shall at least hope to see you soon. For now, I shall go to bed. This unexpected departure has made me rather cross, I must say. Why I am doomed to always hop and skip to the whims of some brown-haired girl, be she lovely or not, is more than I know. Have a care, brother, or you will find yourself dancing to the tune this one calls, and in a most demeaning way."

"I am not worried about that. I have no doubt who will be master once she has given her consent. Making her pay the cost of her perverseness will be half my pleasure in the marriage, I am sure."

At this point Tomazina heard sounds that suggested that the Ashleigh brothers might be coming out into the hall. She gave up her plan to speak to her sister that night and stole back to her room. Her self-reproach had abruptly dissolved.

The words of the Psalmist came to her: *They encourage themselves in an evil matter: they commune of laying snares privily; they say, Who shall see them?*

She undressed, put out the candle, and lay down on her bed. She forgot about Mr. Hugh Ashleigh and his brother; her thoughts turned—it seemed her whole body and soul turned—to Samson Esterbroke.

"*The Shulamite,*" she said to herself under her breath. She somehow felt certain, though the proof was weak, that Samson had read, even studied, the Blue Book. Her fascination with the Song, which was so evident there in her having copied it out at full length in both Hebrew and English, must have encouraged him in choosing that subject.

And if he had read the Blue Book, how had it affected his thinking about her? Had it been one of the reasons he had been repelled by her? Or was it not rather one of the reasons he had felt drawn to her?

Then it struck her that perhaps he had only lately discovered it among his possessions, only lately read it. Did it have anything to do with this odd change in his manner? Had it only increased his pity for her, his regret at his not being able to love her?

It was not until the early hours of the next morning that she finally slipped into sleep, hearing over and over again a confused stream of words in her mind. The two fragments of that half-dreamt and half-consciously scripted speech that dogged her the longest were "The Shulamite" and "Samson Esterbroke, R.A."

Chapter 45

The wicked shall be cut off from the earth.

—Proverbs 2:22

The following day began so very badly that Tomazina's justifiable expectation of it was that it could get no worse; and indeed, there is this to be said for lack of human foresight—that in the throes of any given day's commencement, difficult though it may be, we do not have to suffer any anticipatory horror for the infinitely worse way in which that day may in fact end.

Rose Elizabeth was very ill at breakfast—would have vomited, except that she could not bring herself to eat—would have fainted, except that Tomazina had made her lie down—would have caused her companions, against her wishes, to postpone their journey home. Mr. Ashleigh, of course, seized on the circumstance and forbade any thought of their departure, a decision he announced to Tomazina with great satisfaction.

Mr. Hugh Ashleigh, who had come to the house early in order to see them off, added annoyance to the very real concern and discomfort of that hour by sending a maid to Tomazina every five or ten minutes to beg her to see him in the parlor. She had no doubt that overnight he had formulated some arguments against her going home, and that their sophistry would gain in zeal from the accomplished fact that her plan was in ruins.

The victory of the Ashleigh brothers was short-lived, however. Rose Elizabeth improved very rapidly. By eleven in the morning, even before Tomazina could be compelled by common courtesy to descend to the parlor to see Mr. Hugh

Ashleigh, she declared herself to be feeling perfectly fit. "It was just a little spell," she said, with a perfect appearance of innocence; and there was no talk, even between the sisters, of what that little spell might portend. Mr. Ashleigh, though he seemed to be utterly ignorant of the suspicions of the women of the household, remained firm in his decision that the journey must be put off, and Tomazina could not controvert his reasons, even as her spirits sank at the thought of being confined in London with Mr. Hugh Ashleigh for one more day.

Unfortunately for Mr. Ashleigh's triumph, in the midst of all his self-satisfied bluster against Tomazina he neglected one simple matter; which was to inform Lord Esterbroke of their change of plans. And so at mid-afternoon, when Rose Elizabeth was quite recovered, his lordship arrived at the door, complete with trunks and manservant, ready to go visiting in Hampshire. He was very cross when he arrived, perhaps because he was still suffering the effects of a very late night; and he expressed strong disgust for Mr. Ashleigh when he heard that Mrs. Ashleigh's health—and Rose Elizabeth by then looked in the very pink of it—was to force his lordship to throw over all his preparations and find some other way to kill the remainder of the day. Mr. Ashleigh could not endure Lord Esterbroke's disapprobation—all their undoings were to be undone, the bags and trunks repacked in haste, and they were to set out after all.

One blessing of this urgency and confusion was that there was no time for Mr. Hugh Ashleigh to say his farewells to Tomazina—to hold her hand too long, look with puppyish adoration into her eyes, urge her to think of their future together, or make any of those other fervent protestations in which he was becoming so well practiced. He had already gone off to the club to dine on a good steak and some excellent Spanish wine, blindly thinking he would be able to do all those important things to advance his cause on the morrow.

It was very late in the afternoon before they set out from Park Lane. In fact, by then even Tomazina would willingly have postponed their departure; it seemed madness to her to undertake such a long journey with darkness in the offing; but when she said as much, in somewhat milder terms, to Mr. Ashleigh, he only frowned and answered, "These are the fruits of your unthinking haste to go home, my dear sister. It is too late now to stop what you have set in train; I only hope your impetuousness will take a lesson from it. We shall have to stop in an inn, of course; which will be all at my expense, unless you wish to volunteer the funds." This reprimand was, to say the least, unfair; and she allowed herself the private luxury of briefly rehearsing to herself why it was so. But righteousness is all the sweeter when one only basks silently in its aura. She accepted his reproach without reply, and set it down as another of the indignities she had to endure for her sister's sake.

From the moment they were under way, Lord Esterbroke and Mr. Ashleigh talked volubly, on the same topics that had occupied them for hours on the previous evening in Park Lane. This was at worst only boring; and as the women were neither required nor even allowed to join this conversation, Tomazina was able to turn her thoughts to much more pleasant considerations. In the first few hours she even managed to achieve a dizzy contentment, sunk in a dream about Samson. Her body was lulled into a sweet, half-stimulated sleepiness, as the carriage rocked and swayed and clattered over the road. They traveled at a brisk pace, even as the shadows grew long and the sun sank and set; for the July evening was clear, if rather cool, and a fair moon, quite full, rose in glory on the eastern horizon. From time to time Tomazina murmured a question to Rose Elizabeth—"How are you feeling, dear?"—but her sister always smiled cheerily, even taking her hand and squeezing it reassuringly. From these signs Tomazina knew that Rose Elizabeth, too, was glad to be returning home.

Indeed, Rose Elizabeth doubtless thought that return was not a moment too soon, for reasons of her own.

They stopped for a late dinner at an inn. The gentlemen drank too much and became irrational; and because the moon was bright and full, they were for hiring fresh horses and pushing on all the way to Priedpie Hall. Tomazina again tried to dissuade them; but Mr. Ashleigh only said again, "You wished to go home, my dear sister; now you must pay for your contrariness with a little discomfort." It was Rose Elizabeth for whom Tomazina was most concerned; but her sister had taken dinner with a good appetite, and Mr. Ashleigh was now as convinced that nothing was wrong with his wife's health as he had been certain that very morning that she would not be able to travel for a week.

There were other considerations beyond personal comfort that argued against their setting out again. Night travel was a dangerous business in those days. Hired horses were diurnal in habit, and would protest being put into harness so late in the day; they shied at the shifting shadows of the stableboys and were skittish even when pulling together. The light of lanterns did not cast a useful light very far, and moonlight tended to conceal some defects in the roadway as well as to trick the horses into thinking that other defects were present when they were not. The road was generally not a bad one, as roads in those days went; but 1816 was long before the day when the good work of Thomas Telford and John McAdam had been carried into that part of southern England; and indeed, in that very year the latter's views on road building were just being made known to the world. Furthermore, though England's famous highwaymen had receded into legend, there were occasional incidents in which less romantic ruffians seized on a stray opportunity to plunder innocent travelers. If Mr. Ashleigh cared for any of these dangers, he gave no indication of it. As for His Lordship, Tomazina observed to Rose Elizabeth that he seemed to think he could no more be impeded in his own travel by coach than the

Lord God could have been halted on his way into Jerusalem on the back of a donkey.

As they started out again, Tomazina found it more difficult to block out the prevailing conversation and think her own thoughts. Somewhere in the hours of travel, as she and Rose Elizabeth endured, without any right of protest, the stupid conversation of these two males, she thought to herself: *What an existence! You would think wives and women in general were just so much baggage in the lives of men. Edmund does not treat Mariah this way, nor would Mr. Hanscom ever insult Mrs. Hanscom in such a fashion. And Samson would not treat me this way, either. Men claim we women chatter, but these two great boobies have done nothing but yammer through every second of this journey!*

At some point she dozed off. When she awoke again, she found that Rose Elizabeth had put an arm around her and was holding her upright. That she had succumbed to sleep even briefly in the shaking and swaying carriage was a great testimony to her weariness.

As she shook off her slumber, she realized that the carriage had come to a halt; that this cessation of travel was in fact what had awoken her. Mr. Ashleigh put down the glass and thrust his head out into the moonlight.

"What is it?" he demanded of the coachman.

This fellow, the same elderly servitor who had commented favorably the other day on his master's sister-in-law, was so slow of movement that he did not attempt to descend from the box and come to the door; he only called down, "We seen a horseman ahead, sir. And the minute he seen us, he turnded round, and set off hell-for-leather the way he come."

"Well, what of it?" said Mr. Ashleigh testily.

"'Tis common knowledge, sir," said the coachman in some surprise, and in some weary irritation of his own. "Robbers post just such a watch on the road when they are planning to waylay travelers."

"Robbers!" said Mr. Ashleigh scornfully. Lord Esterbroke laughed harshly beside him. Mr. Ashleigh then said, "What are you, Dakes? Become an old woman, have you?"

"I on'y thought it proper to ask you what you wished to do, sir," said the coachman with ill-disguised indignation.

"Drive on!" said Mr. Ashleigh. Having given that peremptory command, he put up the glass again to end the conversation.

The coachman and the footman traveling on the forward box spoke to one another, but Tomazina could not make out what they said. There was another footman traveling outside as well, in addition to Lord Esterbroke's man and Mr. Ashleigh's valet. They, too, joined in this conversation; but whatever they said, it was but brief, as they realized they had no choice but to obey. The coachman stirred the weary horses; all the technology of leather and wood groaned under the strain and impetus of horseflesh; and the motion of the carriage resumed.

"I suppose you, too, Sister," Mr. Ashleigh said to Tomazina, "are afraid we shall be robbed by Dick Turpin." Lord Esterbroke guffawed again.

"I am not afraid, sir," said Tomazina stoutly. "But I do believe we would have been better to stay at the inn. And it is not too late to go back to find one, I believe."

The men sniggered. "Go back to an inn!" said Lord Esterbroke, mimicking Tomazina's voice.

"Dick Turpin has been dead some eighty years, if I recall his history aright," said Rose Elizabeth, hoping to moderate the tone of the exchange.

"If it makes you feel better," Mr. Ashleigh told Tomazina, "I can tell you that there is another coach ahead of us on this road. I am sure your highwayman will have his fill of plunder from that."

Something about this information was unsettling rather than soothing. "Is that not odd?" asked Tomazina. "It cannot be the regular coach, not if it is traveling at night."

"It is a special," said Lord Esterbroke derisively, "packed full of the ghosts of highwaymen." He and Mr. Ashleigh laughed again.

Yes, laughing at women is such good sport, Tomazina thought. *And we may be fools at times; but never so much fools as you two* ever *are.*

"And did you see this coach, sir?" she asked Mr. Ashleigh.

"I myself did not; Dakes told me about it. It passed us when we were having dinner. Dakes said it was a great unwieldy old thing, stuffed full of passengers, and with many a man clinging to the outside as well—a rough-looking bunch, he said—just the sort of fellows that might give Dick Turpin himself a very hot welcome."

And he and Lord Esterbroke laughed once more.

"I say," said Lord Esterbroke, "The coach did not belong to the Earl of Beelroy, did it? He is down on his luck; he might be moving his household in something like that."

"There was no shield on it," replied Mr. Ashleigh. "I asked Dakes particularly. He said that it looked as if it had once been a commercial machine, but it is now more than a bit broken down."

"It *could* be Beelroy," said Lord Esterbroke. "He would not stoop to hiring such a vehicle. That would explain why he is traveling by night: he does not wish to be seen in such a thing. What luck if it should be Beelroy! He owes me twelve hundred pounds."

"And that would explain why he did not stop to dine with us," said Mr. Ashleigh, with a laugh.

"Yes," responded Lord Esterbroke, but in a savage tone. "But I do not suppose the scoundrel has *got* the twelve hundred to pay me, in any case." And to Tomazina's astonishment, he went on for a full five minutes, complaining about the impudence of deadbeat lords who would not pay their debts of honor.

Finally he interrupted himself to say, "Ashleigh, have you anything about you? I am damned thirsty." Then, somehow observing Tomazina's eyes on him in the dark of the coach, he said, "You see what a tedious journey you have got us involved in, Miss Comstock—not only do we have to suffer the attack of ghosts, but we are tormented by the thirst of those in hell."

She wanted to answer that such thirst was a sensation to which his lordship would do well to accustom himself, but she held her tongue. Instead she contented her irritation with thinking of the aptness of the psalm: *As he loved cursing, so let it come unto him: as he delighted not in blessing, so let it be far from him.*

During this talk, the carriage had gradually resumed its speed, and now they traveled on for another ten minutes as fast as the horses could be compelled to go. Suddenly there was a collective outcry from the five men outside; and this time the carriage did not simply roll to a gentle stop—the dry screech of the brake was heard, and the vehicle, shuddering and swaying, halted abruptly.

"What the devil?" said Mr. Ashleigh. He seemed to think that this disregarding of his orders called for a direct, face-to-face reprimand; he thrust open the door of the carriage, and in an instant he had climbed out. Lord Esterbroke, with a string of his own oaths, more colorful than Mr. Ashleigh's, followed him; and Tomazina and Rose Elizabeth, moving to the open door, peered after them in a mixture of mild alarm and curiosity.

The full moon lit the scene strangely, as its brightness seemed to overpower and bleach and leach away all true colors, creating a distorted chiaroscuro. For a moment, in fact, Tomazina thought of a charcoal sketch, in which a broad palette of colors was reduced to a few shades. The road at this point descended between two low hills covered with grass and furze—it was a curiously wild place, in an interval between villages; the only mark of humankind on the landscape was a milestone giving the distance to that spot from London and Winchester. Their own carriage had turned to the right as it drew up, so that it was now partly athwart the road, and the two women could see the highway ahead of them.

Here, very close before them, was another coach—certainly the very one that Mr. Dakes had described. It had stopped, though there was no immediately visible reason why it should have done so—it had not overturned, to all appearances it had four working wheels, and it had four horses in the traces as well as a spare horse accompanying it. There seemed to be some difficulty, however, for its passengers had descended and were now approaching their own carriage as if seeking assistance.

Or so Tomazina thought at first; but this innocent assumption was immediately dispelled; for without speaking a single word the men seized Mr. Ashleigh and Lord Esterbroke. The latter was immediately pinioned and held immobile; but Mr. Ashleigh had studied the pugilism that was all the rage in those times, and he was a strong man as well; and wrenching himself free, he dropped one of his assailants with a single blow of his bare fist. There was an outcry from their attackers then—they rushed in a mob at Mr. Ashleigh; Tomazina saw a weapon rise and fall behind him (it was a blackjack, though she would not have known the term), and Mr. Ashleigh crumpled to the ground.

Before Tomazina could even begin to comprehend this, Rose Elizabeth had given a cry of terror and sprung down from the carriage. She ran through the attackers and fell on her knees beside her husband, gathering him into her arms, and drawing his head and torso into her lap. Though Tomazina's instincts had not prompted her to assist Mr. Ashleigh, they did urge her instantly to defend her sister, and she too now leapt down and ran through the men to where her sister knelt. In her turn she fell on her knees behind Rose Elizabeth and threw her arms around her protectively.

For the moment, however, no one paid any attention to them. There was a further commotion as several of the attackers pulled the coachman, the two footmen, and the two valets down from the carriage. They cuffed them—almost as if by way of showing threat, without causing harm—and drove them away into the hills, offering a final incentive to flight with a few following cracks of their own whip.

Then all attention turned back to the passengers. Several men laid rough hands on Tomazina's shoulders as if to drag her from her sister, and one pulled her shawl from her, but she clung tightly to Rose Elizabeth, crying out "No!" in protest and defiance.

"Leave them be," said one of the men. "It is not them we want; leave him and his women be." This fellow wore a pistol in his belt, unlike the others, who were armed only with clubs or knives or blackjacks or old fowling pieces, or with their fists and their brawn alone.

"I say we do for 'im, too," said another. "If he's a friend of 'is lordship, 'e's a henemy of us." Even after her short stay in town, Tomazina could recognize his accent as that of the London lower class.

There were many who voiced agreement with this fearful judgment, but the man who had spoken first countered him again; and in a tone of authority said, "No. We'll leave him and his women alone. He won't hurt us after that crack on his skull. Let's get on with what we come for." His accent, by contrast, was somewhat more literate; he seemed of better standing, though rough still, and his coarse clothing suggested he was very down on his luck.

"But *this* one," protested one of the men, seizing Tomazina by the hair and drawing her head back sharply, "This must be his lordship's whore."

The scalp of her head sang with pain, and she looked up into the eyes of the throng of vicious men around her, and at first she thought she might pass out with the sheer horror of it. But then she rallied.

"No!" she cried. "As God is my witness, I am no man's whore!"

Her voice seemed even to her to be clear and silverly on the cool night air. The man who had jerked her head back released it in surprise at her daring. She rose to her feet and addressed herself to the man who seemed to be the leader.

"We are decent women," she said. "We are sisters, and this man here is my brother-in-law. We have been forced by circumstance to travel with Lord Esterbroke. What is your purpose? What is the meaning of this? Let us go our way in peace. We have no quarrel with you, and you have none with us."

"You are *his whore*," repeated the man behind her in a furious tone. "Why should we take pity on you?"

"Let her be, Redding," said one of the men. "She has done us no wrong."

But Redding, the man behind her, was apparently still not convinced; he seized her by the hair once more and jerked her head back again, and held her thus, in sharp pain, unable to move. Out of the corner of her eye she could see his face, taut with unaccountable fury in the moonlight. If she had struggled in the least, he would have struck her down.

"Redding," said the leader, in a stern tone, "Whore or no whore, she is *some man's daughter.*"

And this remark seemed to be devastating to the man Redding. He loosed his grip again; and with something between a furious groan and a sob, he thrust his way out of the knot of men around her. In a flash of a intuition that came to her even in the confusion of her terror, Tomazina guessed that his daughter had been raped or debauched by Lord Esterbroke.

Rose Elizabeth now reached up from where she knelt on the ground and tugged at Tomazina's skirts, wordlessly telling her to sink down to the ground, to grovel if need be, and to let this storm of human hatred pass over them if possible; and she did sink to her knees again, and she clung to Rose Elizabeth as if she could shield her from the clubs and knives of this mob with her own two arms. And in stooping thus submissively to the earth, she seemed to allow the very thought of the three travelers huddled on the ground to pass out of the minds of their assailants.

"Let's get on with it," said the leader again.

The throng turned, with one accord, toward Lord Esterbroke, who was still held fast in the arms of three burly men. The leader of the gang stepped close to him. He was much the smallest of them all, and conspicuously shorter than Lord Esterbroke.

"I know you," said Lord Esterbroke in surprise.

"Do you, now?" said the man in an ironic tone.

"Yes . . . I believe you are—my tailor!"

The largest part of his surprise seemed to be the fact that he knew his own tailor by sight.

"Odd how you never gave me the time of day before," said the other. "There must be something different about these circumstances."

The throng laughed fiercely.

"Yes," continued the man, "I am your tailor. John Smet is my name; and you have made me a very desperate man, your lordship. I have kept you in the finest clothing these five years now; and now I am bankrupt, and my wife and children thrown out onto the street. I would be in prison ten times over if I had had a home where the bailiffs could find me.—You shall pay me now."

"Pay you? What, pay your bill? Is that what this is all about? A mere tradesman's bill?"

"That is exactly what it is all about, your lordship."

"So you say I owe you something?"

"You owe us all a bit of change," said the tailor grimly.

"And how much would that be?"

"In sum, the lot of us—about ten thousand pounds."

"Oh, for God's sake! Do you think I pay my tailors? Do you think I concern myself with grocers and candlestick makers? You must apply to my man in London, Mr. Cheeseboro. He will see you paid."

"We have, all of us, applied to Mr. Cheeseboro many a time these past years; and nary a farthing have we had from all our applications to him—or should I say, from his applications to us of his boot to our backsides."

"Well, do not be ridiculous, man. Do you think I carry ten thousand pounds around in my purse?"

"I am not so foolish as that, your lordship. If you ever got your claws on ten thousand pounds, you would only gamble it away."

"And why should I not do whatever I damned well please with it?—Look, what the devil are you up to here? You cannot waylay a Peer of the Realm on the open highway and demand quittance of your petty debts! You will swing for this, do you not know that?"

"I know it full well," said the man simply.

As he said these words, a chill of new terror went through Tomazina so icy that it left her almost unable to breathe.

"We all know it full well," added Smet, and the men around him voiced their agreement.

"You may have observed that I am not in this alone, your lordship," Smet went on. "You observe these other men. They have the same business with you that I do. You see, your lordship, we made the acquaintance of one another during our long attendance on your Mr. Cheeseboro. We have helped one another as best we could as we went down—as we descended from being prosperous tradesfolk to beggars in the street—as you broke us one by one. And when the last of us was bankrupt, we determined together that though it meant the death of us all, the one thing we should see before we perished ourselves was the execution of the man who brought this upon us in his own greed and heedlessness. We suborned your own household servants, who were more than happy to betray you to us for a few pence—Mr. Cheeseboro does not often pay them, either. We learned this morning of your journey, and we followed you—we went before you— we have been waiting for you in this quiet spot. You are far from help now, your lordship. There are no bailiffs, no officers of the peace, none of your lackeys and toadies about. That is the way we wanted it—just a quiet place where you might shout and protest all you like and nothing could fore-stall us. There is no need for a judgment—that has already been decided. There is only a need now to carry it out."

"You are damned fools!" cried Lord Esterbroke, struggling ineffectually to get free.

"No; we are only damned poor," said the man. "There is nothing foolish about us. That is the trouble with you lords and rich folk; you think that because a man is poor, he is stupid."

"Now, look—I say you *are* stupid, and here is why: Do you see that man on the ground? You may pray you have not killed him! He is to lend me twenty thousand pounds. Twenty thousand pounds! And you could have had your ten and been happy. But now you will swing for it!"

"We should never have got our ten thousand pounds, your lordship. We know that right well. We are past asking for it now; we have come for one thing, and one thing only."

"Well, damn you, what is it?" cried Lord Esterbroke in frustration.

"Only to kill you, your lordship.—Now, come away from the ladies; there is no need for them to see this."

"What?" Lord Esterbroke cried. "For a trifling ten thousand pounds you will cut me down in cold blood? For ten thousand pounds you will go to the gallows? I do not believe it. Tell me your name again, man, and I shall see you paid as soon as I come to London again."

"No, my lord. It is too late now. We have come to our resolve—that no man shall go on living who has so recklessly battened on our labor like a parasite."

Lord Esterbroke was incensed at this insult. "A parasite!" he said. "It is you and all your kind that are parasites to your betters! And if you are not promptly paid, it is your own fault. We are sick of your importunities! What has England come to, when people of your kind no longer know their place?—But you cannot deceive me—you are too well spoken for a mere tailor. You are a radical—that is what you are!"

"I thank you for the compliment, your lordship. I am indeed perhaps a bit better read than the ordinary tailor; but this is the first time *you* have ever seen fit to notice it. Yet I shall tell you this: I never was a political man in my life, until the bailiffs put my wife and children on the street; and then, by God, I became not just a radical, but a revolutionary.— Now, will you come away like a man, and spare the ladies this scene, or shall I blow your brains out where you stand?"

Now, it is a peculiar fact that the innocent think good principles will prevail against wrong (or against wrong disguised as right), even against the most brutal and homicidal wrong, provided only that those good principles are expressed. And Tomazina, raised as she had been in one of the deepest pockets of rurality in southern England, under the tutelage of a father in many ways constitutionally more innocent than herself, and in the company of sisters certainly more innocent, was, in comparison to these fierce radicals and the radically immoral target of their wrath, as spotless as a saint. During her childhood, the death of a dove in the cote had been attended with mourning and the elaborate mimic of a church burial; the discovery that the neighboring squire drowned unwanted kittens and puppies as a matter of course haunted her for years; and even when she grew up and became engrossed in the news of England's patriotic wars, she had little grasp of the horrors they entailed—the callous butchery, burning, maiming, rape, gangrene, sickness, dislocation.

She heard in Tailor Smet's discourse that he was justly aggrieved; this she understood at once. To her it seemed that, being so, he ought not to take judgment into his own hands, but appeal to those who held the punishment of wrong in theirs. She little understood the obstructions to simple justice raised by ancient law and the class system. She saw only that these men, whom she instantly and fervently believed were in the right, were about to put themselves in the wrong, not only in the eyes of the law, but more importantly (for any Comstock) in the eyes of God.

At this point, terror or no terror, she rose to her feet again. The men would not have paid the least attention, but she spoke out, in an earnest, clear voice, which again carried like the tone of a bell on the still air.

"No, sir," she said to the tailor. "You must not do this thing! Have you not read what the Bible says?"

The men now turned to her in infuriated astonishment.

"The Bible!" repeated Smet, as if she had spoken the name of something utterly irrelevant.

"Yes, sir, the Word of our God. Have you not read what the Bible says about what you propose to do?"

He was nonplussed for a moment; and then, as if recovering a memory from his former life only with difficulty, he said, "Aye, I believe I have read something about this in the Bible. I do recall that it reads: *Thou shalt give life for life, eye for eye, tooth for tooth, hand for hand, foot for foot, burning for burning, wound for wound, stripe for stripe.* And believe me, Missy, there are many among us who have lost child and wife to hunger and want and sickness because of this lordling's lies. His life does not even begin to repay what we have lost."

"But that is not the verse you want, sir! That is the Old Covenant, and we live under the New."

"Is that so? Maybe you and your ilk do, Missy, with your fine dresses and carriages; but me and mine live under the Old. Here is another for you: *The wicked in his pride doth persecute the poor: let them be taken in the devices that they have imagined.*"

"Aye!" cried some of the men; and one added, "*That* is the Bible for us!"

In the heat of this terrible moment, verses Tomazina had not heard or spoken for years were bubbling up in her brain. "Nay," she replied to the tailor, "the verse you want is this: *Say not thou, I will recompense evil; but wait on the Lord, and he shall save thee.*"

With bitter inspiration he rejoined: "*Woe to him that spoiled, and was not spoiled; and dealt treacherously, and they dealt not treacherously with him! When he shall cease to spoil, he shall be spoiled; and when he shall make an end to deal treacherously, they shall deal treacherously with him.*"

"Give it to her, Methody John!" said one of the men.

"Aye, Missy," said another, "ye did not know you were up against a preacher, did ye?" And they all laughed harshly.

"Are you then a preacher, sir?" she asked.

"In my time I was," said the tailor. "But that is all past now. Now I have come to give this man to drink of *the cup of the wine of the fierceness of God's wrath.*"

"But *the wrath of man worketh not the righteousness of God,*" she said. "And we are told *Avenge not yourself, but rather give place unto wrath; for it is written, Vengeance is mine, saith the Lord.*—And St. Paul says: *See that none render evil for evil unto any man; but follow ever that which is good, both among yourselves, and to all men.*"

The implacable tailor cut her off. "I tell you," he answered her, "this man has been the cause of the death of many of ours. It is writ: *He that killeth a man, he shall be put to death.*"

"But that applies to you as well," she rejoined. "Do you not see? *Whoso sheddeth a man's blood, by man shall his blood be shed: for in the image of God made He man. If ye do not forgive, neither will your Father which is in heaven forgive your trespasses. Put up again thy sword into his place: for all they that take the sword shall perish with the sword.* If you kill him for his crimes, you will be killed in turn. This man is a wicked, wicked creature, but you must let God have the judging of him. This rash act will only lead to your own deaths, and make widows of your wives, and orphans of your children."

"So be it," said the tailor grimly. And many of the men around him nodded as well, and some repeated, "Aye; so be it!"

But this did not give Tomazina pause. "Do you not believe in the Lord Jesus Christ, risen from the dead?" she asked the man. "He told us, *Ye have heard that it hath been said, An eye for an eye, and a tooth for a tooth: But I say unto you, That ye resist not evil: but whosoever shall smite thee on the right cheek, turn to him the other also.*"

Redding, the man who had held her by the hair before, had pushed his way back into the throng when he heard her speaking; and now he came up to her, full of his rage, and he said, "We shall see how you yourself keep to that saying, Missy!" And before she or anyone could guess what he was about, he dealt her a brutal slap across the cheek with the palm of his hand.

She was thrown from her feet to the ground, where she landed on all fours. For a long moment her head rang and her ears sang. Over the roaring of the blood in her brains, she could hear the outcry of the men around her, some approving, some protesting.

But she kept her wits, if such they could be called, and she rose to her feet again, though slowly, and faced her assailant. He watched her through narrowed eyes, sneering at her triumphantly.

Then, deliberately and calmly, she turned the other cheek toward him.

There was an uproar—again of mingled anger and admiration. Redding himself was outraged. He turned to one of his fellows and, with a bellow of one insulted past all forbearance, jerked from the man's hands the ancient musket that he carried; and the muzzle of this he planted between Tomazina's breasts.

The shouting rose to a crescendo around them. Redding pushed the muzzle hard against her; and either because she was forced, or because her legs gave out beneath her in her terror, or because Rose Elizabeth was dragging her down by the skirts, she collapsed to her knees. The barrel of the gun followed her, as if to impale her, like a pin that holds a butterfly in a case.

The mob caught its breath, awaiting the outcome.

"Now, Missy," said Redding, "we shall pay *you* an eye for an eye and a tooth for a tooth!" And he pressed the muzzle hard upon her breastbone, drawing himself up to his full height; and with a slow, exaggerated motion, he squeezed the ancient trigger bar of the old musket.

The hammer gave a dry, cold snap, but the gun did not fire.

For a long moment, Tomazina did not know what had happened—whether she was alive or dead. Then Redding loosed a wild guffaw, and the men around him joined in. As she realized that he had known the old matchlock could not fire, and that he had never intended to shoot her, she sagged back against Rose Elizabeth, limp with both terror and a sort of numb relief.

Then, in an instant, the pale girl who had defied this mob was forgotten. Bloodlust surged in their veins again. They swarmed over Lord Esterbroke; he struggled and swore at them in vain. On the orders of the tailor, who led the way, they picked their victim up, mocking him and taunting him; and half-bearing him and half-dragging him, striking him with their clubs and brutally kicking him, they forced him away from the road.

As the mob left the women behind, Tomazina got on her knees again and put her arms around Rose Elizabeth. She wanted to say something, but her voice seemed stuck in her throat. Together they watched this deadly procession in horror and amazement, as if seeing something impossible take place before their eyes. And yet they could not doubt it was happening, for they could see everything, since the moon was luminous and the air clear.

"Oh, Mazie," pleaded Rose Elizabeth then, "pray something! Say a prayer for us! It is up to you—I have not a word in my head!"

In response Tomazina began to speak, almost before she knew where the words came from:

> Deliver me, O Lord, from the evil man; preserve me
> from the violent man;
> Which imagine mischiefs in their hearts. . . .

And on she went until she came to the line: *I know that the Lord will maintain the cause of the afflicted, and the right of the poor.*

Then the psalm died on her lips, as she realized that that particular verse counted against Lord Esterbroke even more than it did against those who meant to kill him.

The men had some instinct to take their victim to higher ground—whether thinking it a kind of seat of judgment or a gallows, Tomazina did not know; and so they dragged him up onto a piece of rising heath between the two hillocks, no more than two hundred feet from the carriage. The main part of them stopped short of the crest of this rise. Only four men went onward with Lord Esterbroke, three to hold him secure, and one his self-appointed judge and executioner, the tailor. It seemed to Tomazina that these four must have been acknowledged by all to be the most aggrieved and to have the right of officiating at his murder.

"Oh, Mazie, are they really going to do it?" cried Rose Elizabeth then, unable to believe what she was seeing with her own eyes.

Tomazina whispered back: "Perhaps they are only going to frighten him, dear, as they frightened me. Just to teach him a lesson—as they taught me one."

John Smet went behind Lord Esterbroke. The other three held their prisoner at arms' length to give Smet room; and the tailor struck the lordling over the back of the head with a blackjack. The three who had been restraining Lord Esterbroke now fully released their grip, and he fell to all fours, stunned, but apparently still conscious.

Smet stepped up beside Lord Esterbroke and applied the muzzle of his pistol to his victim's skull. Then he began to speak; and though his voice was as calm and cool as the night air, at this distance all Tomazina and Rose Elizabeth could hear was something about prayers and the Lord and "mercy on his soul."

Rose Elizabeth gave a sob of terror; and Tomazina, now desperately willing that this horror should not happen, said, "It cannot be! They cannot throw away their immortal souls for the sake of mere vengeance—and least of all in such a cold-blooded manner as this!"

But no sooner had she spoken those words than the night resounded with the crack of the pistol. Lord Esterbroke pitched forward headlong on the ground.

The echoes of the shot died away slowly on the surrounding wastes. There was a long, cold silence; and during that hushed moment, it seemed everything was frozen—the watching mob, the tailor-executioner, the very air and moonlight, even time itself. And then the tableau came abruptly to life again.

The murderers swarmed around the body and stripped it of purse, watch, and jewelry. It was peculiar how they then immediately left it, as if they were men of business who had completed a task to which they were inured by long practice; though in fact they were rather so full of contempt for their persecutor and victim that the instant he had ceased to live they cared not even to stand gloating over his corpse. They returned to the coach, led by the tailor, who now approached the little group on the ground. At his coming, Rose Elizabeth, who was still cradling the unconscious Mr. Ashleigh in her lap, drew him tighter against her and leaned over him again protectively; and Tomazina in her turn, upright on her knees behind Rose Elizabeth, held her sister more tightly in her arms and leaned over her with the same purpose.

"And who is this gentleman?" said Smet, indicating Ashleigh.

"He is my husband," protested Rose Elizabeth. "He is Mr. Ashleigh of Priedpie Hall in Hampshire."

"And is he in debt to his tailor, too?" said the man.

"Oh, no! No, sir! He pays his debts faithfully every quarter! He does not live in London, sir—he lives in the country, and he pays his debts!"

The other men laughed harshly at this curious bit of rustic and feminine naïveté.

"Well," said the tailor, "it is not my part to quarrel with him. Let this be a lesson to him, though, not to trifle with those to whom he owes money. As for you, ladies, it were best if you said nothing of what you have heard and seen this night. We know who you are, Mrs. Ashleigh of Priedpie Hall; and we will find your husband out and serve him the same way, if you or this Bible-spouting sister of yours here says ever a word about what you have seen."

"No, sir!" cried Rose Elizabeth.

"Yes, sir!" cried Tomazina simultaneously.

The murderers laughed at the agony of their propitiating fear. Then, without another word either to the women or to one another, the men turned and ransacked the Ashleighs' coach. They broke open the luggage, scattered it in the moonlight, and took everything portable and valuable, including all of the clothing. It was clear that they meant to sell these garments, as they took items too rich or incongruous for their own wear; and it was bizarre to see them striding about in the moonlight clutching hastily gathered bundles of velvet jackets and crisp white stays and silk stockings and muslin petticoats and embroidered French nightgowns. The hard goods they brought to the tailor, and he divided the plunder according to his own instantaneous judgment of their individual needs and deserts; and such was his authority that though the division was necessarily uneven, no one seemed to question it or envy anyone else's portion. To one man he gave a guinea from Lord Esterbroke's purse, saying, "There, Danny, that is for your missus." To the next he gave Mr. Ashleigh's silver-headed cane, saying, "Joe, that should fetch sommat to put in your chillers' mouths." And so on, round the crew again and again, until it was all distributed.

The last item—indeed, the tailor seemed to have deliberately held it back—was Tomazina's Bible, the one she had owned since she was a child, her father's gift. It was battered and plain, but still worth a few pence if it was sold, and a few pence was a lot to these men. When he came to it at last, Smet held it up in the moonlight for a moment and peered at it. "It is a Bible," he announced to the mob; and then he looked down at Tomazina where she still knelt on the ground behind Rose Elizabeth. "Is this yours?" he asked her.

"It is, sir."

"I hardly think you need it," he said, and the men laughed, but less raucously this time.

"Aye," said one of them, "she would make a good Methody preacher-lady herself, that one."

"Sir," Tomazina said to the tailor, "if it will do any one of you any good, to read or to sell, he may have it with my blessing."

The men seemed surprised at her offer, and at the tone of compassion in which she made it.

The tailor considered it for a moment; and then he threw it down on Mr. Ashleigh's prostrate body. It was hardly a kindly gesture, for the book was a goodly quarto.

"Read it to *him*, Sister," he said, using the title for a female colleague that was common in the radical Christian circles of the day.

He took a long look at Tomazina in the moonlight, and she braved his stare, looking evenly back at him.

"And pray for our souls," he said.

"I shall," she answered quietly. "And I shall pray for *his*, too." By that she meant Lord Esterbroke's.

"Do not take the trouble," he answered. "*The womb shall forget him; the worm shall feed sweetly on him; he shall be no more remembered; and wickedness shall be broken as a tree.*"

It was as if he had spoken the truth before when he had said he was an avenging angel—as if this were the final judgment on the condemned soul now hastening on its way to hell. Her mouth opened to reply, to speak some softening word; but in the face of the awfulness and the righteousness of that judgment her voice failed her.

Then it seemed as if the spell that had held the men broke. The ambush they had come so far to accomplish had been successful; their bloodlust was sated, and fear of the law recurred to their minds.

Smet barked orders: the Ashleighs' carriage was forced off the road, and the great coach of the attackers was turned about. The murderers climbed aboard again; the driver whipped up the horses; and the coach lumbered away in the direction of London, accompanied by its lone outrider.

❈ ❈ ❈

Those next few minutes were an eternity, during which Tomazina and Rose Elizabeth could still discern the coach that carried their attackers; but then its dark and indistinct form passed over a hill and vanished from sight.

"Oh, Rose! Rose!" cried Tomazina then. "Does he still live?"

"He must! He must live! He cannot die now—just as we have begun to find one another! And just as I have begun to hope—"

She did not finish her thought; but she did not need to. *A widow with child!* thought Tomazina fearfully. *Dear Lord, do not let Rose suffer that fate!*

She crawled to Mr. Ashleigh's side and helped Rose Elizabeth lower his head gently to the ground. As they did this, he groaned and made an involuntary movement.

"Oh, thank God!" cried Tomazina, and Rose Elizabeth burst into sobs of gratitude. Then Tomazina said: "Look, he is bleeding heavily—he is badly cut where he was struck." She seized her shawl, which had been overlooked by the mob and lay trampled on the ground nearby, and she applied it to the gash in the back of Mr. Ashleigh's scalp, from which she could feel blood running freely. "You must hold this in place, Rose Elizabeth; do you think you can do that?"

"Yes," said Rose Elizabeth in a choked voice.

"Hold it firmly. You must stop the bleeding."

Rose Elizabeth did as she was told. "But what will you do?" she said, sensing that Tomazina had another purpose in mind for herself.

"I shall go see if Lord Esterbroke still lives."

"It cannot be possible!"

"Indeed, I think the same; but we must know for sure before we can determine what to do."

With that she rose to her feet; but Rose Elizabeth, in a fresh panic at the mere thought of being left alone, cried, "Do not leave me!"

"You may watch me every step of the way, dear."

"No, Mazie, Mazie! Do not leave me!" If her hands had not been occupied in staunching Mr. Ashleigh's wound, she would have caught at Tomazina's skirts again to prevent her.

"Rose, I must do this! We cannot leave him to die if there is any way to save him.—Look, dearest, I shall never be out of your sight; you may watch me the entire time. I shall count the steps out loud, so you shall know how very close I am to you. Besides, I assure you we are quite alone here. I think there is no one to harm us for miles about, now that those men have gone."

"What comfort is that? We must get Mr. Ashleigh to a surgeon or apothecary; and how are we to do that?"

"We shall find a way, Sister. Think on it, and hold that shawl tightly to the wound, and watch me till I come back to you."

And so she left Rose Elizabeth and went to see if Lord Esterbroke could somehow be alive. As she had promised, from her very setting out she counted each step out loud. And yet for her, even more than for Rose Elizabeth, the farther she went, and the closer she approached to that dark shadow on the little hill that was her goal, the more terrified she felt; and more than once she considered giving up her purpose. But the effort of counting helped occupy her thinking, and each step led to another as one number to the next, and soon she was too close to turn back; and then she came up on the fatal spot itself, the little gallows hill on which the tailor had committed this terrible execution.

What she saw then in the moonlight was a sight that never left her. The pistols of those days were very large of bore, and the shot had been discharged point-blank. The evidence disclosed by the moonlight was as incontrovertible as it was ghastly: gore, blood, brains, fragments of the shattered bones of the skull covered by scalp and glistening hair, these were everywhere. No one could possibly have survived such a terrible wound.

Thus his miserable luck has at last run utterly out, she thought. He had fallen alone and friendless, without the least thought of repentance or atonement or regret, at the mercy of just a few of his many debtors, whose claims he had so cruelly disdained to acknowledge for year after year.

Terrible it was, horrific and haunting, to consider both his crimes and his punishment. But the ways of the human mind are unaccountable. As she stood there in the night and shadow, with a bloody, murdered man before her on the ground, her brother-in-law injured behind her, and her beloved sister terrified for her husband's life, the first thought that came to her was how Samson would feel at the loss of his cousin. He must feel some sorrow and loss, surely; for he was a man who would love his kin as those of his own line— a line that had included many good men and women as well as this evil one; and she grieved for any grief he must feel.

And then another thought came to her—flooded her mind like a deluge, struck her with a force that was almost physical; and she did in fact physically sway for a moment as it came home to her. It arrived in the form of one of Solomon's proverbs rising up in her well-trained memory.

A man's pride shall bring him low, she thought, *but honor shall uphold the humble in spirit.*

The proud Lord Esterbroke had fallen; but a humble man was now the new Lord Esterbroke. To Samson would come, by inheritance, the title and all the lands and wealth— if any were left—of the man who was lying dead at her feet.

❂ ❂ ❂

The rest of that night played out with all the terror of a suffocating dream. The servants never returned; so it had to be between the two of them, and with some half-conscious participation from the victim himself, that Tomazina and Rose Elizabeth managed to get Mr. Ashleigh into the coach. With a shawl and a sash they tied him upright in the forward seat, and Rose Elizabeth took her place beside him, staunching the blood still. The night seemed freezing by then, and nearly every single article of their extra clothing had been stolen; but as luck would have it, there were a few traveling blankets in the carriage that the mob had missed. Throwing one of these over her shoulders, Tomazina crawled up into the coachman's seat and gathered the reins in her hands.

She immediately chose against going back toward London, a course that would in all probability have caught them up with the murderers; yet that decision meant she must go onward, with no notion of how far ahead the next hamlet might be. What was more, she had never driven anything larger than a pony cart in her life, and the carriage lamps had been stolen during the plundering of the coach. Fortunately the hired horses, though weary, knew that they must go on in order to reach a place where they would be fed and rested; so they were perfectly willing to be directed; and the moon was still many hours from setting.

But as dreadful as the event was—and God alone ever knew how she wept with terror, as the horses surged forward in the moonlight, jerking and jolting at their harness; and as the coach swayed as if it would topple at every curve and hole in the road; and as the half-light seemed to trick and cheat her eyes, which sought forward desperately to make sure she did not run the horses straight off the highway—when she saw ahead in the far distance a light that she guessed might be a village, a different mood came over her.

She felt a kind of exhilaration. She had some hope that the man her sister loved would live and recover; and indeed, aside from the aching of her cheek, she and her sister were unharmed; but beyond these blessings, she was carrying the first tidings to the world of a great change to come in the fortunes of the man she loved.

She could not help thinking how Lord Esterbroke had now certainly lost the wager he had proposed. Now Samson was possessor of everything Lord Esterbroke had ever owned, and in addition he would be able to marry the woman he loved. He would make sure of his fiancée—that would probably be his first act as Lord Esterbroke. And, of course, Miss Doronne would now be glad to get him. But all the same, Tomazina could only rejoice that Samson Esterbroke would rise in the world.

And more than that, the love she felt for him, if nothing else, gave her reason to hope, as she clung to the reins and steered as best she could over the dim road, that she might somehow find a way to convince him otherwise: that in fact the best partner to him, now that he was to be ennobled, might be—not the woman whose love *he* had sought, the woman who had refused him in his days of want; but the woman who, without his seeking, had sought *him*—had loved him and cared nothing that he was poor.